WET

WET

true lesbian sex stories

EDITED BY
NICOLE FOSTER

 alyson books
los angeles | new york

MANUFACTURED IN THE UNITED STATES OF AMERICA.

THIS TRADE PAPERBACK ORIGINAL IS PUBLISHED BY ALYSON PUBLICATIONS, P.O. BOX 4371, LOS ANGELES, CALIFORNIA 90078-4371. DISTRIBUTION IN THE UNITED KINGDOM BY TURNAROUND PUBLISHER SERVICES LTD., UNIT 3, OLYMPIA TRADING ESTATE, COBURG ROAD, WOOD GREEN, LONDON N22 6TZ ENGLAND.

FIRST EDITION: DECEMBER 2002

03 04 05 06 a 10 9 8 7 6 5 4 3

ISBN 1-55583-766-2

LIBRARY OF CONGRESS CATALOGING-IN-PUBLICATION DATA

WET: TRUE LESBIAN SEX STORIES / EDITED BY NICOLE FOSTER.—1ST ED.
    ISBN 1-55583-766-2
    1. LESBIANS—SEXUAL BEHAVIOR. 2. LESBIANISM. I. FOSTER, NICOLE.
HQ75.5.W48 2002
306.76'63—DC21   2002028026

CREDITS
COVER PHOTOGRAPHY BY YVETTE GONZALEZ.
COVER DESIGN BY MATT SAMS.

For all you adventurous girls
who keep taking the plunge

Contents

Introduction

This book is called *Wet* for many reasons. When I first decided to pull together another collection of true lesbian sex tales (following the success of my book *Skin Deep: Real-life Lesbian Sex Stories*), I thought about all of the euphemisms men have for being turned on: hard, erect, turgid, etc. And then I thought about the dearth of similar terms for women's sexuality. How often in films and erotic literature do we see or read about men having a "rock-hard pole" or "big boner"? Way too often, if you ask me. Women's sexuality may be discussed, but rarely do we hear people talk about women's *excitement*. I guess I could have called this book *Hard Nipples,* but that doesn't quite elicit the same effect as *Wet.* I wanted to use something bold, something in-your-face, so to speak. I wanted to celebrate women's sensuality, their ability to get just as horny as the next guy.

I also chose *Wet* because I want these stories to make you, the reader, wet. So I looked for the sexiest, hottest material I could find. While some of these stories celebrate loving, gentle sex between women in a relationship, others are a little crazier and explore the flip side of that equation; thus we have stories set in public bathrooms, an S/M dungeon, a waxing salon, a backyard, a rooftop, and a locker room, among other offbeat places.

The one thing that unites all of these stories, though, is that they are based on the experiences of real women—women who could be your next-door neighbor, your boss, your best friend, or even you. That's what's so great about this collection—and what makes it so sexy. In the pages of this book, you won't find erotic true-life stories that are written to fulfill straight men's fantasies. There are no *Hustler*-type stories of supermodel women getting it on with each other in front of men. There are no stories of wives who sleep with each other merely because they're randy and their husbands are out of town. In my book, a female lover isn't a substitute for a man. That's ridiculous. Women go down

INTRODUCTION

on each other because they love it; they love getting other women off. They fuck each other because they love it; they love the feel of a woman's body. They love getting her *wet*. They love *getting* wet.

So open up these pages and dive in. And don't forget to bring a towel, sweetie. It's gonna be a long, wet trip.

—Nicole Foster

Those Blue Suede Shoes

_____

Jesi O'Connell

When my honey reaches for her blue suede shoes, I know I'm in trouble. Oh, yeah. The really good kind of trouble, the trouble you want to be in during a slow Saturday night after the dishes are washed and dried and the cat's fed and the dog's walked and there's nothing good on TV and you're just a little bit antsy.

Every time those shoes come out I'm in for something—a spanking, maybe. My honey's special disobedience lessons. A trip to the grocery store wearing snug jeans and a slutty black shirt with my newest underthings from the Good Vibrations and Victoria's Secret catalogs hiding beneath: crotchless candy apple-red St. Valentine's Day bikini panties, a silk bra with lace-lined holes for my stiff nipples, a little quietly vibrating toy nestled between my legs, making me squeeze my thighs together and walk in a kind of duck-like shuffle because it feels so-o-o good.

Yeah, that kind of trouble.

My honey, we'll call her Sondra, has a vintage pair of men's size 7 blue suede shoes, just like the kind the King used to wear. She got them in high school, when she used to browse thrift stores after school with her best friend, Lisa.

"That Lisa," my honey says one night, while we're still sitting at the dinner table. She stretches her hands above her head, arching backward, giving me a good view of her breasts straining against the button-down blouse she's wearing. I suddenly notice she isn't wearing a bra. Hello. "Yeah, she used to like to cut class sometimes, just so we could go shopping down on Melrose. Lisa was really into Madonna at the time, and Madonna was into thrift stores, so that's where we went. Bargain," and she slaps her

_1_

hands down on the table, making me jump a bit, staring into my eyes, "basement."

She's giving me that look like I'm a bargain-basement find. Eyes traveling up and down my body, slowing down over the curves, lingering at my crotch, which has gotten a bit tingly. Oh, yeah.

"We stopped into this one store on a Friday afternoon—we were supposed to be in algebra. Right." My honey's eyes capture mine again, and I decide I shouldn't squirm—not yet. Not until I'm sure I'll get good and punished for it. I sit and nod and keep my eyes wide and interested. "There were shoes all over that store. Crazy. Piles of them, sitting in heaps, up on shoe racks, tossed in boxes, on the plastic feet of mannequins with bad '70s hair. And then—I saw them. Those blue suede shoes. Just like the kind Elvis sang about," and she sings me a bar of that famous song in her deep husky voice, and my crotch gets all wet and slippery, and I *know*, without a doubt, I'm in for something tonight.

"You ever seen those blue suede shoes?" she asks me then, in a sexy purr. Her eyes are still locked with mine, and I feel my breath getting short. Uh-huh. "Maybe I'd better model them for you," and she gets up from the table, napkin drifting down to the ground as she turns and heads for the bedroom. After half a step, she turns and says, "You just stay right there like the good girl you are."

Sure.

When my Sondra comes back in the room, she's wearing the blue suede shoes. They're really nice, clean, and practically brand-new. She's got white socks on with them, which always makes me giggle and moan at the same time. She looks all clean-cut like a '50s butch, but I know the thoughts she's thinking are anything but wholesome. Rolled-up jeans, white T-shirt, hair slicked behind her ears. *Rowr.* But I can hardly take my eyes of those shoes.

"Get over here. Right now," she commands, and her voice is soft but her words are so hard that I'm there in a second. She means no fussing around, no long slow lead-up. She means business, and she means it now. Yes ma'am.

"Get down on all fours," says that voice, still soft, still somehow cracking over me like a whip. I obey, and my panties are sopping and my breath is ragged and my head is whirling. "What a good girl you are," she says, and my thighs quiver. "So fuckable." More quivering.

There is a pause. I look up at her, almost ready to start begging, and she snaps, "Look at those shoes!"

Of course, I obey. The blue suede is like the sky. It reminds me of other little adventures that happened when my honey wore these shoes. An impatient sound comes out of my mouth, and she laughs.

"Think you're ready?" Her voice is faintly taunting and enticing at the same time.

"Please?" I say. My nipples are at that stage where they really want to be touched—rolled between her fingers, licked by her talented tongue, nibbled on by her small white teeth. They want to be pulled, played with, flicked with her fingertips until they get so enormous and excited I could come almost from that sensation alone.

"Ooh, I hope you know what you're letting yourself in for."

The sound of the zipper on her jeans being pulled down very slowly sends a rush down my spine, through my legs, straight to my clit. Is she—? Could she be—? I turn my head up to try and peek.

"What did I tell you!" she snaps, and she puts her hand on my head to force it to look down again. Her touch is gentle, though. "Keep your eyes on those shoes. Know that I'll be wearing them—and not much else—in just a few minutes."

Not much else? I distract myself with wondering if she'll take the jeans off or if the denim will just be left crumpled around her ankles when she does something to me. Something delicious, and wicked, and meant to make me hers.

Her jeans slither to the ground and cover the shoes. Then I hear an interesting noise, one that makes my back prickle. I think I know that sound. My body thinks it knows that sound. I get a hot flash, all over, so intense that I feel like keeling over.

"Look up," she commands.

I do, and that's when it really hits me how much trouble I'm in, how much trouble these shoes are going to get me in tonight. I am so slick between my legs, so plump and waiting, when I see what my honey has in store for me. I am going to get fucked tonight.

My honey is packing. It's big, it's crystal purple, and it's already glistening in its little spot nestled in her dark, curly hairs. I notice the bottle of baby oil tipped on its side on the floor behind my honey, my Sondra, my lover who is going to make me remember who wears the blue suede shoes in this family.

"Remove my jeans," she orders, still standing. I can hardly tear my eyes away from the huge dildo poking out in front of her. She's already covered it in oil. This is the special toy, the one we bought just for us. Or rather, the one she bought just for me. I think about its thick length burrowing deep inside me with my honey guiding it in, and I get weak in the knees. Did I mention I was already dripping wet?

"Remove," she says more firmly, grabbing my chin in her hand and tipping my face up to look at her, "my jeans." She's stern-looking, as stern-looking as a woman can be with a purple dildo strapped on.

I comply, somehow. Her jeans are flared a bit at the bottom, so I manage to shrug them over the blue suede shoes. Delicately, my honey steps away as each leg is freed. She's already naked from the waist up, her small breasts white against the rest of her tanned skin, the dark nipples erect. I want to take one in my mouth, but she shakes her head. Very slowly, knowing I'm watching her, my Sondra runs one finger along the veined side of the toy. Her finger comes away gleaming, and she runs it down her chest, between her breasts, through her little curly hairs between her legs, around the dildo, into herself.

I can tell she likes the way that feels by the way her breath catches in her throat. I can tell I like it by the electric sizzle that shoots down my thighs, making me clamp them together and start to throb. Then she pulls her finger out and licks it, running her tongue around it suggestively. This time I do keel over in a little flop onto the ground.

"Take your clothes off." No problem. I strip so fast I pop a button on my shirt.

"All fours again," she says in that dangerous voice, the one that means she is just barely holding herself back. "And don't drip on my shoes."

The blue suede shoes and the purple dildo—my, what a sight my honey is. I can hardly take it, and I feel my heart beating more quickly. Carefully, I roll onto my hands and push myself up to my knees. Soft suede runs next to my ribs, over my back, dances over my bare butt as she rubs me with a foot. I shiver. Then I barely have time to take a breath before she is on me, the dildo pushing insistently against my legs.

"Let me in. I know you're wet enough to take it," she growls into my ear. "I know I didn't even have to put the baby oil on it. You want it."

"Yes," I sort of whimper, and I move my legs apart so she can get between them. And then she does, and her hand is on my crotch, then her fingers are stretching apart my folds, and I can hear myself making a little sucking noise, it's so wet down there.

"Mmm." She sounds appreciative. "You want it really badly, don't you?"

"Oh, yeah," I moan, and I lean down on my arms so my ass is in the air. "Please, please," I beg, and I know I sound pathetic, and I don't care.

"OK." And she is amused at my desire.

The dildo shoves against me, and she opens me more with her fingers, and from my position with my head down looking between my legs back at her I can see her blue suede shoes on her feet, and they turn me on so much that she suddenly just slides right in, I am that big and slippery and wanting it. It feels huge but just right, and my muscles close around it. We both sigh, and then she starts to pump.

"Don't move!" she says in that commanding tone again. "I want you to take it like a woman—feel me against you—can you feel how good you are to be so open for me? Huh? Can you?"

Her voice is starting to sound a bit out of control, rough around the edges. I can't answer her, because I'm concentrating on not moving, on staying still like she told me to, on not rocking with the motion and giving in to it. The dildo is plunging inside me with no resistance, I am not tight at all—and then her hand starts to play with my clit, just lightly brushing it, then fondling it, then tweaking it gently. I groan and tremble, but I still don't move. Then my honey starts to rub it in just that right way, circles, round and round until I almost feel dizzy, I feel so full, and I can hear my wetness as the slippery purple thing goes in and out.

"Aah," my honey mutters against my ear, and I grin, I can't help it. She's getting close herself, the harness is rubbing her as she's ramming into me. I can still see those shoes, upside down, between my legs, and I connect them with fucking, and being fucked, and my Sondra moaning into my ear, and all the wetness that's dripping down my legs, filling the room with a pungent scent that is heady.

"Now," my honey says in low, guttural voice, and she grabs my hips with her hands, holding me firmly as she still rocks back and forth into me, almost slamming against me, and I gasp when her fingers leave my clit. But it doesn't matter anymore, because I am so close I will come anyway, just from being fucked and hearing her moan and knowing that she's about to come too. She does come, right then, I can feel her fingers tighten on my hips and she pauses for just a moment, like it's too overwhelming to move. And then I come, and it's a good one, the kind that starts with a little tingle and gets bigger and more and everywhere, all over, so you hardly know if you're right side up or upside down, spreading from my little tiny clit through my legs and then over my whole body, up to my head, which just wants to explode. My honey shrieks my name, starts rubbing hard against me with the dildo again, massaging herself and trembling and almost puncturing my eardrums with her voice.

After a long while more, we finally stop moving, and we silently crumple together into a gasping little heap, sweaty arms and legs and hair all tangled up. I am still faintly throbbing, and I jump when my honey runs her hand over my exposed thigh. We stay quiet for a while longer, steadying our breathing, before she speaks.

"Mmm," she purrs in a throaty rumble. "I just knew you'd like my blue suede shoes."

"I always do," I manage to say, and she kisses my neck and rubs the soft suede of a shoe against my calf.

The Regular

Stephanie Holinka

Pool with the girls, upstairs at Girlbar. Same bar girls, same tables, same as all the weekends before. Since I'd broken up with the ex and taken to spending as little time at home as possible, the itinerary varied little: hang out, drink, play bad pool, and watch the new women show up. And on Friday night all kinds of women showed up: thin, fat, goth, country, big-haired girls from the burbs, urban digerati, and tourists of all kinds. Most of the regulars waited for some fascinating woman to arrive and make their Friday night waiting ritual worthwhile. For several months I waited to see the same woman.

Kathleen crossed to the other side of the table to take her shot, and I glanced up just in time to see that woman walk in. Every Friday night for months I'd seen her standing in the doorway and pause as her friends gathered, waiting for them to come to her. She'd hold court at the tables nearest the bar, a consistent flow of women saying hello, whispering in her ear, or wrapping themselves around her—women far gutsier than I. I couldn't blame them, since she really was incredible: tall, solid, and tan with an unstoppable aura and strong hands that could fix cars, lift heavy things, kill bugs, or rub tired shoulders. Tight ringlets of sun-streaked blond curls clung to her scalp, refusing to lie down. She wore carpenter's jeans, black Doc Martens, and a vintage light blue mechanic's shirt with MEL written on an oval patch over her right breast. When she laughed I could hear her from across the room.

The Friday night crowded parted before her, and she surveyed the room the way an architect views a skyline or a historian browses the Smithsonian: proprietarily, with a practiced eye and, perhaps, an agenda.

Heading through the packed bar, Mel parted group after group of gathered women, trekking toward the bartender. A few feet away from me, she suddenly changed direction and headed my way. Smiling at me, she swung herself around and landed expertly on the couch at my side, bypassing the flirting couple to my left. Pleased with herself, she flashed me a big grin. The twinkle in her blue eyes seemed to come from a light source outside of the dingy bar.

"Why is it I've been here so many times and yet I've never seen you?" Mel asked.

Momentarily stunned, I tried hard to both remember my own name *and* form words. "Clearly you weren't looking hard enough. I've seen *you* before."

"Really?" Humor and mock perplexity played across her face as she feigned amazement.

"Really," I somehow said. "Of course, we've never spoken,"

"Why on earth not? Clearly I should have spoken to you a long time ago." Those eyes again. Was I still blinking? Was I still breathing? Thank God I was sitting down; even sitting I felt a little wobbly.

"Clearly." A second of awkwardness as my mind blanked again. Why did the dork in me have to come out *then*?

Mel settled in next to me. I tried to relax and breathe regularly while we talked. She said she was in the military, an explosives expert in training. She was in town only for a few months, on leave from her program in San Diego. In addition to working for a furniture moving company, she was here to think about whether the military would be a full-time career option. Part of her reason for not wanting to go back was a rather ugly-ending relationship with one of her team members. I told her about my ex, whom I was desperately trying to get over, and all the life decisions I'd been reevaluating and my thoughts about chucking it all and moving back west.

I started to talk about my job when Mel interrupted my descriptions of the media business and pointed behind me. "Who's that woman?"

I looked up, and Kathleen's glassy eyes burned on me. Right after my ex left, Kathleen and I had shared a brief, uneventful dating thing that early on revealed itself to be totally wrong. I tried to sidestep the entire issue. "Just a friend of mine."

Mel was unconvinced. "She doesn't look at you like you're her friend. She looks at you like you're her girl and she's pissed."

"We dated for a short time. She and I are different people. We decided that dating wasn't the best plan for us."

"Well, *you* might have decided 'lez be friends,' but it's pretty clear *she* didn't."

I'd noticed Kathleen's jealous glances before but didn't want to deal with all the mess behind them. "If she has boundary problems, I can't help that."

A tiny grin edged up one corner of Mel's mouth. "True. We could help her along with her little boundary problem. For her own good, of course."

My smile joined hers. "That would be nice of you. How do you propose to do that?"

Her big baby-blues glittered with just a hint of malice. "I could kiss you right now."

Surely she could see my heart thudding in my chest. Perhaps even hear it. Heck, the bartender could probably hear it over the jukebox. "You could," I agreed.

Drawing my face to hers, Mel kissed me softly. My pulse pounded in my ears. I tasted her lips, cool and soft, slightly sour from gin and tonic. Each tiny kiss flowed and deepened into the next, and the noise and crowds and smoke dissolved until all that remained was Mel and her lips and Janis Joplin singing in the distance and maybe my incessant heart racing.

"That worked out well," Mel said. Her cheeks were flushed and her lips reddened. "Perhaps we should go somewhere more private."

Even though I had never used them, I knew about Girlbar's many hidden corners. "This place wasn't exactly designed for privacy. I'd say we could step out onto the deck, but it's really cold—not exactly deck weather."

Mel pointed at a woman chatting up the bartender. "My friend over there is holding my coat. I'll put that on you. I'd hate for you to be cold."

My face was flushed all the way to my ears. "I don't think cold will be a problem."

She grabbed her coat from the woman at the bar, placing it tenderly on my shoulders. We stepped out onto the terrace, which was too cold to be open now. The door pushed a few inches of early-season frost and snow to the side, but the sky was clear and the city lights and the stars lit the patio.

Making sure we weren't locked out, Mel closed the door and led me to a corner protected from the elements. She pressed her whole body against mine, her fingers playing with my hair and traveling the length of my exposed neck. Out of the corner of my eye I saw Kathleen through the window, hurt and furious. But as Mel nibbled gently on my left earlobe, all thoughts of Kathleen flew far away.

After a time the patio door opened. Kathleen stepped out, her mouth a tight line and her eyes refusing to meet mine. "It's time to leave," she gruffly mumbled at the floor.

"I think I'm going to stay." It was colder than I'd expected, but I was sick of playing these games—sick of walking on eggshells, sick of worrying about hurting her when I'd already laid out my feelings and my intentions.

Mel spoke up. "I'll see she that gets home OK."

Kathleen shot Mel a look of pure rage. Mel remained calm, clearly still in control. She was right: The "friends thing" was not an option. This pretty much sealed it. Kathleen slammed the door behind her, and a tiny bit of snow and frost fell from the roof, twinkling on its way to the ground.

Feeling free and suddenly bold, I suggested that we too should head home. My home. "Though I usually don't take women home," I told her. OK, *never*.

"Well, I don't usually go home with strange women, so we're about even," Mel said.

I wasn't sure I believed her, but at the moment it didn't really matter to me.

"I always go home with a strange woman," I said. "Sadly, it's me."

Mel laughed and led me from the deck. I grabbed my coat and we left, heading for my place. We were pretty silent in the car, enjoying the lights of Lake Shore Drive on the left and the vast lake on the right.

Nervously, I jiggled the key into the lock of the front door, trying to remember if I'd cleaned at all recently. So much of my routine had fallen by the wayside since the ex had left. One thing I really missed was the cleaning guy.

Mentally, I breathed a sigh of relief at my first glance inside: no dishes on the coffee table and no mail scattered around the house. I guess at some point I'd remembered to at least clear off the top layer of clutter.

"Cute little place you have here," Mel said, looking right at me.

"How would you know?" I asked. "You haven't looked around yet."

"I don't have to see anything but you. And I could go for seeing a lot more of you."

"I think that can be arranged," I grinned.

She pushed me hard against the wall leading to my bedroom, her mouth on mine, our thighs touching.

How did we get from clothed and in the hallway to naked and writhing on my fluffy white comforter? All I remember is lying outstretched on the bed with Mel kneeling between my ankles, tearing her shirt off over her head. Her unveiling revealed the muscle she'd built up; she was solid and compact. Highlighted by her farmer's tan were thin, silvery parallel scars, five or six of them on each of her biceps. No one with even one psych class could mistake those scars for anything but what they were: the marks of a cutter. They made her look all the more dangerous.

I pulled Mel down on top of me. Though she was clearly no stranger to hard work, her skin felt soft and silky over the solid muscle that she'd built up moving furniture and blowing things up. We lay together and kissed for what felt like hours, rolling and exploring and laughing. I was fascinated by the fragile places on her body: her delicate ears usually hidden by her hair, her tiny breasts with their firm nipples that responded to the slightest touch, and the belly she'd probably picked up from too many Friday nights at the bar.

Growing impatient, Mel rolled on top of me and sat up. She

stared at me for a long time, her eyes roaming over me from head to toe. Reverently, she ran her hands over every inch of me, her lips following her hands, pausing at my breasts, the hollows of my collarbones, the curves of my hips, before kissing the inside of my thigh while dipping her strong fingers into the warmth of my pale thighs. Gasping, I realized that one small touch was all it was going to take. I felt my legs tremble, and I don't know if I screamed or said anything because things seemed to slow down and go black for a split second.

When I regained some kind of composure, I looked at her sitting next to me, watching me. Her cheeks were flushed, and her eyes were bright. I reached for her, to pull her back, but she gently stopped me.

I was shocked and a little hurt. "But…"

She laughed. "Sometimes just watching a beautiful woman come underneath me is all I need. Besides, it's almost dawn. How about a small nap?" She curled around me and I fell asleep.

I woke up with Mel's curls tickling my neck and her breath gently warming my back. Remembering some vague notion about her having to work, I woke her up as gently as possible. We were both pretty quiet, not uncomfortable, but still at a bit of a loss.

I took her to breakfast and watched her eat an astonishing amount of food. Guess all those muscles required some intense feeding. After countless cups of strong black coffee, we took off and I dropped her off at her job.

She left me her phone number, and I called once or twice, but I never heard from her again.

It wasn't until later that I learned how little I knew about her. She was in the military, and I think the family stuff was all true—certainly the scar tissue didn't lie—but her falsified military ID said she was a good five or six years older than she was, which meant she was too young to even *be* in the bar. It was true that she was in town for only a few months, but she'd already apparently decided to head back to San Diego to continue blowing things up. And waiting in San Diego, in addition to Uncle Sam, was her longtime girlfriend, whom she'd never broken up with and who probably never found out about Mel's adventures.

Perhaps Mel hightailed it back to San Diego early. Maybe

she just found a new bar for the remainder of her time in the city, but I doubt it. Even in big cities, it's hard for women like us to truly disappear unless we die or suddenly settle down with "the one." It would have been nice to see her again, but I certainly didn't expect anything substantial to come of it. Still, for a short time, someone came around and made me feel beautiful at a time when I really needed it. That doesn't happen often in the midst of a bad breakup. Rushing into something new really wasn't the point anyway; nobody meets "the one" at a bar and lives happily ever after. But sometimes, if they're lucky, they get a great evening.

Three in a Bed

Nicky Donoghue

I had been single for a while, and I was horny as hell. One night I went out dancing with my friends, Cathy and Kelly. We all got pretty drunk, but Kelly was by far the most intoxicated. She had driven us there, so when it was time to leave, I suggested we take a cab. My friends agreed, which surprised me, since Kelly was a major booze hound and it was hard to get her to agree to anything, let alone when she was so loaded.

Cathy and Kelly had been girlfriends for a couple of years, but they always flirted with me when not together. Cathy would make sly comments about my breasts, and Kelly would say things like, "Well, Cathy's out of town, so if you get desperate tonight, come on over." I never knew when either of them was joking.

When the cab came, we piled into the backseat and gave the driver Kelly's address. "You can crash on my couch," she said. "I'll make sure you get home in the morning." My head was spinning a little, so I agreed. I didn't feel like taking the cab all the way back to my place, which was about four miles from where Kelly lived.

It was about a 15-minute cab ride to Kelly's, so we three drunken fools made idle chitchat, talking about the women at the bar and how I'd been single way too long. Kelly and Cathy were groping each other a little, caressing each other's thighs and such, and I was getting turned on watching them. "Like what you see?" Cathy said through a big smile. I just nodded, then Kelly started stroking the inside of my blue-jeaned thigh. If I hadn't been drunk, I probably would have protested, but I'm not sure. These girls were both gorgeous: Cathy a high femme with shoulder-length red hair and Kelly a soft butch with short golden-brown curls. I fell somewhere between the two: an average-looking tomboy with short dark-brown hair and glasses. Kelly shoved her hand up the back of my shirt and caressed my skin. I felt a puddle of wetness between my legs, and I was glad when the cab pulled up to Kelly's apartment.

Kelly paid the driver, and we all tumbled out. When we got inside her place, Kelly and Cathy just grinned at each other. They both grabbed my arms and led me to Kelly's bedroom. "We've been wanting this for a while, Nicky," Cathy purred. "Mmm-hmm," Kelly echoed.

They wasted no time getting my clothes off, pulling my sleeveless tee over my head and unfastening my bra. Kelly helped Cathy out of her little black dress, and Kelly pulled off her own clothes in no time. They hopped onto the mattress with me. There we were: three naked women in a bed, the smell of whiskey and cigarettes surrounding us. Kelly started sucking on one of my tits as Cathy went down on me. She circled my clit with her tongue and probed my hole with two fingers. Kelly bit and nibbled on one of my breasts, groping the other with one of her large hands. I looked up at the ceiling in disbelief as I gripped the sheets beneath me. As Cathy ate me out, Kelly moved up to my mouth and kissed me hard on the lips. She took off my glasses and set them on the nightstand, then ran her tongue down the length of my body. When she got down to my crotch, which Cathy was still going to town on, she lifted Cathy's head gently and kissed her. "I can taste you on Cathy's mouth," Kelly said to me, which made me so hot I thought I would come right there.

Just then, Cathy repositioned herself and put two fingers inside me. She slid them in and out, then added a third. "I can tell you like this," she said. "You're so hot and wet. It's like a waterfall in there." She pulled out her fingers and put them in her mouth, licking off my juices, and then ran her fingers over her full, gorgeous lips. "And you taste so good." She put her fingers back inside me and increased her speed and force. Kelly sat on the bed and watched, groping one of her breasts and furiously rubbing her clit. I didn't know who to look at: Cathy who was fucking me hard and fast or Kelly who was masturbating and looked just beautiful in the lamplight. So I alternated my gaze between the two, getting wetter and more turned on by the second.

"Fuck this," Kelly said, then climbed on top of me, straddling my face as Cathy slid her fingers in and out of me. I felt my pussy clench her fingers, and there was a wonderful, sweet pounding in my clit and cunt. As Cathy fucked me, I ate Kelly out like she was my last meal ever. Her pussy was sopping wet and tasted sweet and tangy. I focused my attention on her hard bud, which I took into my mouth. I licked under the hood and around her clit, then flicked it back and forth with my tongue. I slurped on it as I continued to flick it, then moved down and licked her hole. Kelly gripped the headboard as I tried to jam my tongue in, but I couldn't get it in all the way, so I just licked the perimeter of it, then moved my mouth back up to her clit.

Just as I did this, Cathy went down on me again and licked and sucked me into ecstasy. Kelly and I cried out in pleasure at the same time. She climbed off me, and as a huge orgasm traveled through my body, I watched as Kelly shivered and shook with the effects of her own climax. It was a sweet sight to watch this beautiful soft butch in so much pleasure.

Kelly and Cathy and I went at it for a couple of hours. But toward the end of the night, Kelly seemed to get a little jealous because Cathy was paying me so much attention and practically ignoring her. So after a while, she asked me if she could call a cab to take me home. Cathy protested, though, so we all fell asleep in the bed together, in a drunken haze, smelling like pussy and cigarettes and bourbon.

In the morning, Cathy drove me home, and we spent the afternoon fucking at my place.

We're girlfriends now, and Kelly is in A.A.

Kim Like Bob

Lynne Herr

In South Korea the roads are dragster alleys, the bargoers play smoky macho games, the restaurants reek of fermented cabbage, and the beautiful women are *everywhere*. Almost all are sexy and sleek by nature—even the shy girls, the young girls with their Hello Kitty hairpins and flared legs and perfect bangs. Waiting to marry so they can leave home.

Then there's the Korean dyke. The fringe element, often sacrificing family and sometimes the entire family's honor to meet, smoke, and dance in quiet, dangerous spaces. At least that's how it was five years ago, when I flew into Seoul as an English teacher. Five years ago, when I thought some of my friends were cute but assumed the feelings were isolated incidents...

Jana, a fellow teacher who always wore hats to cover her misguided foray into white-girl dreads, grabbed my hand late one night and tugged me from the American area downtown (drunk soldiers and burger joints) to "the only dyke bar in Korea." She knew I'd been to the Egyptian Room in Portland and even kissed a few drunk girls, talking about how nice they smell, how much I dug drummers...but I didn't know if I was queer enough to be going to the *only dyke bar in Korea*.

"Shush. Do you speak Korean?"

"No. I can only read—"

"No need," she said, the purple threads in her skullcap picking up her nearly purple lipstick. "There're two female symbols out front on this tiny neon sign. I just want you to talk to this one girl for me. She speaks good English, but not enough to get my jokes. My Korean is fucking awful..."

She hailed a cab, gave the driver the cross streets, and sat back with me, talking about her crush. I watched our cabbie pinball through the crowded masses, nearly colliding with three drunk businessmen and a long BMW. The backseat smelled like Soju and old shoes. Sticky brown pleather. Some things are universal.

"Her name's Ming and she's so hot. We danced last time. A waltz or some shit," Jana laughed.

The club sat between a "Coppee House" and a barbecue place where you cook your own meat on grills built into each tabletop, scoop it into lettuce leaves, add a hunk of garlic, some sprouts, red pepper paste, and blanched spinach, then eat. Lettuce, taco style.

"Hungry?" I asked, staring at my curly red hair reflected off the window, my ragged wool sweater and torn leather jacket. No makeup. Sneakers. Not exactly the kind of girl I thought would appeal to the standard impeccably dressed, fashion-conscious Korean lady.

"I'm not hungry. Stop stalling. I know you dig chicks. Let's go," she said, grabbing my hand again.

We walked down a small side alley to a brightly lit back door, where two drag kings greeted us. One eyed Jana up and down as we walked down the hallway to the bar. Jana looked over her shoulder playfully, her butt wiggling more than I'd ever seen. "It's still a little old-school with the butch/femme thing," she whispered.

"So what are you?" I asked, looking at her skirt *and* boots.

"Femme. Femmes get free drinks." She smiled back at the taller king.

At the end of the hallway, we reached a huge windowless room where about 15 women were scattered around, most of them smoking. Hip hop blared from crackling speakers high up on the paneled walls. A heavyset woman with a pompadour and black suit served drinks from behind the cherrywood bar at the far end of the room, k.d. lang posters framed behind her.

"Hello," a gorgeous, bobbed boy-girl to my left called out. She stretched out her hand as if she were the owner.

"Hi. I'm Lynne. This is Jana," I said.

"I know Jana," she said, giving me a friendly look. "Come here," she winked, towing me to the bar for a mai tai, on her.

"That's OK. I got it," I awkwardly mumbled, offering some won.

"No, not *date*. Just friendly only," she smiled.

Jana had already struck up a conversation with some "Westernized" women along the back wall; one knew a friend of hers from New York. "Small world," Jana said—then explained what the saying meant. They laughed, holding their fingertips together in the shape of tiny world globes.

One of the women smiled at me with her head half bowed, but her eyes met mine. She wore a small plastic choker around her neck, black patent go-go boots under a sheer black skirt, and a baby tee. Rings on her thumbs. Fidgeting with the filter of her Marlboro Light.

I thanked my temporary host, then joined Jana.

"This is Kim and Sue. Kim and Sue, this is Lynne."

Korean schoolchildren take English names for class and often keep them when speaking to foreigners as adults. It's easier for foreigners to remember names familiar to them.

Sue also taught English, but in Pusan. Kim, the go-go boot chick, was off to college in Australia next week. She was drinking a red cocktail with yellow cherries and said her favorite movie star was Jodie Foster. "Of course," I laughed.

Kim and I sat down and started talking. She told me about the difficulties of being gay in Korea, how she decided to study international marketing as a way to leave her country but not her people, how she hoped someday to marry a gay man. Maybe even a gay Korean man. These things weighed heavily on her mind because she was, after all, nearly 28 years old.

"I'm too much a girl to live like a man," she told me—gesturing to the woman who'd bought me the mai tai. "She work with men and live like a man. But she left her village and her family."

Some funky Asian dance music blasted on, prompting all the ladies to hit the small dance floor in the far left corner. To me, most Korean dykes looked androgynous; I could only identify the "butch" chicks by whether they drank cocktails or beer, sat with their legs together or apart, laughed quietly or out loud. Kim drank cocktails, sat with her legs apart, and laughed quietly. Two out of three. A versatile girl. What luck.

She held my hand while we danced. Swinging arms and smiling to the electronic drum beats, like a 1950s love story with the wrong soundtrack. Telling me she'd like to kiss me. She had only kissed two other women before, and they were both Australian.

"Oh—so that's why you're moving there."

"No," she giggled.

I leaned in and kissed her. The bartender clapped. When the song ended, she bought us both a shot of tequila. Said we looked sexy.

But sexy or not, it was time to close. The bartender yelled something to everyone as the lights came up.

"She is telling us to be careful. Last month a girl was hit when she left here. A very boyish girl. It can be bad."

"Where do you live?"

"Five kilometers away," she said, watching my mouth with her dark almond eyes.

"How do you get home?"

"I am staying tonight with Sue. Very close. We take a taxi."

"Oh…" I wondered if the underlying sense of duty and shame that pervaded most of South Korea's culture still held on to the foundations of even these fringe rebels. "Um…" I fumbled, not wanting to insult her but knowing she would be gone in a week. I had to make my move.

"Where do you live?" she asked.

"About 15 minutes away by cab."

"By cab…oh, yes. Alone?" she asked, her face flushing as she reached for another cigarette from her black bead handbag.

"I have a roommate, but she's in Japan this weekend."

"Ah…"

I lit her cigarette. The crowd moved out.

Jana tugged my arm. "My girlie Ming wasn't here. Oh, well. We headin' out?"

"Su-u-ure…"

Jana looked back and forth between us. "OK. How about I meet you out front. I'll be the only one outside alone." It's true, you hardly ever see anyone walking alone in Korea.

After Jana left and the 100-watt bulbs showed all the burns and scars on the dull wood floor, Kim kissed me again. A long, deep kiss. The kiss of someone ready to break open.

"Would you like to come home with me?" I finally asked.

"Yes," she whispered, this time keeping her eyes on the ground. Then she grabbed my hand, quickly kissed my knuckles and walked ahead of me up the back stairs into the damp fall air. My stomach flipped.

Jana was both pleased and disappointed I was taking Kim home. "I feel manic, and now I have to go home and talk to my cutouts." She had to leave her cat in the States, so she taped photographs of him on her wall.

We grabbed a cab in no time. Kim translated my address and off we flew. She sat flat against her side of the cab, afraid to touch me. I wondered what she'd say when we starting having sex—what words in what language.

She leaned forward abruptly and told the driver to stop then ran out without looking back. What the hell was that all about? I jumped out and ran after her after dropping too much cash on the front seat.

"Kim?" I called after her, bumping into people, stepping on discarded Coke cans.

I peeked in and around the crowd, following her with my eyes as she slowed to brisk walk and turned down a small alley. I found her leaning against a dirty wall behind a dumpster. Bar goers poured out by the mouth of the alley, oblivious to us. We heard music cut off in the coffee shops and restaurants around us. Cabs honked.

"Kim?"

"I'm sorry. I can't. I want to, but I am afraid…if anything happens, then I would not go to Australia."

"I understand," I told her, standing with my hands in my pockets.

She pulled me in to her. I put my arms around her waist, feeling the black bead bag poking from the back of her skirt. We kissed slowly, timidly at first, each of us listening for footsteps or windows opening above.

Then the kissing intensified, and she drove her tongue into my mouth. I gingerly moved my hands down the hem of her skirt.

"Don't go slow. I want this," she instructed, her eyes shining.

"OK." And I took control, acting like I'd done this a million times. I moved my hand slowly under her skirt, wiggling inside her tights, pulling them down a bit in the front. She gasped.

Her hands moved quickly up the front of my sweater, rubbing my hard nipples through the wool. She sucked on my neck.

"Touch me," she whispered.

I felt her wetness through her underwear as I rubbed her clit up and back. Kim grabbed my shoulder with one arm and ran her hand up my sweater with the other. She groaned quietly. I could feel she was hard enough to come, so I stopped.

I kissed her again, this time moving her hand to undo my zipper. She shoved her hand deep inside my jeans, imitating what I'd done to her. I started jerking her off again with the same beat.

Her hand stopped; she was too distracted by her own feelings to concentrate on me. I reached down and picked up where she'd left off, rubbing her with my right hand and myself with my left. She watched me intently, leaned back against the wall, and spread her legs farther apart.

Touching her while I touched myself felt almost like I was watching myself in a mirror, feeling exactly the way she felt. I imagined coming into her. She mumbled something in Korean, grabbed my nipples hard and pulled me close to her. I stopped, thinking I'd heard someone at the mouth of the alley.

"Go…" she said.

She braced herself against the wall, sucking in shallow, fast breaths with closed eyes. I leaned my forehead against the wall, feeling urgent and hot and dizzy.

I moved my fingers from myself and put them in her mouth. She lapped up the taste of me while I circled her swollen clit until she came, teeth against my fingers. Then I took a step back and jerked myself off with her leaning against the wall, lighting a cigarette, telling me she likes to watch me…

We smoked together on the slowly emptying street corner, waiting for separate cabs. She told me she had a wonderful time. "It was crazy!"

A cab pulled over for me and I hopped in. I told her I'd write a story about the experience someday. Kim asked me to change her name, then she laughed. "Oh, I am like Bob in the United States!"

"You're not like any Bob I've ever known," I said out the window as my speed-racer dragster screeched away.

The Bet

T. Green

"I bet I can get a girl to wave at me before you."

That was what my friend Lou said to me one summer morning as we sat on a bench in the pedestrian mall. Every morning we got up around 8 and met each other to grab doughnuts and coffee downtown. We liked watch women walk by and see who could get the most hellos. It was sort of childish—well, boyish actually. Maybe "baby dyke-ish," if that's a word. Sometimes Lou was a little more perverted than I expected him to be, but I figured he just needed to get laid or jack off more often.

One morning we sat at our usual bench, close to the edge of the ped mall, next to the phone booths. We were talking about the 1970 Honda 350 I had just bought. I needed to take it apart and clean the carburetor and then detail the whole bike. I was really excited to fix it up and ride it for the rest of the season. During our conversation, we kept our eyes peeled for good-looking women. People passing by would've had a hard time understanding our discussion. One second we'd be saying, "Whoa! Check her out! Shit!" Then "The hose clamps…" Not very intellectually stimulating.

That day was so beautiful. There was a slight breeze, like you'd feel on an early fall morning lying in bed with only a sheet covering one leg and maybe a cotton comforter to keep your feet warm. The sun was shining and there wasn't a cloud in the sky. As we sat talking and sipping our coffee, I caught a glimpse of this gorgeous woman. I stopped talking and stared at her. I swear my mouth dropped so far I felt like I had lockjaw. She had long, almost black, shiny hair down to her shoulders. Big brown eyes. She was about 5 foot 5 and not too skinny but definitely not overweight. I smiled at her and waved with my arm close to my side. I don't remember whether I said hi or if I just thought about saying hi. She waved back.

I was in pure shock. Lou said my face was as red as a fire truck. How embarrassing. I wanted to go talk to her, but I was too shy. A "tough" dyke, ha! I was almost peeing in my boxers. I turned to Lou and said, "Shit, did you see that? She waved at me!"

Lou was very reassuring. "Go for it," he said, jabbing me in the ribs with his finger.

But I couldn't get up enough nerve. Lou and I stood up to go back to my house and work on the bike. But first we had to walk past her. We meandered in her direction, where we saw her sitting on the ledge of a flower bed. When we walked by her, I said hi, kind of quiet-like.

With her brown eyes wide open she responded, "Hello."

I almost melted. Her voice was sensual, and I felt I was in a very surreal moment. I had never heard a voice as sexy as hers. Low and unforgiving. For God's sake, all she said was hello! I was a kid again. Giddy and scared. Jesus! I might as well have pretended I was a dog and put my tail between my legs.

The rest of the day I thought about her. I imagined myself having done things differently that morning. I imagined that I just went up to her and grabbed her in my arms and kissed her passionately. We made out in the middle of the ped mall, no worries or concerns of others around us. It was very intense. I'd daydream for a while, then go back to cleaning my motorcycle. I couldn't help spacing out about her. All day I had a silly smirk on my face.

Later that evening I heard a knock at my door. I peeked through the door window and saw her standing on the steps. She knocked on my door again. I took a deep breath and opened the door. "Uh…hi," I said. "What do I… How did you know where I live?"

She smiled and looked down at her hands. She was holding my wallet. "You left this on the bench this morning. I thought you might need it."

I reached out to grab the wallet, but instead I wrapped my hand around hers. It was greasy from working on my bike, but she didn't seem to care. I asked her to come inside, and after she did, I shut the door and turned around to say something, but before I knew it our bodies were slammed together. As we touched each other, fast and vigorous, our hearts were beating as though we were on cocaine. Our tongues intertwined. We stopped. So suddenly. The look in her eyes pierced into mine. Staring deep into my eyes, she moved a step closer. I stepped back and ended up trapped in the corner of my living room, trapped with a gorgeous woman. She leaned in and kissed me gently on the lips. I felt my face grow warmer; I knew it was beet-red.

I couldn't breathe. I wanted her bad and she knew it. Yet she decided to make me suffer and wait. She placed her hands on my belt; her fingers moved millimeter by millimeter and eventually unbuckled my belt. She pulled the belt out of the loops, then looked up at me. I tried to kiss her, but she moved her head back too fast. She slipped a sassy little smirk onto her face and looked down at my pants again to assess her fancywork. She unbuttoned the top button of my Levi's and then the next one. I was getting into her groove when she ripped the rest of my fly open as if it were a Band-Aid on a hairy arm.

I grabbed her and we kissed wildly, on the lips, neck, and shoulders. I reached to caress her breasts while at the same time trying to get her shirt and bra off. She lifted her arms, and I quickly pulled her shirt up over her head. She grabbed my shirt and flung it across the room. We held each other tight, feeling our breasts touching. Sweaty, hot, pulsating vibes ran through our bodies. We felt the need to feel every crease, every curve, and every muscle on our bodies. Somehow we ended up in the bedroom.

She pushed me and I fell onto the bed. She put her leg between mine and leaned down toward my stomach. She kissed it, moving around to my ribs and back to my lower belly. Then she put her hands on my breasts and her mouth onto one of them. She cradled them in her hands and sucked fiercely. I was in sheer ecstasy.

I wrapped my arms around her back and rubbed her all over and down to her pants. I opened up a space so as to let my hand move freely around inside. I grabbed her ass and squeezed it. We couldn't stop; we were going crazy. I flipped her over to her back and placed my leg between hers and then laid my hip upon her crotch. Back and forth we ground into each other. She put her hands on my hips and pulled my jeans down until they hit my knees. I took my boots off, using only my feet as a guide, because I didn't want to stop kissing her and my hands were too busy unbuttoning her pants.

Finally I got my boots off and then slipped out of my jeans. I leaned down and unzipped her pants with my teeth. I rubbed my face and nose into her lower belly. With my teeth I grabbed her underwear and pulled them down, just a little. At the same time I pulled her jeans off. I threw them across the room but decided to take my time with her underwear. I wanted to eat her out really bad, but I thought I should wait a while before I did— just to get her even more excited.

I was taken by surprise when she took her foot and pushed me in the stomach and I fell onto my back. She jumped on top of me, and once again we started grabbing and kissing each other all over. We were sweating so much that we slid across each other like two sticks of warm butter.

She reached down and put her hand on my crotch. "You're really wet," she said. I put my hand down and touched her hand at the same time and felt to see how wet I really was. She guided my finger across my clit. I was so horny. "Fuck me. Please. Fuck me!" I told her.

She smiled and kissed me. I turned my hand around and put my fingers inside her. She was smooth and creamy. We fucked each other harder, back and forth, breathing heavier and heavier. Sometimes it felt, the way she had her hand on me, like she had a dick. In fact, it was sort of a turn-on for me to think she had one. She stopped and kissed my breasts. I knew she was going to eat me out when she moved slowly down my chest. She sat up and moved her hair out of her face. We looked at each other. Leaning down, she put her fingers on my crotch and separated my lips to get a better view of my clit. Then she put her mouth on my crotch and ran her tongue up from my hole to my clit.

"Oh! Like that, yeah…" I said as I put my arms above my head and closed my eyes; I wanted to feel everything she did to me. Every once in a while I'd open my eyes and watch her. I felt her suck my clit and slowly put her fingers inside me. She added another and another, moving back and forth while sucking my clit. I moved around so much she had to hold me down. I wanted her to fuck me harder, so I urged her on "Fuck me!" I yelled. "Come on…fuck me harder!"

She complied and moved her hand as fast as she could. I was in such bliss. I ended up moving back so far on the bed that my head draped over the edge, almost to the floor. I didn't care, though—I just wanted to feel her inside me. I couldn't see, I couldn't breathe. But I could hear her trying to breathe inside me; her breath was heavy and tired. I was almost there. "Fuck me-e-e!" I screamed. My legs clamped together. I had her head smashed between my thighs. I flipped her off me. I couldn't help it—I wasn't in control of my body. She got loose and watched me flop around on the bed, moaning in enjoyment. I finally stopped to catch my breath.

Her mouth was red. We were drenched with sweat and come. I reached my arms up to her, and she came over beside me and laid her head on my chest. I grabbed a couple of cigarettes and lit them. We just lay there and enjoyed the cool breeze that came from my window.

I never did learn her name. I wasn't sure how to ask her since we did just fuck. *Oh, well,* I thought, and I decided she would tell me when she was ready.

A Bottle of Moscato Allegro

Emily Beller

Billy arrived modishly late as usual, but to make up for it, he brought the wine bottle that started it all that evening—the divine, naughty bottle of Moscato Allegro. My lover, Christa, and I were at dinner on a Friday night with our married friends. There were five of us, all told; the two couples and our dashing unattached wine-bearer, Billy.

"I brought a libation, cookie," he announced to no one in particular when he whirled in the door, air kissing everyone and showing off his shiny new black Kenneth Cole shoes. Billy does have a flair for both fashion and the dramatic. He's what you might call a flyboy's gay man: fluffy and insubstantial when the time calls for it but soulful in a Zen meditation way when you're questioning the meaning of everything. He also has impeccable taste when it comes to the good things in life, and that 15-year-old bottle of Moscato Allegro was definitely a sure sign of his style. Mine and Christa's too, as it would turn out—our style in bed, that is.

The second Billy pulled out that bottle, our hostess, Marianne, who had just sat down to her plate (Billy was late by almost an hour, so naturally we'd finally served up and dug in), made a suggestive sound and said, "Wow. What a great shape that bottle has." Her husband widened his eyes and sort of flapped his lips at her in surprise. So naturally, we all stared at the bottle. Turns out she was right. Have you ever seen Moscato Allegro? The bottle is elegant and long, slender from rim to base without that sudden curve inward as it rises to the top like most bottles have, and pearled, giving it the appearance of a swanlike model swathed in some gauzy, see-through wrap. When it's breathing, getting ready to be poured down thirsty gullets, little water droplets shimmer delicately all over it.

"I meant," Marianne said, rolling her eyes at her husband, "flowers would fit beautifully in there. Sunflowers, maybe." Marianne has little sense of humor.

But my Christa, though, is full of humor. My lover leaned over to me, rubbed her bare foot along my leg, and murmured, "I know where that would fit."

I just about choked on a bite of salmon.

"Up your hot, dripping wet cunt," she said even closer to my ear, although the others were laughing at some joke Rob, Marianne's husband, was telling and couldn't possibly hear her. Even so, I coughed and instantly got a hot flash that raced down my spine and landed somewhere in the vicinity of the part of my anatomy she was describing in such crude terms.

Suffice it to say that dinner was delicious, the wine was smooth perfection, the company sparkled, and Christa and I got out of there as soon as we decently could—with my girl toting home, like some sort of prize, the empty bottle of Moscato Allegro. She managed to take it surreptitiously, but I still wonder who might have noticed that the bottle disappeared with us. Maybe I was dreaming, but I could have sworn Billy winked at me when we left, and I think Marianne looked almost wistful.

Since we live just down the block from Marianne and Rob, we had walked. On the way back, we shivered in the chilly early March air and looked up at the stars that were rolled across the sky like a kid's shiny marbles scattered over the blacktop of a school playground. Christa walked right next to me, one arm slung over my shoulders (it has always been my bane that I am so much shorter than she is, but I think she likes being the tall, butchy half of our equation), bottle clutched firmly in her other hand, hip bumping mine in an unmistakable signal. I know when my girl is horny—not like I couldn't tell, what with all that bottle stuff. I was still a little shivery between my legs from her earlier remark.

"So," she said, "where do you think this bottle will fit?"

"Am I going to find out?" I asked in the most flirtatious tone I had.

"Mmm-hmm," she said in this sort of growly voice, which I felt from my eyeballs to my toes. I walked faster, and she laughed.

When we got home, I expected at least a moment's breather. Hit the bathroom, brush the teeth, all that pre-nooky stuff I usually get to do. Nothin' doing. The second I tried to step into the bathroom, which is off our bedroom, Christa grabbed me from behind and threw me onto the bed, landing on top of me with her enjoyably strong body. There are definitely times I like the fact that she can sort of control me with her size.

"Hey—" was all I managed to get out before she laid a finger across my lips.

"Let me do the talking, darling," she whispered, and I shut up fast, more because her fingers were busy with the fly on my jeans than because of her order.

My jeans were kicked off the bed, but she left everything else on, since it was cold in the bedroom (our house is badly insulated) and she didn't want me to get distracted. About two seconds after my jeans were off, my underwear followed, and then I felt my lover's tongue brushing the insides of my thighs.

"Christa—" I managed to gasp, but she immediately stopped what she was doing and muttered in a low voice, "Didn't I tell you to be quiet?"

Normally I would have argued with her and pointed out that she'd merely said that she would be talking. However, as her tongue went right back to my thighs, licking over them in great wet strokes and making me tremble and jump from the sensations, I stayed quiet. This was getting right to the point right away, and I decided to enjoy it.

Christa's tongue traveled slow circles around my thighs, first one, then the other, as if she were a cat. The methodical licks made my blood sizzle in my veins. Ever since I had fallen in love with this woman two years before, she had been able to send tingles along my skin and shivers up and down my spine when she touched me like she was touching me now. When her tongue swirled closer and closer to that hot, dripping wet cunt of mine, I thrust my hips into the air and moaned. She paused long enough to mutter roughly, "You like that, huh, bitch?" before getting back to work.

I have to admit that no one had ever called me "bitch" before Christa—at least not in a way that I liked. But every time my lover says that, I feel myself just open wider, feel the juices start to flow from deep inside and come out my aching hole, trickle down my thighs, which tremble and clench, just like they did at that moment.

Abruptly, her tongue found its way to my curly hairs, burrowed in among them, and dove into my deliciously full, pulsating cunt. Like a soft little torpedo her tongue flicked in and out, every now and then curling up to touch my clit with a quick lightning strike that left me wanting more.

"That's it," she said encouragingly, and I realized I was moaning and grunting as I heaved my hips upward to meet her. Then her mouth descended on me again, lips, tongue, hot breath all working together to lick my engorged labia and encircle my sex and make me feel light-headed, as if I were spinning around in a zone of pure bliss. My head felt full of static, as if it might blow off from the increasing pressure and pleasure.

Then her fingers started to go in. First one, gently, then more vigorously, from side to side, as if trying to expand me. Then two, rolling and rubbing a delightful tango deep inside me. Then three, then four. I felt filled and huge, and I still wanted more inside.

But then, just when I was at my wettest, plumpest, and readiest, my lover stopped and drew away.

"No!" I protested, forgetting the edict against talking. Christa stretched herself over my body and kissed me to silence my cry. I could taste myself on her, all over her mouth and face. It was creamy and a bit tart and very desirable. She kissed me good and long to make sure I got every drop before pulling back.

"Don't move," she commanded, and she slipped off the bed, reached down to grab something from the floor, and, keeping the object hidden from view, went into to bathroom. I lay in an interrupted agony on the bed. All my nerves were screamingly alive. I was trembling from head to foot, desire gripping me. What the hell was she doing at a time like this?

I heard water run for a while and an odd clanking sound. All of sudden, it dawned on me, and I practically came on the spot.

The bottle. My Christa was warming up the bottle of Moscato Allegro for me. Just for me and my aching, greedy little cunt.

"Here we go, sweetheart," she said as she turned around and came back into the bedroom. "All for you and that nice, wet cunt, which is just big enough for this to fit into," she crooned, holding up the bottle for me to see with wide eyes.

I opened my legs as wide as possible and lifted my hips from the bed. For good measure I reached down with my hands and spread apart my lips, which were still plumped out and wet from her earlier ministrations. Christa's mouth curved up into a wicked smile as I did that, which made me whimper with impatience.

"Oh, yes," she said. "That's right, bitch. Show me how much you want it," and she came forward with that bottle. It was gleaming a bit, with water sparkling along its sides. I wondered how much of it would fit inside me. When Christa reached the bed, she slipped her free hand under me and slapped my upraised ass, which drew a sound from me that was undeniably wanton. "Good," she said, more softly. "Very good."

Very carefully this time, my lover lowered herself next to me. Gently, for someone who had just been calling me bitch and smacking my ass, she rubbed the bottle next to my skin, the fingers of her other hand playing with my nipples, tweaking first one, then the other, and rolling them around. The bottle was warm and slippery from the water. Slowly she stroked it back and forth against my thigh before running it over my hipbone. Then she nuzzled the mouth of the bottle up against the slick curls sheltering my needy cunt. A shivering sensation started deep inside me and worked its way out. It felt like a thousand tiny fingers were fluttering against the lips of my sex, tingling and arousing me even more, if that was possible.

"Yes, girl," she crooned again, and I realized I was grunting and moaning, louder this time. "This is all for you."

"Now?" I couldn't help begging, looking at Christa hovering over me, teasing that bottle against my thickened folds of flesh. I thought I might go crazy if she didn't thrust it inside me soon.

"Since you asked so nicely," she said nonchalantly, and abruptly pushed the bottle into me. Hard and warm and so smooth, it pressed its way in, insistent and unimaginably filling. I felt the little ridge around the mouth tenderly slide in, and then the long neck, and then the flare where the bottle widened. Then Christa pulled it out again, almost all the way, and I yelped in frustration. She laughed and pushed it in again, deeper this time. Then out, so slowly it was like an excruciating yet exquisite torture. In, out, in that classic rhythm. Christa knew full well that I needed clitoral stimulation too in order to come, and she was deliberately withholding. I was beginning to feel more than frustrated; an urgency gripped every inch of inflamed skin and accompanied every exhilarating drive of the bottle.

"Now, Christa," I demanded in a rough tone. "Now!"

"You're not being very nice," she tut-tutted, and stopped all motion of the bottle for an unbearable few seconds. "You should ask more properly," she whispered in a dangerous voice.

"Please!" Every muscle in my body was tense, anticipating. "Please—fuck—me," I said between gritted teeth. "The way I like it."

"Now, that's more like it," my lover said in satisfaction.

Instantly, the bottle was moving again, penetrating deeper and deeper each time, it seemed. And then—oh, delightful bliss—Christa's mouth descended on my soaking wet folds, found my clit, and went to town. Her tongue swirled over my flesh, teasing out of it the sensations I had been longing for. I began a ragged, nonsensical chant in time with her licking and the bottle's thrusting and the movement of my own hips rising to meet everything. Then Christa began sucking my clit and making wet slurping noises, and it started to drive me over the edge. First it was slow, but I felt it building like a huge summer thunderhead in the sky gaining momentum and volume and darkness until you just know the rain is about to come pouring out with a booming clap of sound in a glorious drenching rush.

"Uh-huh," I vaguely heard Christa say between my legs, but it was mostly lost in the surging motion of the bottle and the frenzied circles she made with her tongue over my clit and swollen lips. And then, suddenly, I was teetering right on the brink. And even though I always come from my clit, the deep plunges of the bottle were going to make me explode right then, with each powerful charge lifting me higher and making me more acutely aware of each sizzling nerve ending in my body, all spiraled down to that one point deep between my legs, inside me, a core that was utter pleasure.

"Chris-ta!" I exclaimed when I was suddenly and unceremoniously pushed right over that edge, and I thundered loudly all right, yelling and shrieking and moaning as the wave gripped me and throbbed and pulsed for what seemed like endless, breathtaking moments. My head was filled with light and my hips were uncontrollably lifted into the air and my hands were clutching the sheets on the bed. Christa's tongue stayed right on me, sucking out every last delicious bit of my orgasm until it got to be too much and I begged her, finally, to stop.

We lay in a heap on the bed, tangled together. My breathing filled the room, hitching once when Christa carefully removed the bottle from my grasping interior. It slid out with a very quiet little pop—"Like a cork," my lover murmured into my ear. She dropped the bottle onto the rug beside the bed and curled herself around me.

"So. Was it good?" she asked. I could tell she was smiling.

"Mmm-hmm," I said sleepily.

"Think the others were jealous?"

"Hmm?" I asked, confused, already drifting off into sleep.

"Billy. And that Marianne. She was definitely jealous. Knowing you got to sample the Moscato Allegro tonight," she said playfully, nuzzling me under my chin. "Very special reserve. Only for sweet little bitches like yourself."

"Mmm-hmm," I answered, and the last thing I heard before falling asleep was Christa saying, "Bet I know a fun way to wake you up later."

Late Edition

Danni Kellerman

"Hello, this is Claire," I say into my headset. "How can I help you?"

I notice they waver on the other end of the line. Something in my voice gives them pause. I know what it is too. It's sex. It's how I feel today. Don't you ever feel like that? Like you could take the world's greatest lover, flip her on her back, and surprise the heck out of her? Some days I wake up with sex weighing so heavily on my mind, I feel like I'm wearing a neon sign and it's flashing, "Now. Now. Now." And, of course, being single, there is no relief. Just me and Melissa, and every time she screams for someone to bring her some water, I silently nod an amen.

So it stands to reason that the unsuspecting folks who happen to catch me on the line while calling in for their newspapers get, let's just say, a bit more than they bargained for.

Sometimes it's fun. Sometimes you get a very cool woman on the phone and you forget what she called for and you talk and talk and talk, about life, about circumstances, about regrets. And I want to forget that I'm here to do a job, that this is how I make my living—uh, until the "big break" hits, that is—and that the landlord expects his monthly meal ticket and the two fuzzy, four-legged things that hog the bed at night also need to eat, as do I. It's just me and the voice across the telephone lines. And she needs something from me, which is always nice. Always good to be in a position of power that way.

I document all the vitals: name, age, address, members of the household. Amazing what people will tell a perfect stranger over the phone. And I keep thinking how each sentence can easily be transposed with another, equally significant one: What is your full name—what is your pleasure? Are you the head of the household—will your husband, boyfriend, lover be home tonight? Or do you spend your nights pining for another like I do? Where would you like me to ship this—will you tell me where to touch you so I can drive you insane quicker, or must I negotiate the uncharted terrain of your body and find my own path to the river?

"Did you hear what I said?" You break through my longings.

"No, I'm sorry. What was that?"

"I said I've called and complained to your customer service department several times already. I have been trying to get home delivery for some time now."

"Well, I—*we*—would be only too happy to oblige." I snicker silently at my own double entendre.

"I was hoping you'd say that. Will you be bringing the paper by personally?"

"Personally? Uh…well, uh, we have a service for that, actually.." I retreat into cowardice.

"Now that's what I'm talking about: service. Businesses nowadays forget what that word really means. Used to be people took pride in their work. Personal attention to detail was a mainstay, not an added bonus. Now, if you were to deliver this personally, say, around 7, I would have a whole new image of your periodical."

I look up at my supervisor, who happens to be monitoring my call. He nods menacingly in agreement, to my outward annoyance and secret angst.

"I'll have to check with my manager. This isn't actually our policy," I say, my eyes never leaving his. He nods furiously at me, but I pretend not to notice.

"You do that," she says, "I'll hold." I have a sistah on the line, but old Douglas Brown, with his pocket protector and the hair, or what's left of it, slicked back on his nearly bald head, can never know this. He can never know about me, not because I'm ashamed, but because I refuse to feed into his sleazy little fantasy life, which is where, I'm certain, my life story would end up if he ever got wind. His little amoeba brain could never wrap itself around the thought of two women together. So I play the game and talk to him in his language. Into the phone I grumble a raspy "Hold, please" and turn my attention fully to Brown. I push just enough buttons to make him feel he's still the boss and able to control me, an ability he's never had, while this power gives me more freedom than I could ever steal.

"Now, Douglas, I was not hired for this. I'm strictly a phone operator. This house call business is above and beyond the call of duty."

"Nothing is above and beyond the call of duty here."

Really? I'm glad you see it that way, I think and make a mental note to memorize that line verbatim to be used at a later date.

"If this client wants home delivery today, we'll give her home delivery today. You do this one now and we'll set her up with a regular carrier tomorrow."

"And what do I get?" I hammer away at him enjoying seeing him squirm.

"You? You get to get out of the office for an hour and 'our thanks.'"

An hour? This will never do. I click the phone off mute and ask a question to which I already know the answer, just to make my point.

"What was the address again?"

"7135 Maple."

"Hold please," I click the mute button again. "It's at least an hour one way, Douglas. And with traffic…" my voice trails off. "Better allow for three, just in case."

"Three?" he's sputtering. I can see the missed calls and missed sales racking up in large numbers before his eyes.

"Or you can have John do it. I'm sure we can get her on his route by, say, early next week?"

"Think she'll wait that long?" he asks hopefully.

"To be honest, I doubt it," I tell him. "She's pretty peeved. She's been paying for the last three months and we've not gotten the deliveries there on time once, and sometimes not at all. I think it's now or…"

"Or?"

"Or we lose her to *USA Today,*" I say getting irritated.

"Screw them *and* their 10-cent maps made at goddamned Kinko's."

I knew that'd get him. Old Brown's archenemy is his perceived direct competition through one of the leading newspapers in the country. The only reason he perceives this competition is because he tries to copy their every page down to their "10-cent maps" that he tries to make himself—which brings me to his second archenemy: Kinko's, which customarily refuses to photocopy, mimic, or in any way reproduce copyrighted material. Which is why our paper is floundering and presently in need of phone sales operators. This is where I step in.

"Ms. Hall?" I say determinedly.

"Mmm?"

"I'm on my way."

She hangs up without a word. I make a big show of being annoyed, logging out with great cursing motions. Secretly, my heart is beginning to race. I wonder what she looks like. What she smells like. Will she let me hand-deliver it into her Beverly Hills home, or will I have Jeeves to contend with? Will she let me come inside and meet her face-to-face? And know her. Will she let me...?

The drive from downtown L.A. to Beverly Hills is a nice one this time of day. I consider taking the side roads to enjoy the warm spring evening, but decide I'm in too much of a hurry. Entering the 101 freeway I suddenly become Mario Andretti, downshifting from fourth to first, stopping on a dime, hanging precariously between the gears until I see an opening and then going from first back to fourth gear in 0.3 seconds. I hate L.A. traffic and love it all at once. On the radio, Whitney is belting out "I Will Always Love You" set to a newly remastered techno beat. I see my exit and dart for it, cutting over three lanes of traffic and pissing off more than one already-annoyed driver. They say road rage is on the rise. My contribution to it today is a necessary evil: I have a mission.

Ten hours later it seems, with the starts and stops of street traffic, I pull up in front of 7135 Maple. A magnificent site, to be sure. A Mediterranean-style home, complete with circular drive, what my real estate friend would call a "sexy house." The entrance is gated, and I have to pull up and buzz in. I wonder tentatively if I should just leave the paper by the gate, but my curiosity gets the better of me. I ring up.

"Yes?" a familiar timbre greets me.

"Ms. Hall? It's Claire. With your newspaper? Shall I leave it by the gate here?" Long pause. For a second I wonder if she heard me. I look up toward the house for some clue and notice that fewer lights are on than before, or is my imagination playing tricks on me again? This is ridiculous. I'm like some testosterone-filled schoolboy hanging around the playground hoping for the popular girl to grace me with a glance. I'm too old to play this game, even at my ripe ol' 25. I pick up the paper and hang it out the window of my car. Slowly I let it slide out of my hand, giving her every last chance to respond.

"Come around the back," the voice suddenly appears again. And with that, the gates swing open slowly. Great. I lunge out the window after the damned thing, but too late, the paper lands in a small puddle that formed from the rain we've had for the last two days. I swing open the car door and pick it up, shaking off the excess water. Just great. I had one simple thing to do and I blew it.

The gates begin to close again. I shift into second just in time to make it through before they shut me out for good, all the while wiping the moisture from the paper on my car seats and passenger carpet. No use. The paper's dimpled and wavy but hopefully still readable. The front page is all excerpts any-way, I console myself.

Stepping out of the car I edge slowly around the back of the estate. This side, while still magnificent, with a flowing garden and gazebo, is less formal and so less ominous. Never say we don't bend over backward for our readers. This little stint proves beyond the shadow of a doubt that we'd stoop to any depths to steal away subscribers—or keep our paltry existing ones.

I walk up to the back door and raise my hand to knock when I notice it's slightly ajar. Hm. I push it open tentatively. Inside, a walkway illuminated by candles stretches out before me.

"Ms. Hall?" I call uncertainly.

The flickering light gives off hardly enough power to help me grasp my surroundings. Vaguely I'm aware that I'm in a kitchen. My hand touches cool tiles of the wall, and I'm grateful for their chilly reception. As I pass through the doorway into the next room, I allow my hand to trail along the walls for balance. My forehead is beginning to feel as damp as the paper I'm holding. My outstretched hand comes to rest upon a smooth surface. I trace the outline of the object and notice that it's a stack of newspapers, as tall as my chest. This is curious. The stack is neat, untouched, perfect. As if someone is collecting it for posterity and not for reading pleasure. I stoop and bring up one of the candle lanterns on the floor to get a better look at the stack. It's a copy of the paper I work for, the same one I'm holding in my hand. Except this one is perfect, not waterlogged like mine. The name on it reads "Loren Scharf." *Why does that name sound so familiar?* I wonder.

"I don't understand. What was the point?" I mutter to myself.

"The point was," the voice from the dark startles me, and I struggle to save the candle from falling and creating a reprisal of *Gone With the Wind*. Finally steadying the damned thing, I allow my eyes to search in the direction of the voice.

She stands illuminated by the candlelight. Her tall frame is oddly familiar. Dark locks etching her face bring out the best of her finely chiseled features. She walks slowly toward me and I am reminded of my favorite Byron poem: "She walks in Beauty, like the night / Of cloudless climes and starry skies / And all that's best of dark and bright / Meet in her aspect and her eyes...." I stand dumbfounded, forgetting my mission all together.

"The point," she says again, smiling kindly, "was to get you here."

"Me?"

"Yes."

"Do I know you?" I scour my memory banks.

"Don't you know me?" Ms. Hall. No, Ms. Scharf, I keep chanting in my head. Ms. Loren Scharf. Why does that sound so familiar? And then it hits me. A memo sent around sometime last year about the buyout. Scharf Enterprises...foreign conglomerate... It's coming back to me, slowly. I was a fresh recruit at the time, so it didn't really affect me or my day-to-day. I still had Douglas Brown to contend with.

Loren walks gingerly toward me, her dark eyes huge pools in the light. "I'm glad you came, Claire." She raises her hand and traces an invisible line down the center of me from the tip of my head to the tip of my nose, taking extra care down the middle of my lips, to my neck, to my sternum, to my navel, and she comes to rest her hands on the waist of my jeans.

"I've been watching you for a year. You're an excellent worker. You've saved more than three dozen accounts in the past quarter, and for that we're grateful. I believe you're in line for a promotion."

"A promotion?"

"Yes. Douglas Brown has become…obsolete." "We need fresh blood. We need someone who is hungry, and I believe that you fit the bill."

"Replace old Brown?" I could have told her he was obsolete a year ago, but my mind is still having trouble grasping all this information at once.

"Thank you for the vote of confidence," I say and begin to relax a little.

"Not so fast. You haven't got the job yet. I think you're quite good at what you do. Yes. But you haven't proven yourself sufficiently. It takes more than the mechanics of sales to be a manager."

"Oh," I stammer. She paces in front of me like a lion in too small a cage.

"Oh, yes. The ideal candidate possesses, tact, adheres to strict protocol, and…"

"And?"

"And, most important, the ideal candidate interacts well with executives."

"Well, I—" I start defensively ready to enumerate my strong points, but she dismisses all that with a wave of her hand.

"Now, my partners aren't as sold on you. There have been several names bandied about for this position." She runs a tentative finger over the first button of my fly and stares deep enough into my eyes to make the hairs on the back of my neck stand at attention. "Convince me I'm not wrong."

Like an automaton reacting to a verbal command, I take a step forward hypnotically and crush her finely manicured naked toes with my motorcycle boots. She recoils in pain.

"What a clod," I rasp, angry for a break in the mood. "I'm sorry."

"No, you know what," she says recovering. "Maybe this was all a mistake."

"No!" I growl. Enough cowering. I won't be dismissed so easily. "Fuck the job. I don't care about it."

"Then why are you here?" she says hotly. I step forward carefully, and she steps back, hiding her feet. I raise my hands in surrender.

"Must you ask?" I say. With hands still held high I kneel before her. Her cunt is inches away from my face. Her eyes sparkle with anticipation though she tries to give away nothing. Slowly I lower my hands to her tight hips. The silk peignoir covering them feels cool to my touch. I trace her long legs and aerobicized thighs to her ankles and small feet. My hands slide under the silk hem and she leans her crotch into me as I bury my head in her center. I'd give anything to be a cubist Picasso right now, replacing my fingers with my tongue as it slides up the length of her exposed limbs. I reach her taut buttocks and slip my fingers into their warmth.

On my knees I edge forward and spread her legs farther. She can't clasp them together now with my figure supplanted between them.

She strokes my hair and rocks me gently. My fingers slide along the baby fine skin separating her anus from her cunt. She moans with suffused pleasure and tangles her fingers painfully in my curls. I begin to slide in her wetness. The rocking has created one entity out of us two. One entity, one mind, one desire.

Someone moans softly, though I'm not sure who. My voice in her throat, my fingers in her cunt spreading her wider, tracing ever-tightening circles around her clit. Her nails dig painfully into my shoulders, as I know she wants me to do from below, but I tease. I know what this one needs, and she needs it desperately.

This one who is always in control—and always tired of it. A lass like this needs that control stripped from her, to be cut down to size, humiliated a little—just so she can breath a sigh of relief, if only for a moment. I place one hand on each of her nether lips. She bucks, but my shoulders between her legs won't let her go.

Through sheer will I hold my position, nearly lifting her off the ground. She steadies herself on my form in this delicate ballet we're performing. With rough hands I pull her open, slowly, painfully, so she can't pretend this isn't happening, allowing the cool air in the room to stroke her gently. She squirms, the thin, fragile muscles of her lips willing to close around their riches but desperately unable.

"Stop," she begs me.

"When I'm damn well good and ready," I say, and pull her more open still. She begins to buck harder, trying to impale herself on thin air, trying desperately to close the distance between my mouth and her flesh.

"Please," she groans. "Please," she whispers.

I smile secretly to myself. Who says I'm not management material? I'm the ultimate negotiator; with the lightest touch I having them eating out of my hands.

"All right, darlin'. If you insist," I say, and bury my mouth deeply within her folds. I drink her pungent sweetness, swallowing deeply as she orgasms over and over into my mouth. As her spasms begin to subside I slide my tongue back up to her clit to tease her further, then commence drinking, like a nomad rescued from the brink of dehydration, until I drink her dry.

She totters on wobbly legs. I give her clit one last hard, teasing stroke and am smacked on the top of the head for it. I disentangle myself from her peignoir and stand facing her. Her eyes open slowly and immediately zero in on my wet lips. I swipe the lingering moisture off my face, then suck the remnants off my finger with a loud smack. She raises her hand to slap my face, but I catch her in mid stroke and wiggle an index finger at her.

"Now, what kind of way is that to treat your new floor manager?" I smirk, needling her a little.

"Honey, with moves like that, I'm recommending you for V.P."

I chuckle and pick up the newspaper I'd brought. I wad it up in a tight roll and smack her lightly on the ass.

"Same time next week?" she says.

"Yeah, but next time I get to play boss lady," I say, and toss the paper in the trash on my way out the door.

Poor ol' Douglas Brown. You'd think he'd catch a clue; Wednesday lunch hours are getting longer and longer.

Hitting the Showers

Anna Avila

I had just moved to San Francisco two weeks before, but I had already joined a gym—a women's gym, in fact. "Those all-girl gyms are crawling with hot babes," my friend Becky had advised me. I had left Chicago after a bad breakup; I wanted to start fresh, and even though my heart was still a little tender, I was ready to find someone new, someone who wouldn't be so obsessed with settling down. Someone who wouldn't want to just snuggle all the time and not get down and dirty. Someone who wouldn't call me at work 10 times a day or wonder where I was every second—which was exactly the kind of person my ex Rachel was.

So there I was on the treadmill, just minding my own business, jogging along to the Bronski Beat tune on my Walkman (it was 1987, after all), when I caught the eye of the most delicious butch woman I'd ever laid eyes on. She was around my age (mid 20s) with closely cropped brown hair, pale skin, and sparkling green eyes. She had a swimmer's body, lithe but muscular, and was wearing a men's tank undershirt (what they call a "wife beater" these days) and baggy boxers. A snake tattoo wrapped around her tight biceps.

I swear to God I couldn't take my eyes off her, which I guess she picked up on, since she ended her bout with the free weights and ambled over in my direction. "I'm Chris," she said, extending her hand.

I took my headphones off but still kept my pace on the treadmill. I couldn't believe she was being so bold. Back then I would never have had the guts just to walk right up to a woman like that and introduce myself. Still, I went along with it—she was totally hot! "Hi, I'm Anna," I said, and her handshake was firm, her palm warm.

"You're new here, aren't you?" She smiled as she said this.

"Yeah, I just joined two weeks ago. I'm from Chicago."

"No kidding!" she grinned. "I'm from Milwaukee. Another Midwesterner."

Chris told me that she'd lived in San Francisco just about a year, that she was enrolled in the MA program, studying history, at San Francisco State. I told her I was a graphic designer, but I didn't go into the whole breakup discussion, and I didn't tell her I hadn't found a job yet. What was the point? We learned too that we only lived about a mile from each other—but I neglected to mention that I was living with my friend Becky until I found a place of my own. Again, what was the point?

"Since you're new in town and all," Chris smiled, "would you like a tour guide? Or at least a date?" Wow. I'd only gone to this gym four or five times and already I was hooking up. I realized I should take Becky's advice more often.

"Yeah, a date," I grinned. "A date would be nice."

We decided on dinner that Saturday night and exchanged numbers.

Chris went back to her free weights, but I decided I'd had enough of the treadmill for the day, so I went to the locker room to hit the showers. I was at my locker when I looked up and saw Chris standing right beside me smiling. "Hey, done already?" I asked her.

"Well, see, that's the thing," Chris began. "I thought maybe you'd like to get to know me a little better a little sooner." She didn't need to explain what she meant. Still, I was stunned—and turned on—by her bold, cavalier approach.

"You mean, right here?" My eyes grew wide.

"I know where we can get a little privacy." She pointed toward the shower stalls. The expression on her face was nearly lascivious.

I crammed my stuff in my locker and locked the door. Chris led me to one of the showers, and we both entered and drew the plastic curtain closed. Thankfully, the locker room was fairly empty, so I don't think anyone saw us go in together.

Immediately, Chris peeled off my sweaty tank top and sports bra. She swooped in on one of my nipples, which was hard and begging for her hot mouth. Without any words, she worked that nipple good and hard, taking into her wet mouth and feasting on it, licking it all over, making little slurping noises. Just then she pulled back and grabbed both of my breasts in her hands, kneading them like bread dough. She gazed straight into my eyes, and the look on her face was like that of an artist concentrating on her work, admiring its beauty and form. She continued to caress and massage my breasts as she leaned in and kissed me hard on the mouth. She was fully of urgency, of lustful need, and I was obliging her with no qualms. "You're so fucking hot," she said between kisses. "So fucking hot."

Her tongue was forceful and wanting, and I opened my mouth even wider to let it in. She ran it over my lips, my tongue, bit my lower lip playfully.

I helped her out of her wife beater, then grabbed both of her small, firm breasts in my hands. (She wasn't wearing a bra.) Her nipples were dark brown and very hard and erect. I pinched one of them, teased it with my fingers, and she cried out softly before I licked and sucked it. Then she rammed her hand down my sweat-drenched shorts, teased my clit through my underwear. It was hard for me to tell how wet I was, because I was so sweaty. I remember a definite sweet odor in the air of sweat and come and saliva, though. The air was tinged a little with chlorine, which wafted in from the pool that was adjacent to the locker room.

My clit was throbbing now, so much so that I couldn't stand it anymore, so I grabbed her hand and shoved it under my panties. She rubbed my drenched pussy—up and down, up and down. Over my shorts I positioned her hand so that it was right on my clit and moved her hand in circles. As she continued to work my red-hot clit, I looked at her body: sculpted, tan, and hairless. She was absolutely gorgeous, with rock-hard abs and firm biceps. "Yeah, baby, like that," I groaned, and I heard a light smacking sound of her fingers and my pussy juice and my clit all moving in rhythm together. "Faster, faster," I said as quietly as possible, so that no one would come in and bust us.

Just then, Chris yanked down my shorts and underwear and turned me around so that I was facing the shower wall. I knew where this was going, and I was thrilled: She was going to fuck me from behind. I braced my hands against the wall and stuck my ass out toward her. She grabbed my left thigh and slowly put what felt like two fingers inside me. I felt my cunt walls expand and then contract around her fingers, and I heard a slurping sound as she fucked me hard and fast. Her left hand moved up to my ass, squeezed it, then slapped it lightly. "Yeah, that's it. Oh, my God," I told her.

"You're so wet. You feel so good, like silk," Chris responded. She moved her mouth down to my ass and nibbled and kissed it forcefully as she slid her fingers back and forth. I looked over my shoulder and saw her get down on her knees. As she kept finger-fucking me harder and faster, she buried her face into my ass and started to lick my asshole. I'd never had a woman do that to me before, but I eagerly welcomed her warm, wet tongue there. My entire body was electrified, and I swear I saw tiny stars before my eyes. Just then, I guess she located my G spot, because I felt like I was going insane. Blood filled my hard clit and my entire cunt, and my fingers and toes were tingling. Chris massaged my G spot forcefully. "I wish I had my dick with me," she said. "I'm not properly equipped."

I could only grunt in response. But then I mustered up some words: "Right there. Please. Keep doing that."

My hole was gushing now, and I kept hearing those wet smacking noises—which turned me on uncontrollably for some reason—and felt Chris's strong hand grip one of my ass cheeks. Just then she brought me over the edge, which was like wave after wave hitting a sun-drenched shore. Hot ripples coursed through my body, and my cunt was pounding in a combination of exquisite torture and pleasure. "Oh fuck, oh fuck, oh fuck," I moaned, and my entire body shook with release.

Just then Chris slowly pulled out her fingers, stood up, and turned me around. I grabbed her sweaty head and pulled it toward mine, ran my fingers through her wet, dark hair, and kissed her passionately. I kissed her neck, her beautiful collarbone, placed tiny sweet kisses on her forehead and the bridge of her nose.

"So about that date…" I laughed.

"Are we still on?" Chris smiled as she took my breasts in her hands again.

"Yeah, but instead of going out to dinner, let's eat in."

"My place?"

"Exactly what I had in mind," I said with a devilish gleam in my eye.

And that's just where we went.

Summer

Connie D. Brown

One beautiful summer afternoon I was walking along the shoreline. I could hear the ocean waves crashing against the rocks and the birds singing in the sky. The water washed across my feet. It was cool and soothed my skin, which was hot from the sun. The beach was relatively empty of people, which wasn't unusual because it was a weekday, when most people are at work. I didn't mind, though, since I had come here to relax and get away from it all.

I came across an area cut out of the rocks that seemed to be created from years of the ocean's mighty waters crashing against the huge rock formations. It was like a barrier, making me feel as if I were alone with the ocean view. But when I walked farther into the depths of the cove, I discovered I wasn't alone. Lying on a blanket, reading a book, was the most beautiful woman I had ever seen. I felt as though I had intruded into her private space, and I was trying to retreat quietly when she sat up. "Hello," she said. Immediately I found myself looking at her voluptuous breasts. I noticed the cool ocean breeze had caused her nipples to harden.

Several moments passed before I was able to manage a mere hello. I was fumbling around for the slightest thought; a two-word sentence would suffice, anything, just some words! I finally managed an attempt to apologize for my intrusion. "Sorry. I didn't realize anyone was here," I told her.

"It's all right," she replied. "I've been reading here alone for a while. Some company would be perfect right now." There was a pause. I knew I should say something, but the words wouldn't come.

"What a beautiful day this is," she said. "Don't you think

this is the perfect spot to relax? I come here a lot, and I must admit that during the week I've never had anyone find me in my little cove."

I was so mesmerized by her soothing voice and her beautiful face that I must have seemed rude. All I could do was answer her questions with a simple yes or no.

She had a basket filled with some grilled chicken breasts, cheese, and crackers. In a cooler she had some wine, and she offered me some. I told her I didn't drink, so she offered me some bottled water. I took the water, which I really needed because of the heat and all the walking I had done. I opened the bottle and tilted my head back, taking long, hard swallows of the cool water. Some of it escaped my lips and ran down my chin to my neck and between my breasts. I felt the ocean breeze blow across my wet chest, which made my nipples hard. They must have been very visible, since I had on only a muscle shirt and wasn't wearing a bra. As I reached to wipe the water from my chin, I realized she was watching me. This beautiful creature was staring right at me! The moment our eyes met, she quickly turned away and looked out at the ocean.

She told me she was here hiding from life. From an ex-husband she loathed. From a job she actually enjoyed from time to time and from her daughter, who was her greatest joy of all. When she spoke of her daughter her brown eyes sparkled and her voice became soft and soothing, as comforting as the sounds of the waves crashing onto the shore.

As she spoke I couldn't stop looking at her, absorbing every inch of her body. Her long red fingernails, the way her fingers held on to her wineglass. Her silky smooth skin glistened with moisture from the ocean. I wanted to reach out and touch her. I wanted to feel the softness of her gorgeous golden-brown skin.

She must have felt my eyes tracing every inch of her body, because she looked at me and smiled. "What are you thinking right now?" she asked.

I felt my face redden with embarrassment. I'd been caught. "Nothing, really," I told her.

"Come on, you can tell me."

The funny thing was, I felt I *could* tell her. Her voice was mesmerizing. Again she said, "It's OK. You can trust me."

I took a long, slow drink from my water bottle. I was seriously thinking of telling her how attracted I was to her. As I lowered the bottle from my lips some of the water spilled once again down my chin. Before I knew what was happening she was right next to me, licking and sucking the water from my skin. "Tell me, tell me your thoughts," she whispered. Her lips were against my ear. "Tell me," she whispered again as she gently licked my ear with her tongue. I couldn't even think a complete thought except that I wanted this woman. And I knew I didn't want her to stop what she was doing.

As suddenly as she started licking and sucking she stopped. She sat back and said, "Tell me your thoughts right now." Somehow I managed to open my mouth and tell her how beautiful she was. I could tell she liked the sound of my voice. Her eyes were closed, her head tilted slightly to one side. And I could tell she was visualizing everything I said. I was somewhat apprehensive about telling her what I was really thinking, but I began anyway.

With each sentence I became a bit more daring. I began by telling her she had a beautiful smile. I told her I wanted to rub my hands all over her smooth brown skin. Then I got a little more brave and said, "I want to lick every inch of your body, beginning with your toes and working my way around and ending with your clit." The second I said "clit," her head tilted back. She took a deep breath and let out a deep moan, slowly allowing the air to escape her lungs. If I wasn't aroused before, I sure was now. It was obvious this woman wanted me to make love to her right there. It seemed a great idea to me as well!

I moved closer to her and kissed her neck. Her skin was like velvet. Gentle little kisses at first, up and down her neck. Then I sucked and bit her neck just behind her ear, guiding my mouth to the next section I'd devour with my lips.

This went on for a few minutes before I traced her ear with my tongue. "Oh, that feels so good," she softly moaned. She took another deep breath as her body shuddered. All of this made me so full of passion that I began to caress her body. From this point on I was no longer in control of my actions. My body reacted to hers. I rubbed her nipples and gripped her firm breasts. With a simple twist of my fingers, the top of her swimsuit fell away to the sand and exposed her erect nipples. My heart and mind were racing; I couldn't believe I was about to make love to this gorgeous woman. I began to suck each breast. I felt her pull me closer, her fingernails digging into my flesh. I heard her breathing grow heavier. I bit slightly on her nipple and she gasped, pulled my head closer to her breasts. I licked her stomach, sucked and caressed her with my lips.

I stopped for a moment to lay her down on the blanket, then removed my shirt to expose my breasts. I saw desire and hunger in her eyes. I saw a fire deep inside, a fire I was about to extinguish. I positioned myself on top of her, then lifted my body up just enough to allow our nipples to touch. She let out small moans from deep inside.

I watched her face, such beauty. I could tell she was absorbing everything at once: the sound of the ocean, the cool breeze, the sensation of our nipples rubbing together, everything. I leaned closer to her and kissed her gently on the lips. One tender, brief kiss. I repositioned myself so that my thigh was between her legs. Our eyes locked as I pressed my thigh hard against her wanting pussy. Much to my surprise, I felt how wet she was. "I want to fuck you so very hard," I whispered in her ear. "I want to eat your sweet pussy. I want to feel it tighten as I slide my fingers deep inside." As I spoke I continued to move my body so that my thigh slid up and down against her wet pussy. Even though she had on her swimsuit bottom, I could feel the heat and the moisture of her pussy. With one hand I pushed her thong bikini past her knees.

I sat up beside her, drinking in her gorgeous body, her silky smooth skin. Oh, how I wanted to taste her, but I didn't want to rush this. I wanted to savor the moment for as long as I could. I positioned myself back on top of her with my thigh between her legs. She raised her hips eagerly, welcoming my thigh against her pussy. This time I felt the flesh of her hot wet pussy against my thigh. I moved my hips up and down, her arms wrapped around me, her legs interlaced with mine. We were making a sort of music together to the rhythm of our passion and heavy breathing.

With one hand on either side of her I pushed myself up so I could see her face. Her pussy was getting wetter and wetter. Again I leaned down and our lips met in a soft tender kiss. I pulled away only to have her pull me back. I kissed her again gently. Her lips parted and her tongue brushed against my lips. We continued this way for what seemed like hours; it felt as though time itself had ceased to exist. It was only us, the rhythm of our passion, and the waves rising and falling in sync with our lovemaking.

I pinched her nipple and pulled it slightly. She arched her back and moaned with pleasure. I ran my hand down her stomach to her cunt. It was soaked, dripping with her sweet juices. I made little circles around her growing clit, felt it harden at my touch. Her wetness was turning me on so much I wanted to bury my mouth in her pussy and drink her up. As I slowly guided my fingers deep inside her, her fingers dug into my back. The deeper my fingers went, the harder her nails dug into my flesh. I slowly pulled my fingers almost all the way out, then pushed them in again. Out then in, out then in. Like the waves against the shore, in then out, in then out. "I want to fuck you so hard and so deep," I whispered as I thrust my fingers deep inside her.

"I want to feel your pussy on mine," she whispered as she unzipped my shorts. I pulled my fingers out of her to assist, then repositioned myself so that my fingers slid easily inside her pussy. I felt her fingers brush against my clit. That single action took my breath away. My clit grew bigger and harder with each caress. She quickly thrust her fingers deep inside me. The feeling was so intense my whole body went limp. She began to finger-fuck me, matching my rhythm.

I couldn't take much more, so I pulled back and lay on top of her. I spread her legs wide and placed one over my shoulder. I managed to arch my back enough so that our hot, wet clits were now touching. I moved my hips in a circular motion so that our clits caressed each other. I felt as if I might come all over her hot pussy right then and there. But as badly as I wanted to cum, I also wanted this to last. I felt my orgasm build; I pulled away so I could prolong this a little more.

I slid my body down and stopped with my breast just over her pussy. I spread her legs and ran my hardened nipple across her clit. I lifted myself up; my nipple was soaked. The wetness mixed with the breeze from the ocean made my nipple even harder. I went back up on her and placed my pussy-soaked nipple in her mouth. She eagerly sucked and licked every drop off my breast. When she had licked off all of her juices, I went down on her again. She tasted sweet yet a little salty from the ocean air. I took her pussy lips and clit into my mouth, sucking deep and pulling back the length of her labia. As I did, she thrust her hips to match my rhythm. I placed two fingers inside her as I continued to eat her out. Her thrusting increased in speed, and so did I.

She gripped my shoulders and ran her fingers through my hair, pulling my head closer to her. She moaned loudly, and that's when I remembered that we were outside and that anyone could come along and see us. But I quickly forgot that thought because I felt her pussy get even wetter and the walls of her cunt tighten against my fingers. I could tell she was close to climaxing, so I placed another finger inside her and pushed deep, which made her entire body shudder. "Oh, shit!" she moaned, letting a deep breath escape her lips.

I kept pumping my fingers deep inside her while I sucked her clit. All of a sudden, she grew quiet and very still. What was going on? Then she began moving her hips again slowly. She grabbed my head, pulling me hard. Suddenly her whole body shook and she screamed, "Yes, I'm coming, yes!" She let out one last scream as the orgasm continued to ripple through her. I tenderly kissed the inside of each of her thighs, then worked my way up—licking and sucking all around her sweet pussy; kissing her beautiful breasts, her neck, her ears, her lips. We wrapped our arms and legs around each other in a tight embrace. Our bodies were wet with sweat from our passion and the heat of the day. The breeze from the ocean felt cool against our bare skin.

I held this beautiful woman in my arms, allowing her

explosive orgasm to subside. After a while I rolled over onto my back, and she snuggled in my arms with her head on my breast. I ran my hand along her spine and caressed her back. Her fingers moved up and down between my breasts.

She ran the tips of her fingers across my nipples. I was still very turned on, and it wasn't long before my breathing grew rapid again. I closed my eyes and listened the cries of the seagulls, the waves of the ocean. I breathed in the ocean air, felt the sun beat down on me. I felt her hand trace the hairline of my pussy. I realized she was moving her hand closer and closer to my hot clit. I was still very wet from making love to her, but I felt myself get even wetter. She kissed my breasts, then my stomach, then moved to my inner thigh. Oh, how I wanted to feel her lips on my pussy. She rubbed my clit, causing it to harden even more. I felt her tongue so close to my pussy, I felt her breath on my clit. She gently guided her fingers inside me. I gasped as her tongue brushed quickly across my clit. Again I felt her tongue on my inner thigh, licking, sucking, teasingly close to my wanting pussy. The anticipation was driving me insane with desire. I needed to feel her tender, soft, sweet tongue on my clit. I placed my hands on her shoulders.

As she sat up she took my hand and placed it on my clit. She sat facing me, looking deep into my eyes, then slowly entered my pussy with her fingers. "I want to watch you," she said in a sultry tone. My first thought was to protest, but it's not like I'd never masturbated—I had just never done it in front of a beautiful woman. She placed her hand over mine to help me to begin. I watched her watch me. With her fingers inside me, her hand on mine, how could I not give in? I circled my clit with my fingers, felt the heat and wetness of my pussy. My clit was engorged as I stroked it faster. Her fingers felt so good deep inside me. With her breath on my clit and her fingers probing deep inside me, it took everything I had to keep from coming.

My orgasm was building faster as my fingers pressed harder against my clit. I moaned loudly, and my breathing grew rapid. "I'm going to come!" I cried out, and as I did, she thrust her fingers deeper inside me. Suddenly I felt a wave of complete release and my head tilted far back into the sand. My pussy gripped against her fingers as they slid in and out of me. My passion climbed as she continued to fuck me hard. I felt my body anticipate the explosive orgasm I was about to have. "Yes! Oh, fuck me! Yes!" I moaned. I felt her tongue so close to my clit, and as I continued to stroke myself, she licked my hand. This only heightened my desire to feel her tongue on my clit.

She kissed and licked my fingers as I masturbated. I wanted to say, "I want to feel your tongue on me," but before I could speak my body exploded in orgasm. At that moment I felt her tongue and lips replace my fingers, which brought me to the height of the most incredible orgasm I'd ever had. I felt her fingers inside me and the warmth of her tongue on my clit. My head pressed against the sand as my toes curled with the waves of my intense orgasm. Sensations zapped every nerve in my body; I was hardly able to take a breath. As my orgasm subsided, my body went limp, exhausted from the last two hours of making love. She licked all around my pussy, sucking up my sweet come, then kissed me gently on the lips.

By then, my mouth was dry and I was famished. My pulse and breathing began to return to normal, and I began to remember where we were. We lay there in a deep embrace, relishing the afternoon's events. Finally I said, "What's your name anyway?"

She just smiled and said, "Are you hungry?"

"Aren't going to tell me your name?" I asked again.

She handed me a bottle of water. "Do you like chicken?"

As I dressed, she prepared a snack from the items in her basket. We sat on the beach feeding each other cold chicken and crackers. We talked about many things, but remained nameless to each other. The sun began to set across the great ocean—a beautiful sunset to end an exquisite day. We sat in silence watching it unfold before us.

Wrapped in my arms, she kissed my ear and finally broke the silence by saying, "What are you thinking right now?"

Putting on a Show

Marla Carter

The first time it happened, the Sparks' WNBA championship game was sold out and I just wanted to pick up a couple of tickets. I'd met this really hot girl, Trina, at a dyke bar the night before. Amazingly, she was just as big a WNBA fan as me. I'd told Trina I had a couple of tickets to tonight's game—I had season tickets—but I'd forgotten that I'd given them to my coworker Diane, who wanted to take her girlfriend Tammy out for their fifth anniversary.

There was no way in hell I was going to let Trina down, though. Five feet six inches, 160 pounds of pure womanhood, cute short 'fro, beautiful cocoa skin, and breasts as soft as a baby's butt. (I'd discovered that last bit of trivia when we went into a toilet stall for some one-on-one.) She told me that women's basketball made her horny, and now, with the memory of her warm, slick tongue sliding in and out of my mouth, her plump breasts in my hands, I'd find some extra tickets come hell or high water. I had just four hours before our date.

So I went online and scanned the sports chat rooms, scrolled down for what seemed an eternity: Hockey Fanatics, Nuts4Soccer, GoCheeseheads!!! I was near the bottom of the list and hadn't seen any Sparks rooms. Despondent and horny as shit, I was just about to log off when I spotted B-Ball in L.A. The room was empty except for one woman. It was a slim chance, I thought, but I'd try my luck.

"Hey, there," BadGirl6548 typed.

"Hey," I typed back.

"So what's a golf fan like you doing in here?"

"Huh?"

"Your screen name—HoleNOne."

I had completely forgotten I'd logged in under that screen name. I usually only used it for my online sexcapades. Most of the time I went by Marla0808. So I lied.

"I golf a little."

"So do I. What kind of clubs do you use?"

Oh, shit. I had no clue about golf. In fact, I considered it the most boring sport, second only to fly-fishing and shuffleboard—if you can call those sports.

"The same kind as Tiger Woods."

Before she could respond, I quickly checked her profile:

Screen name: BadGirl6548
Real name: Jackie
Location: West Hollywood, CA, BABY!!!
Occupation: trainer
Hobbies: ass and pussy play, spectator sports, nasty encounters, working out, dancing 'til dawn, gettin' down with other sistahs
Quote: "Bring it on."

Well, apparently in the interlude, BadGirl had also checked my profile, which of course, had zilch to do with golf. My hobbies included "long, slow grinding," "making love to beautiful women," and, sadly, needlepoint and latch-hook crafts. (My gay boyfriend Craig had added that one night when we were both smashed on some really bad rum we'd mixed with grape juice out of desperation, and I'd forgotten to remove it.)

"Knit one, purl two," BadGirl wrote.

"Oh, God," I typed. "Listen…"

"Or is it knit one, do me?"

"I'm just in here trying to pick up some Sparks tickets for tonight."

"What are you wearing?"

"Clothes. Now, listen, do you have any tickets?"

"Actually, I have season tickets," BadGirl wrote, "but I'm not going tonight."

"GREAT!!! Is there any way I can buy them off you?"

"BadGirl does not accept cash. Only TRADE."

"What are you saying?"

"Where are you in L.A.?" she wrote.

"Near the Beverly Center. Why?"

"Are you home?"

"Yes."

"Then it'll take you about 10 minutes to meet me at Astro Burger on Santa Monica. I'm 5 foot 8, shoulder-length hair, 26, fit and trim. I'm sure you won't miss me. People rarely do. You got a Sparks T-shirt?"

"Yeah."

"Wear it."

"I can't just…"

"I'll bring the tickets."

"Hey!" I typed, but she had already logged off.

I didn't know for sure what this woman had in mind, but I was fairly sure she didn't want to eat. Well, she wanted to eat, but nothing that was on the menu at Astro Burger. What choice did I have, though? I was aching to see Trina that night, to feel her body good and close against mine after the game, get to know her a little better, if you know what I mean. And part of me didn't want to ask her to go to a movie or hang out at my place. I wanted this night to be kind of special, because even though I play around a lot, I was kind of sweet on this one. Still, if Jackie (a.k.a. BadGirl) was a dog, I could just bolt out of the place. And if she was a hottie, well, I'd get myself a little nooky, get my tickets, and be a little more revved up for Trina. I figured I didn't have much to lose one way or the other. And God knows, I've always been a risk taker.

So I pulled on my Sparks T-shirt and hopped into my pick-up truck and headed for West Hollywood. I pulled into the parking lot with a mix of nervous agitation and eager anticipation. When I walked into the restaurant, I spotted her right away, sitting in a booth and chewing on a straw. Damn, that girl was not lying. She was F-I-N-E fine. She looked like Angela Bassett in *What's Love Got to Do With It*. Black tank top covering a slim, toned body. Pumped arms and full lips. As I walked up to her booth, she grinned real wide. "Hi, HoleNOne. Damn, you are hot."

I smiled my prettiest smile and said, "I try to keep in shape. So what do I have to do for those tickets, sweetheart?"

"Follow me," she said, and went into the ladies' room. She locked the door, then turned her gorgeous face toward mine. She reached into her purse and pulled out a fat blue dildo. "I'm sure a stud like you knows what to do with this."

"No problem," I said as I reached for her beautiful body.

"You got it wrong, girl," she said, pulling away from me. "I want to watch you use this on yourself."

"What? You've got to be kidding me." She was so tasty I wanted to eat her up, and what did she want from me? She wanted me to put on a damn show.

Just then she pulled out the tickets from her bag. "Remember these? Come on, baby, show me what I want to see and they're all yours."

I was so turned on just looking at her that the thought of that big blue prick inside me sent shivers all over my body. *All right,* I thought. *I'll give her what she wants.*

I stood against the wall and pulled down my jeans and underwear. I left them around my ankles. Then I spread my pussy lips apart and slowly pushed the cock inside. The dark curls near my labia were glistening with my juices. I started out slow at first, taking the long dick inside me centimeter by centimeter. I looked over at Jackie and she stood there smiling a smile a mile wide. Then she licked her bottom lip and said, "Yeah, just like that. Now finger yourself too."

I did as instructed, placing two of the fingers of my left hand on my warm, hardening clit. "Push it in farther," she demanded, her voice a little huskier now.

Again, I followed her order and slipped the dildo in farther and deeper, the whole time circling my clit with my other hand. Jackie kept licking her lips, then she put her hand down her panties and started jacking off while watching me get off. I had no idea watching someone do that could get me so horny. My vagina was throbbing, my clit pounding, and I could tell she was totally turned on. She kept groaning and moaning and saying things like, "Yeah, that's it. That's the spot. Sweet kingdom come." I didn't know if this girl was crazy or just a horny bitch, but right then I didn't care, because that cock was so far inside me and I felt powerful knowing I could drive a woman wild without even touching her. But man, did I want to reach out and touch her, grab those juicy tits in my hands, lick her sweet pussy, dine on her whole body.

I closed my eyes and thought about doing just that, as I kept pounding myself with that dirty little dildo and rubbing my hot love bead over and over. I thought about doing this fine woman from behind, poking her hard with the very same cock I was using on myself. I thought about taking her titties in my mouth and licking and biting her dark brown nipples. I imagined burying my face in her sweet, sweet cunt as she straddled my face and cried out, "Marla, oh God, Marla."

I opened my eyes and saw her with her hand still down her pants; she was up against the wall, writhing and moaning, and her hand was moving quickly. Just then she cried out, "Woman, you are too much," and her body shook with release. That was enough to bring me over the edge. I felt blood flowing hot and heavy throughout my body; my nerve endings were on fire. I was sweaty and my pussy was practically squirting out juice. As that powerful orgasm rolled through me, I pulled out the dildo. Jackie grabbed it from me and put it in her mouth, giving it a hot and heavy blow as I kept circling my clit with my fingers. Just then it was too, too much, because I cried out, "Oh, shit," then practically fell into a heap on the floor.

Jackie pulled me up with her strong hands, then kissed me tenderly on the neck. "Here you go, doll." She handed me the tickets as I pulled up my panties and shorts. "And there are plenty more where these came from."

I didn't regret hooking up with Jackie one bit. And, truth be told, my sex with Trina that night was hotter than I'd imagined possible. Still, when we were doing it, I kept thinking about Jackie watching us. I envisioned her sitting in the corner of Trina's bedroom, looking on as I pumped her pretty pussy, saying, "Yeah, that's it. That's the spot."

I guess that's why I came back to her for more.

Sapphic Pleasures

Melissa Dunn

Sexually I was a late bloomer. At 19, I had finally lost my virginity to a 27-year-old guy who waited tables at a pizza dive where I worked to support myself through college. He was certainly more experienced than I, and he would frequently tell me about the fantasies he had about being with two women. Often he propositioned me for such an encounter, pending our agreeing on the other woman. Eventually our affair ended, and nothing came of our hypothetical plans.

Six months later, Alicia started working there. Initially I hated her. She was a year younger than me, a senior in high school. She had long, dark hair, sleepy blue eyes, dark skin, and large breasts. All the guys at work wanted her, and I was incredibly envious of all the attention she got. After working with her for a couple of months, however, I began to warm up to her.

She seemed harmless enough. And truthfully, I got more of her attention than any of the boys did. When a group of us stayed after work to drink, she'd always sit next to me, whispering in my ear or letting her leg rest next against mine. At work she'd ask my opinion about her outfit or how her hair looked. My responses were always flattering and flirtatious. In fact, my flirting may have been what gave her the confidence to start confiding in me that her girlfriends at school had been fooling around with each other. "They always fool around in front of me," she blushed. "They've even propositioned me to join in one of their little sessions."

"Have you ever thought about it?" I asked.

"Well, yeah, I guess I have," she said, as her face reddened. "But I guess I'd want it to be special, you know. With someone I really trusted and felt comfortable around." She smiled and placed her hand on my arm. I began to get the impression that she was just as curious as they were.

I ignored the first of her advances, partly because I still harbored some resentment and partly because I still wasn't brave enough to act on my curiosity. I knew she had a boyfriend, and I assumed she meant to tease me. After a couple more weeks of flirting and innuendos, we went dancing with some other girls from work. Even though neither of us had fake ID's, getting free drinks from bartenders came easy for attractive underage females.

We danced close all night, occasionally letting our hands linger on each other's breasts or crotch. With alcohol to help weaken my inhibitions, it was hard to resist touching her in her tight-fitting, short black skirt and low-cut, lacy black shirt. By the time we left, Alicia was drunk, and I had to drop her and her friend Jennifer off at Jennifer's car.

When we arrived in the parking lot, I got out of the car to open the trunk so that the girls could get their things. Alicia met me at the back of the car. She pulled me close and whispered in my ear, "I wish I were going home with you." And with that she pulled me tightly to her body, pressed her crotch to mine, and began grinding her hips gently. I kissed her cheek and then her forehead, and let her go to Jennifer, who was now calling her to the car. I decided that Alicia was a sure thing.

She quit her job at the restaurant the next day, since her parents didn't want her working while she was still in school. When she came to get her paycheck, she seemed disappointed to be leaving.

"I hope we'll still hang out and stuff." She looked at the floor when she said this.

"I'm going to visit my friend Ed in Athens this weekend," I told her. "Why don't you come with me? It'll be fun. There's always a keg party going on."

Her face lit up. "OK."

She gave me a long hug before she left.

I picked her up Saturday afternoon, and for most of the hour-and-a-half trip we sat in silence, anticipating what might happen. When we arrived, Ed was shocked to see Alicia with me. I didn't have too many female friends, and everyone thought Alicia was extremely attractive.

When Alicia left the room, Ed turned to me. "Did you bring her for me?" he asked in a suggestive tone.

"No, for me." I winked.

He rolled his eyes. "Whatever."

Alicia and I flirted in front of Ed and his roommates to get attention. Out of nervousness, I started drinking early in the evening. Another guy I knew from high school was there and offered me a hit of mescaline. I decided I needed all the bravado I could chemically muster and took the pill without telling Alicia.

Alicia and I went with Ed and his three roommates to an empty pool hall near his apartment. We were both fairly drunk at this point. While the boys played pool, Alicia stepped outside to smoke a cigarette. I watched her through the window, and the drug started taking effect. She moved in slow motion, and the reflection of the streetlight in her eyes twinkled like Christmas lights. The cherry of her cigarette sparkled around her face. I walked outside, lit a cigarette, and stood beside her, mesmerized by the lights. We chatted about something—I can't remember what—and after a few minutes, our eyes had locked.

"Can I kiss you?" I asked, leaning in close.

She answered by grabbing the back of my head and pressing her open mouth to mine. Her lips were soft and firm, her tongue deliberate. The harder we kissed, the wetter I got. She was sitting on the edge of a brick wall. She turned her hips to straddle the wall and face me. I did the same, but instead of letting my legs dangle on either side of the wall, I wrapped them around her hips so I could feel her breasts pressed against me.

We heard the door of the pool hall open, but we kept kissing. I looked up eventually to see an audience of men standing around us, and I pointed them out to Alicia. We decided it was time to leave. So we walked back to the apartment hand in hand. The boys followed closely, watching the entire time in hopes of catching us in another act of passion. But the passion wasn't a display for them; it was ours alone.

When we got back to the apartment, others had gathered in

the living room to smoke pot. I suggested that Alicia smoke some to relax a little. I watched her in anticipation as I felt the strong chills and tingles from the mescaline course through my body. I went into the bathroom, which was connected on either side by adjoining bedrooms. When I opened the door to exit, Alicia stood in front of me with a smug grin on her face. She walked over to the bedroom door and locked it from the inside. I locked the bathroom door behind her.

I felt sick to my stomach. The nervousness and excitement were overwhelming. Alicia looked into my eyes, and I placed my hand around the back of her neck and tilted her head to one side. Her tongue moved feverishly in my mouth, and I felt my nipples harden as they rose against the seam of my bra. I placed my hands on her breasts to see if her nipples were as erect as mine. They were.

We walked slowly over to the bed, trying not to interrupt our intense kissing. She lay underneath me and I straddled her, but not before using my hand to rub between her legs. She was wearing thin cotton pants; the crotch was warm and moist. I rubbed in rhythm with our kissing, and she rocked her pelvis back and forth to match my rhythm. In the meantime, she had unfastened my bra and was cupping my breast, occasionally rubbing my nipple. I pulled my shirt over my head and lowered myself over her, thrusting my breast into her mouth. She sucked hard and I moaned with intensity because it was as painful as it was pleasurable.

"Did that feel good?" she asked.

I answered with a kiss and placed my hand up her shirt to feel the soft flesh of her breast and her tight, erect nipple. She moaned and kissed me harder. She grabbed my hips and pulled them to flip me over. Once I was on my back, she lifted her shirt over her head. Her large breasts fell against her rib cage. The sight of them was very arousing, and without thinking, I thrust my pelvis up to grind against hers. She rested her breasts on mine and moved back and forth as we continued to kiss. I felt her nipples slide across my chest, a feeling that made my nipples so tight they ached.

I moved my hands across her breasts. I pulled my mouth

away from hers and flicked my tongue back and forth over one of her nipples. She placed her hand on my crotch and rubbed slowly, separating my lips through my pants. After a couple of minutes, I got light-headed. I reached to unbutton my pants but didn't stop sucking her breast. She promptly rolled off me and lay beside me on the bed. I turned to face her. I licked a trail from her nipple, up her neck, as she slid her finger between my wet lips and stroked my clit. I moaned and gasped for breath as I felt the first tingles of an orgasm coming on. From my hips to my thighs, I was throbbing so intensely I could hear pounding in my ears.

Someone banged on the door, and we both jumped. "Let me in. I need to get something." Up until this point, I had been caught up in the moment. Everything had seemed natural, but now that I was thrust back into reality, I felt a sick anxiety in my stomach.

After putting my clothes back on, I walked over to the door and opened it slowly. The other guys in the apartment stood behind him, trying to see inside the bedroom.

"What do you need?" I asked, knowing he didn't need anything.

I looked at Alicia lying on the bed. She had dressed quickly. Her hair was messy, and she had a faded stain of lipstick surrounding her mouth.

"You guys go back to whatever you're doing. I'll be out of here in a minute," he said through a grin. The moment was lost, so we went back into the living room disappointed and frustrated.

That night Alicia drank too much and had to go to Ed's house and lie down. The mescaline kept me up into all hours of the night. I wondered if there was any particular way I was supposed to feel. Did the fact that I was so turned on mean I was a lesbian? Or did the fact that I felt sick and guilty mean I wasn't?

Ed joined me outside his apartment. "So, um…what was that all about?" he asked.

"I'm not sure," I admitted.

"Well, do you still like guys?"

"I think so. I mean, I don't dislike them." I had hoped he might have the answers.

"Is this gonna be a regular thing?" I couldn't tell if he was curious or just hopeful.

"I don't know."

I woke Alicia up with a kiss on the back of the neck. She was a little disoriented from her hangover, and I wondered if she remembered the night before. When we got into the car, her silence answered my question.

We drove home in the same silence that we had arrived in. There was some chitchat about the music on the radio or work. But we said nothing of our encounter.

I pulled into the driveway of her parents' house and popped the trunk. When I handed her her overnight bag, she smiled. I smiled back. She leaned toward me, gave a quick but sensual kiss on the lips, and whispered, "Thank you." We never saw each other again.

Junior Achievement

Karen Ann Sikes

I met her selling lollipops.

The year was 1982, and I was a shy outcast in my high
school of 1,200 students. I didn't have a lot of money or expensive clothes like the rich kids, so I was pretty much ignored by
the popular students, especially because I was a nerdy tomboy.
I had a few friends, but they were outcasts too—real science
and math geeks. To make matters worse, I had a chunky shag
haircut and wore my sister Jean's hand-me-downs from the
1970s, while all the jocks wore Izods or Polos with turned-up
collars and the girls donned monogrammed sweaters and plaid
skirts. On top of my sister's hand-me-down shirts, I wore my
cousin Mark's old army jacket, which, needless to say, didn't
increase my popularity one iota.

My dad was a foreman for a construction company, and my
mom worked full-time at a Sizzler-type restaurant. The youngest
of five sisters, I was the one expected to make something out of
my life, because the rest of them hadn't and I had the most
brains in the family. My sister Laurie had gotten pregnant when
she was 16 and dropped out of high school then hightailed it to
Detroit with her boyfriend to avoid the wrath of my mother; my
sister Cindy was an underachiever who became a secretary for a
lawyer whose paychecks bounced half the time; Lisa was a
chronically unemployed pothead; and Jean had gotten married
straight out of high school to a no-good bum. Unfortunately, like
my sisters, I also had very few aspirations—well, at least feasible
ones, since I knew for a fact that when I graduated in a year I
wanted to ride around South America on a motorcycle just like
Che Guevara. Boys didn't interest me either (I'd known that
since seventh grade), so it wasn't like I could find a rich husband

after high school to placate my parents—well, I *could,* but I'd be pretty miserable.

It was mid November, and my parents had gotten a flier in the mail about Junior Achievement, an organization that helps kids nurture their entrepreneurial skills. "This is just what you need, Karen," my dad said, fidgeting with a Winston Light. "It's about time you did something besides listen to records in your room. You know, get some goals."

"But Dad, all those J.A. kids are snobs. Their dads are all lawyers and doctors and stuff. They'll just give me crap." It was true, but I knew there was no arguing with my dad once he'd made up his mind.

"If you don't make something out of yourself, who's gonna take care of me and your mom when we're old geezers?" he'd constantly say, which he did just then.

So the next week, I went to my first J.A. meeting after school. As soon as I walked into the classroom, I knew it would be pure hell.

"Hey, Cory, did you get laid this weekend?" Bart Farland, the lamest jock in school, said to an equally moronic football player.

"Oh, man, you should have seen her tits!" Cory the lunkhead was all smiles. "They were out to here!"

This is bullshit, I thought, and I was just about to get up and sling my backpack over my shoulder when something stopped me in my tracks—well, *someone,* really: the most beautiful girl I'd ever seen. She had short blond hair and green eyes, and she was stocky and a little on the rough side. OK, to be honest, she looked like a big dyke. And this was something else, because *no one* at my school looked like a big dyke, except for the girls' tennis coach. No way was I going to leave now—things were starting to get interesting.

Just then, a creepy guy with a skinny mustache and a horrible mustard-colored tie came in carrying a briefcase. I think he introduced himself as Larry Perkins or something equally sleazy—whatever it was, it sounded like a name that should be followed by "Used Car Bonanza." He definitely looked like a shyster, with his wrinkled shirt and greasy comb-over.

Larry brought the room to a hush, then told us all about his fabulous life: He was the son of a factory worker, and everyone in his family had expected him to work at the cannery too, but he knew from a young age that he was destined for something better. So as a kid he spent hours upon hours coming up with crazy inventions, ranging from an electric mop to wrinkle-free cotton dress shirts (obviously, he hadn't employed this concept himself). When he was 18, though, he hit pay dirt with some lollipop molds he had created. They were just your basic shapes: hearts, stars, flowers, etc., but he included recipe booklets with them, and he claimed to have gotten rich selling them to school organizations that were looking for ways to raise money. The whole time Larry was giving his spiel, I kept looking at the big blond girl, who sat in the corner looking bored and trying to covertly read from a paperback she held under her desk.

"So that's what you kids are gonna do," Larry grinned. "You're gonna sell my lollipops. And whatever profits you make will go to the school's college scholarship fund." Something told me that a lot of that dough would be going to Larry's checking account as well.

Larry had us introduce ourselves, and everyone did, including the jocks, who usually ended with some obnoxious remark or belched. Then the blond girl stood up. "I'm Joanna, but my friends call me Jo," she said. "I just moved here from Chicago."

Just then I heard Bart Farland whisper "lezzie" to Cory, and they both cracked up. *Well, we'll just have to see about that,* I thought.

After Larry talked for a while longer about his crappy lollipops, he had us pair off into selling teams. So I mustered up all the courage I had and went over to Jo. "Hey, since you're new and all, why don't you be my partner?" I smiled. (This was long before gay and lesbian couples used that kind of cornball terminology. To this day, when a friend introduces me to her partner, I can't rid my mind of the image of two dykes lassoing calves on a ranch.) "I'm Karen," I said, and offered my hand.

"I know," Jo said in a husky, sure voice. "You introduced yourself to the class 10 minutes ago." She shook my hand firmly, her grip like a vise.

"Oh, yeah." My face turned three shades of red.

"OK, why not," she chuckled. "I guess you couldn't be any worse than the rest of these losers."

Man, had city life made her that hard? Still, part of me liked her forthright demeanor, her acerbic attitude. In fact, it sent tingles throughout my body.

At this point, Larry dismissed the group, but not before informing us that we had to get together with our partners at least once that week to devise our sales strategy. And even after knowing her for all of 90 minutes, I knew right away that I'd be devising my own strategy for Jo. So we exchanged phone numbers and planned to talk that weekend. "Don't call us. We'll call you," she laughed, and swaggered out of the room.

All week, I was a pile of nerves waiting for Jo to call. In fact, I was hovering around the phone like a freakin' hummingbird. But she didn't call. Then, around noon on Saturday, my mom called out to me when I was taking out the garbage. "Karen!" she yelled. "Some boy named Joe is on the phone for you!" *Oh, God,* I thought. *I hope Jo didn't hear that.*

"Hello?" I timidly said into the receiver.

"So your mom thinks I'm a guy, huh?" Jo said.

"Uh…sorry about that. My mom's pretty lame."

"Well, it wouldn't be the first time someone's made that mistake. Don't sweat it." I was surprised she was taking this so lightly.

"So do you want to get together before the next J.A. meeting?" I asked her.

"Do I *want* to? Well, not really. But I guess I don't have much of a choice." Her brusque demeanor had quickly returned.

"Um, you could come over tomorrow night if you want," I offered.

"That's cool."

We decided on 8 the following night, and I gave Jo my address.

"Hey, I only live a couple of streets over," she said. "On Woodbine. Cool."

"See ya then."

"Cool."

The next night, I was even more nervous waiting for Jo's

arrival. In fact, the night before, I hadn't been able to fall asleep until 4 A.M. I kept imagining Jo's rugged hands all over my virgin body, her taking the lead and pinning me to the wall, biting my neck fiercely and pressing her girth against me. I envisioned her as the leading man, swooping me up in her strong arms and carrying me off to bed, where she'd ravish me and whisper gruff things in my ear: "Yeah, baby, I like it like that." Or, "Give me some lovin'." My sexual experience had been limited to a night of backseat groping with this skinny guy Kevin I knew from English class. I don't even know why I did it; I definitely wasn't interested in him, but I guess the idea of someone finding me attractive was enough to get me going. We'd both been drunk on a bottle apiece of André's pink champagne. Fortunately, I threw up before we could go all the way. The next day at school, I was mortified and avoided him in the hallways and cafeteria. But even though that night had been a bust, the idea of making out with Jo had my entire body on fire.

Around 8:10 that night, the doorbell rang and I rushed to get it. My mom and dad were in the living room watching TV, and I didn't want them to see Jo and put two and two together. I mean, Jo definitely stood out as a huge dyke, and I didn't want any accusations flying. When I opened the door, there she was in all her glory: short blond hair, messy and cut like a boy's; plaid flannel shirt over raggedy jeans; red Nike tennis shoes. My dream come true.

"Hey," she said.

"Hey," I said back. "Come on in."

"Cool."

"Just a friend," I yelled into the living room. "From J.A." I knew the J.A. part would make them happy and would shut them up if they were thinking of saying anything. They were so happy that I was actually doing something they considered practical.

I led Jo quickly to my bedroom, then told her I'd be right back. I went to get us some snacks.

I came back with a couple of cans of Coke and a bag of Chee-tos. Then I shut and locked my bedroom door. I handed a Coke to Jo, who was sitting on my bed, and opened up the bag. "Cool," Jo said, for like the hundredth time. "Thanks."

I looked her straight in the eyes and she looked at the floor; she seemed really nervous. What was going on? Where was the tough, rough-and-ready dyke from before? Where was my mannerless leading man?

She opened up her Coke can and just sat there drinking it as we sat side by side on the bed. We were both silent. Finally, after what seemed a year, I said, "Want some Chee-tos?"

"Yeah. OK," she said, and I handed her the bag.

So there we sat for what seemed another year. I realized then that I'd forgotten to bring in any napkins, and you know how Chee-tos leave that gook all over your fingers. I looked at Jo's cheese-covered fingers and got a very bold idea. "There's cheese crud all over your fingers," I said.

"Yeah, I guess there is," she replied, and just sort of stared at her left hand as she held it suspended in the air.

"Let me take care of it," I told her.

"Yeah, some napkins would be good."

I just raised my eyebrows at that and leaned over and boldly took her hand in mine. Thick finger by thick finger I licked off the cheesy stuff. She closed her eyes and leaned her head back, and then I went in for the kill, kissing her straight on the mouth. "Put a record on," Jo said. "You know, your parents…"

I booked over to my stereo and put on the first album I found: *Al Green: Greatest Hits*. The first song was "Tired of Being Alone." How fitting. I cranked up the volume. I sat back on the bed and looked Jo in the eyes, and again she dropped her gaze to the floor. What was with her? Well, I'm sure you've heard the saying "Butch on the streets, femme in the sheets." Looking back now, this was definitely the case with Jo. *I* would have to be the leading man. I didn't mind, though, since my entire body was raring to go, and I was going to bed her one way or the other, even if it transformed me into something I didn't think I was: an aggressor.

"Come here, baby," I whispered, and she looked at me with sweet puppy-dog eyes. She moved toward me about an inch, then I just decided to go for it, moving up to my knees and straddling her as I positioned her upright against my headboard. She gripped my waist in her hands, and I lowered my head and planted a firm kiss on her lips. I guess that's what Jo needed to get going, because she reciprocated, tonguing my mouth like there was no tomorrow, ramming it in forcefully and quickly. Granted, her kissing skills definitely needed some fine-tuning, but what did I care? I was finally kissing a girl. Sure, she was a girl who looked like a boy—but that's how I liked them. With each kiss, her grip on me grew harder, until I had to peel her hands off me. I thought she was trying to make orange juice out of me or something. "Take it easy," I said. "It's OK. I'm with you here." Al Green was still belting out his soulful tunes, and his sexy voice and the look in Jo's sweet eyes were turning me on like crazy.

I slowly unbuttoned Jo's flannel shirt, then looked down at her enormous breasts, which were covered in a plain white bra. I tossed the shirt onto the floor, then reached around and fumbled with her bra clasp. Finally I unhooked it and she helped me remove it. It went on top of her shirt on the floor. I looked at her big tits, and my eyes practically bugged out at the sight of them. She certainly did have a talent for restraining them underneath all that flannel. Her bra size must have been in the double D's: Her tits were as big as cantaloupes. I wasn't about to complain, though. I pulled my ratty Led Zeppelin T-shirt over my head and quickly undid my bra. Jo slid down so that she was flat on her back, and I lay on top of her. Now we were breast against breast. Her warm skin felt good against mine; she was so smooth and soft, and her flesh was like bread dough.

I didn't really know what I was doing, but I forged ahead, because I knew everything was up to me. I certainly couldn't rely on Jo to be the dominating one. I buried my head into her cleavage and licked the length of it; she tasted salty and sweet. "Oh, Jesus," she whispered, almost like a prayer. I rested my face between her gigantic breasts for a moment, and her chest was heaving, her face flushed. When I rubbed her pussy through her jeans, her eyes nearly rolled back into her head, and she opened her mouth and moaned softly. I kept doing that, just rubbing back and forth, then licked her navel, gently nibbled on the soft, warm skin surrounding it.

Just then I heard a knock on my door. Jo and I both froze in terror. "Having a good time?" my dad yelled over the music.

"Um, yeah, this J.A. stuff is really interesting," I yelled back. Then I whispered to Jo, "He'll go away in a second. Just be quiet."

"Let me know if you need anything," he said, and then I heard him tramp off down the hallway.

"See?" I said to Jo, but I could tell she wasn't too convinced, because she had a look of utter terror on her face.

"Maybe this isn't such a good idea," she said.

"No, it's OK. Really. I'll turn the stereo up." When I got up to do just that, Jo was already putting her clothes back on. I was dejected.

"It's not you, Karen, I swear," she said, and I think this was the sweetest I'd ever seen her look. "I'm just scared. I've never done this before. Maybe we could wait and take it more slowly?"

"We could go on a date or something," I offered. "And we can still be J.A. partners, right?"

"Cool," she said. "Very cool."

So even though Jo and I didn't go all the way that night, and we both said fuck it to J.A. after two weeks, we ended up—over time, of course—being girlfriends for the rest of the school year. I ended up playing the role of the sexual aggressor throughout our relationship, which taught me my first real lesson in lesbianism: Big butch girls aren't always aggressors; sometimes they want *you* to take the lead.

Lesbian Singles Party

Hilary Watson

Every woman in the house—and trust me, when I say every woman, I mean *every* woman—was wearing a blazer. A few had the sleeves rolled up. Some wore wife-beater tees underneath. But they all wore blazers. And they were all old. We're talking *way old*.

I had on an outfit I felt sexy in—a sleeveless blue velvet top with black stretch pants and heels that brought me up to about 5 foot 5. I stood in the entryway at the back end of a long line of excitedly bobbing mullets, still holding the hip little flier that had been handed to me by a very cute chick on the campus of the University of Texas. "Hundreds of Hot Lesbian Singles!!!" it read. "Prizes, Tarot Readings, Dancing."

Where was that cute chick? Was she just part of an advertising ploy? The old bait and switch? She was probably out right now at the really hip Austin lesbo party. A party where 20-somethings like myself could mingle and compare tattoos.

A 40-ish woman in a bright red blazer, with a face like my mother's, sat behind a table. One by one she greeted and registered the guests, and guest by guest the space between us shortened. When I finally reached her, she raised an eyebrow at me.

"Name?"

"Hilary."

"Two l's in Hilary?" she asked filling out my name tag.

"Whatever you think's best," I said, and began to cry.

Not that I didn't totally have the best reason. I was 21 and my best friend, Trudy, who also happened to be "the love of my life," had just told me she was in love with my other best friend, Rachel—who happened to be "the love of her life." Trudy and I used to take ecstasy and make out all the time, and it was always so perfect; we just never went any further because neither of us knew what to do. OK, we *knew* what to do. We just hadn't done it before. And I guess neither of us was willing to look like a dork.

"What's the matter, honey?" asked the woman. Bless her for her soft demeanor because I was full-on crying.

"I'm only 21—this isn't the way it's s-s-supposed to h-h-happen."

"Don't worry, honey. There's a whole house full of beeyootiful wimmin here to cheer you up." With that happy phrase, she handed me the two items she'd dished out to every poor single lesbo who registered at her post that night: a daisy and a name tag. Both would have looked great in the lapel of my blazer—if only I'd worn one. Oh, well.

Once in the hallway, clutching my daisy, I wiped my eyes and tried to locate a good place to chuck my name tag. Suddenly, a woman with brown hair and bad posture sidled up to me. She was wearing a tan linen blazer, but at least the cut was semi-stylish, and that alone made her sort of attractive. Juxtaposition is sometimes everything. She grabbed my arm and pulled me into a corner. "Hi, I'm Mary. If you say you're my date, we'll get a prize."

My eyes dried out. I tucked the daisy in my hair and tossed my name tag into the pot of one of several ficus trees. I let Mary walk me back to where the red-blazered mother figure was staffing the party admittance desk.

"You again!" the woman laughed.

"We just met! And we have a date next Friday!" announced Mary. She seemed quite proud.

"Wow, that was fast." With an exaggerated flourish the woman extended a lime-green slip of paper, which Mary snatched and held to her nose like she was inspecting a counterfeit bill.

"All right! A weekend at Nocona Hot Springs! " Mary howled.

"And a free massage for two, " the red-blazer woman piped in, wriggling her salt-and-pepper eyebrows.

Queasily, I followed Mary off into the living room where she continued to peer at the paper. Eventually she remembered my presence, or at least she got tired of inspecting the paper, and when she looked up, there I was. She squeezed and rubbed my arm, which felt like it had gotten a little bruised. "Hey, thanks," Mary said. "Great prize, huh? Excuse me, I gotta go to the bathroom."

She moved off to the bathroom, and I moved toward the patio, where I hoped to find a younger crowd or at least some kind of strong drink. Just before I stepped across the threshold, I overheard Mary introducing herself to someone. "Hi, I'm Mary. If you say you have a date with me, we can get a prize."

Once safely on the patio, what did I see?

More blazers.

Damn, this party sucks!

But at the far end of the yard was a bar, and at that bar was a beautiful spiky-haired blond—my God!—in a cobalt-blue minidress. She was easily more than six feet tall, and as she accepted a glass of wine sweetly by the stem, she looked up and out over everyone. When she saw me, she stopped looking, and then she smiled. And then she drank.

I thought, *Wow! Is it the wine or me you're drinking?*

It's you—now get over here. Her eyes were blue, like those of a timber wolf. Soon we were sharing a bottle of merlot. "Are you some kind of gymnast?" she asked. "You remind me of a gymnast. Your arms are so muscular, but your body language is so soft."

"I'm a dancer," I told her.

"A dancer! Well, what kind of dance do you do?"

I bit my tongue about erotic dancing at the Peppermint Unicorn to support my X habit. Instead I told her I did modern and that I had choreographed and performed a solo and had been chosen to perform it at a national competition in Washington, D.C. I told her I had a videotape of it back at my apartment. All of which was true.

Then I told her that I liked her lips and her cheekbones and her shoulders.

"Your eyes are like nothing I've ever seen before," she said. "They're so amazing. They're spaced so far apart." She moved her finger back and forth from my left eye to my right, to the left to the right. "So wide apart," she repeated, then, "Oh, Jesus. I'm drunk."

"You don't seem drunk to me," I lied.

"Well, I am," she said. "I'm very drunk, and you're very young and you've never even been with a woman before."

I drove her back to my apartment, which was just a mile or so away, ogling out of the corner of my eye how her skirt hiked up on her thighs and the dark shadowy zone between her legs.

My place has a lot of cool stuff to look at, props to make me look artistic and sexually sophisticated. She wandered around looking at my collection of erotic photography books, and I went out on the back porch for a smoke. After a while she shouted at me from inside, "Hey, what are you doing with this?" It was a book by Anne Rice—writing as A.N. Roquelaure. She held the book in her hand and smirked. "What are you doing with *Beauty's Punishment?*"

I told her I loved that book.

"So, a little perv, are you?"

"Yes."

"This could turn out to be a fun evening."

"Yes."

She dove back into my things while I finished my cigarette. She dug through my CDs and pulled out Prince's *The Hits* and, smiling, came up to me with it.

"You like Prince?"

I blew smoke up at the stars. "No, I *love* Prince. I love love love love love Prince."

"I'm becoming kind of bored by Prince—but I do like that one song 'Erotic City.'"

I took the CD out of her hands and told her I wanted to go back to the party.

When we got back, the crowd had thinned and everyone had taken off their blazers, so there was something newly sexy in the air. I put "Erotic City" on the CD player, walked myself to the middle of the living room, and closed my eyes. When I finished dancing, I looked over at her and she just stood and stared. Then we went back to my place.

The first thing she did was kiss me while pushing my body into all these poses, and I just went with it. "Your spine is so flexible. Your body just goes whatever direction I ask it to." She kissed me and put her hand in the small of my back, and I let my back fold over and she bent with me. She used her hands to move me everywhere. She took my shirt off and pulled the edge of my bra aside to reveal my nipple. Her face flushed red as she looked at it. "So tight and brown," she said. Then she kissed it with a sweet, soft brush of her lips. The door to the patio was open and the night air blew in across my skin. "Feels good," I said, shivering some.

"Are you cold, honey?"

"No. I love it," I told her.

"Good," she said, and took my nipple in her teeth. As the sharp pain went steadily through me, she turned me in her hands like a toy.

My eyes rolled back in my head, and for a while I didn't even know where I was.

When she stopped, we were on our knees facing each other. I reached under her short dress and lifted it over her shoulders to expose her black bra and ripe curved breasts—two perfect spheres, lifting and falling with her breath. And I saw her soft, flat stomach and her cheap black nylons with a run down the inside of one thigh. I threaded my fingers into that run and, when her blue eyes widened, ripped for all I was worth. I tore those crappy supermarket stockings right off her as she fell back and laughed and helped by kicking her legs. Together we snatched up scraps of ripped nylon and threw them all over the room.

She was naked except for her bra.

She reached both hands behind her back and popped the clasp. Then she stretched her arms out in front of her and the bra slipped down to her elbows. I gasped when I saw her breasts. Greedily, I dragged the bra down her arms the rest of the way and flung it to the wall. Then I stared. She had perfect, large, beautiful breasts with tight, clay-colored nipples, and she had a glossy look in her eyes that made the room spin. I lowered my head, and her hand came behind it as she twined her fingers deep into my hair.

I bit down on her nipple, then tried to bite again, but she pulled my hair so I couldn't, and I moaned. We shared a smile. "Bite harder," she said. And so she teased me like that for a while, urged me to bite harder, suck harder, forced my face into her breast, forced me to stuff my mouth with it. Ordered me to lick lightly, held my hair so I had to lick lightly. She squeezed her breasts together so the nipples were kissing each other. I put both of them in my mouth, tonguing and gnawing.

The moan she let out—I still hear it at the strangest times of the day.

Then we were kissing again. Soft perfect kisses. Her hands moved confidently over my body. She brushed the crotch of my panties with her fingers.

"Oh, you're damp. I can feel how damp you are—you're soaked."

That's when I got stage fright. This wasn't some choreographed performance or some sordidly structured lap dance. This was real. She really meant to fuck me. I freaked inwardly as her hand slipped inside the waistband of my panties.

I whispered, "I don't like penetration."

"You don't?" She paused.

"I've never even let guys do it."

"Why, baby?"

"I don't know…" (And I really didn't; something had always just stopped me.)

She looked at me quizzically, trying to digest this new incongruent information. But then she smiled. "You're scared, that's all…but you *are* getting fucked tonight." And it was said in such a way that I felt fine. Our tongues danced together like old lovers, her taking the lead.

Her soft mouth wandered down my stomach, my belly ring clicked against her teeth. Then, with an exquisite hovering tease of lip, tongue, saliva, teeth, she was on my clit. Her finger entered me, then held still, then it was just that tease again, that teasing mouth. It was just her finger, but I felt terrified. I didn't know what I was going to feel. But then I just felt…amazing.

"Oh, my God, " I said. "What are you doing?" I felt so innocent. And I had been afraid of feeling that way. Through the haze of sex, I realized I had created this artificial girl, this vampy sophisticated sexpot who read erotica and danced at a sex club, but she climaxed alone on her vibrator every night. I didn't want to be that person anymore.

Now, innocent felt perfect with this big safe Amazon fucking me and soothing me at the same time. She had her hand on my ass and rocked my pelvis for me, rocked me over and around her finger, rocked me into and across her mouth. She lifted my legs over my head, then held them—straight-armed, one hand cupping my heels, and her mouth staying with me, her finger staying with me, one finger and her mouth staying with me.

I came hard. So hard. Hard on her mouth—and that one finger.

That was the start of everything, of letting go.

Later that night, she had me fuck her with my hand. She made me fuck her hard, and I was scared I was going to hurt her, but she told me not to be afraid, and it was like she was teaching me not to be afraid of things down there, least of all a woman's hand or fingers. She showed me what a pussy can really take.

"I don't want to bruise you!" I said.

"That's OK. I'd like to know you were there. I'd like to feel it driving home to L.A. tomorrow morning. It'll keep me from falling asleep at the wheel."

The next morning was little awkward. She woke up shocked about how young I was. I felt somehow guilty that she had no panty hose left and had to borrow a pair of my boxers (which she never returned, thank you very much). I got a postcard from her sent from some shit town in Arizona where she'd crashed for a night. It said she'd stopped and had peach ice cream at the place I told her to and it was as good as I said it would be. That was all I needed to know.

Hank, Just Hank

Toni Chen

A few months ago I went to my second drag king show where I had my first boning by a bona fide drag king. His name was Hank, Just Hank, and he wore baggy black jeans, orange Vans, a loose T-shirt, and sunglasses. Hank was the surfer-cowboy of the group who played it cool in the background to songs by Southern Culture on the Skids and the Violent Femmes.

Each king had his own personality: the leather daddy, the bespectacled academic daddy, the butch bottom, the Latino, the inked rockabilly boi, the white trash boi with the missing tooth, and Hank. Hank's shtick was dildo performance art; during the first show he tied fishing wire to his "purple marauder" and went fishing in a yellow mop bucket, throwing his line back in after he caught two plastic fishes and then (after a tug and a yank) pulled out Barbie. Hank clutched Barbie to his chest and walked, smiling, off the stage. It was hysterical, and I was smitten.

During the second show, the emcee announced that Hank was going to paint portraits with his strap-on and asked if anyone would like to volunteer. My hand flew up, waving madly while my friends pointed at me. Hank smiled and nodded to the emcee, who chose me.

I sat on the stage while Hank moved his rubber dick around in globs of finger paint, then slapped it on a canvas to create a likeness of me (emphasis on "likeness"). After he was done, I held it up while everyone applauded, but when I turned around to thank him, he had already sneaked up the back staircase to the green room.

The paint was still wet, so I laid the picture down in the backseat of my Volvo, then rushed back inside a few minutes before intermission. I downed a shot or two, grabbed a pair of

Coronas, and pushed my way around the room until I finally saw Hank's straw hat from a distance. He was talking with a tattooed daddy in chaps and a wife beater; for a moment my resolve faltered. Perhaps Hank wasn't quite what he appeared—perhaps he dug rough trade, not skinny geek girls like myself.

Then I figured, screw it.

I decided to open with something noncommittal, casual, friendly, coy: "Hey, Hank, that was so hot." Well, it was friendly.

"Thanks." He dipped his head down and blushed. Nothing cuter.

"Here's payment for the picture," I said as I handed over the beer. "So, um, what's your last name?"

"Hank, Just Hank. Well, I guess then in that case Hank is probably my last name."

I wasn't sure if he was kidding. "Yeah?"

"Yeah," he laughed, drinking half his beer in one gulp. "It's ironic, but crowds make me nervous," he said, looking around at the glitter and epileptic lighting. "Want to go up to the green room? We're each allowed one guest…"

"Sure," I answered, a little too quickly.

The green room was littered with crunched-up Camel packs, strips of facial hair, scissors, socks, and kings waiting for their next act. "Hey, Hank," the rockabilly boi smiled over at us. Hank grabbed my arm and led me out on to the roof, away from the snickers of his friends.

"Smog sure makes for pretty sunsets," he said when we found a fairly clean area on the flat roof to sit down.

I looked over and watched him gazing out over the city, his light brown sideburns and goatee perfectly matching his real hair color. I'm not quite sure what the appeal of the drag king is, really; it's not the masculine, necessarily. Maybe it's the taboo, the girl-boi. Oh, who knows, who cares—it's all gender-bending fun.

"How do you keep your facial hair on?" I asked him

"This theatrical glue. Comes off pretty easily with cotton balls and rubbing alcohol, except on your upper lip. It's rough there."

"But you have a full goatee."

"I suffer for my art," he said with a smile.

"So what's in your pants?" I asked, not even attempting small talk about movies or George Bush's latest blunder.

"Well…" He downed the rest of his beer. "Usually socks."

"Socks?" I asked. "Where's the marauder?"

"He's too…excitable to wear all night long."

"I see…" I said, then began looking around for discreet places to make out. I completely dig kings and have always dreamed of making out with one, and I don't know why, but I felt like Hank's invitation to the green room was his way of telling me that we were going to be boning on the roof before the second act. Or maybe that was the Jägermeister talking—those two shots I had were kickin' in, and I was feelin' randy and hoping soon to be feelin' Hank.

"I need to put him away soon…" Hank said in a low voice, never taking his eyes off mine.

"So you're wearing it now?"

"Check and see."

For being so shy in public, Hank certainly did find his *cojones* in private.

I put my hand along the inside of his pant leg. "Wait, come here," he said. Hank grabbed my hand and pulled me over behind the air-conditioning unit on the far end of the roof. "I'm not in any numbers until the last song, so we have some time. If you want to spend some time with me…"

I stood facing over the city, my back to Hank, looking over the air-conditioning box that came up waist high. Hank reached his hands under my skirt and pushed aside my underwear to make room for his fingers.

He kissed the back of my neck and brought one hand up to gently rub my nipples through my powder-blue T-shirt. His hands were strong and steady, increasing pressure until he was rolling my nipples between his thumb and index finger. Biting the back of my neck. Making his way inside my panties with his other hand. I leaned back, pushing his fingers inside me while I gripped the edges of the dirty metal.

I wondered what he looked like as a girl; then an odd image flashed in my mind of him fucking himself as a girl. Of me fucking him as a boi.

I felt his rubber dick against the inside of my leg as he moved a second finger in, pressing out toward my stomach to find my G spot. "Do that with your dick," I whispered. "Please..."

"Bend over," he ordered sharply. So I did.

Hank rested one hand on his cock, then slid it inside me gently. I felt myself open up. He began fucking me in one continuous motion while his other hand continued working on my nipples up to where he was twisting and pinching them. I sucked in a quick gasp, but I liked the pain, so I didn't tell him to stop. I banged up against the air-conditioning unit, not caring about the noise or the bruises as he hit my spot over and over again until I felt a tingling deep inside. "Do you like this?" he asked.

I moaned and rammed back onto him, wanting every bit of force as he twisted my nipples until they burned. "Harder...fuck me harder..."

I bent over more and braced myself while he pounded me over and over until I felt my belly tighten. I touched my clit while he hit me from inside, sending waves of heat deep inside me.

All the sensations jumbled in my head: my hand on my wet heat, his dick pumping deeper and deeper inside, his wetness under that dick. I wondered if the cock was positioned well enough to hit his clit. I hoped so.

I spread myself open a tiny bit so I could access my hard clit better, then clenched around his cock and grabbed on to the metal box as I came in waves. Finally, Hank slowed down and stepped back, tucking his rubber dick back in his pants.

"I knew you were hot," I said, still shaking and blushing.

Hank nodded and offered to buy me a beer. "Do you come to all our shows?" he asked. "Because there are a few different views of the city available from this rooftop..."

"I think I'd like to see them all." I said, grabbing his arm. "Maybe I could even show you a few new ones..."

"Maybe," Hank smiled from under his hat.

Teacher's Pet

Romy Newton

My arms tightened around her waist as she pressed on the accelerator of her tiny maroon Vespa. As we headed downtown, I pondered how the hell I'd gotten there in the first place, legs clinging to her firm thighs, erect nipples pressed into her delicate back, as we careened together down Sun Yat-sen Road.

It was the end of the summer, and I was about to head back to the United States, where I was a graduate student in Asian studies. I had arrived in Taipei 2½ months earlier, exhausted from a year of intense studying and depressed from missing Steve, my boyfriend of four years. The last thing I had wanted to do was spend the hottest months of the year studying Chinese in sweltering Taipei. But when I received a grant that paid the fees to the best Chinese language school in Taipei— as well as my living expenses—it was too good an opportunity to pass up. So I packed my bags, said goodbye to Steve, and hopped on a direct flight to Taiwan.

The language program was very intense, and I had little time to do anything that summer but study. All my teachers were excellent and somewhat strict, but the teacher of my first class of the day was especially fierce. I could almost never speak a full sentence without her making me stop and repeat it again and again. Interestingly, her appearance belied her ferocity. She was petite, shorter even than my own 5'3", and slender with delicate, tapered fingers. Her hair was thick and black and reached her shoulders. Her eyes slanted into a wide, white smile. She was not only the fiercest of the teachers but also the prettiest, and I realized about a week into the term that I was terrified of her.

One morning, as she made me repeat a sentence pattern for the umpteenth time, my eyes fell on an area slightly below her neck. I was startled to find myself imagining my finger tracing a route from that point along her collarbone and down to where her low-cut lacy blouse began. Her skin there looked so pale, so smooth, so soft… I began to wonder about the roundness beneath that blouse.

"Hey—you're spacing out!" she barked accusingly.

I leaped out of my chair and blushed furiously. "Uh…sorry," I muttered in Chinese.

She shook her head and told me in front of the rest of the class to write five extra sentences for that night's homework. I nodded mutely, ears aflame. But my embarrassment came not from being called out in front of the class, but rather from the disturbing image I'd had. Never in my life had I thought about touching a woman, and suddenly there I was thinking about touching my Chinese teacher, a woman who moved like Tinker Bell but talked like a drill sergeant. I knew nothing about her, not even whether she had a boyfriend or was married.

That night I had difficulty concentrating on my homework. I thought about my relationship with Steve. I missed him but was gradually getting used to the idea that I wouldn't see him for a couple of months. Was our relationship missing something? I didn't think it was. We communicated well, and the sex was good. Well, most of the time it was. Sometimes I felt intimidated by his size and dominating nature in bed. He was always pressuring me to be aggressive with him and especially to talk dirty. But while I tried, it just didn't come very easily to me. I'd halfheartedly squawk out a few words—"Fuck me…fuck me silly with your big strong cock"— while he pumped vigorously above me. Afterward I'd ask "How was that?" "OK," he'd answer. "But I think you can do better."

As I lay in bed, I tried to do what I usually did during those lonely Taiwan nights: fantasize about grabbing Steve by the hair and ordering him around in bed. Then I would touch myself until I came, then fall asleep. But this night was different. The image of my teacher's soft red lips and the mole that lay just two centimeters to the left of them was imprinted on my confused brain. Would those lips be soft? I imagined kissing the mole and running my tongue along her lower lip. The image disturbed me, and I tried desperately again to picture Steve. But it was no use. When I slipped my hand down to my crotch, a word I find disgusting, I discovered that my pussy was sopping wet and my clit engorged practically to the size of a small olive. And I knew it wasn't Steve who was having that effect on me. I abandoned myself to the image of my teacher's head between my legs as I rubbed myself to a tumultuous orgasm. But after that, I slept fitfully, tossing and turning. When I walked into class the next day, I was so freaked out I could barely look at my teacher.

Things were pretty weird for me for the rest of the summer. I thought about my teacher constantly and even found myself staying after classes ended and working in the library at the school because I knew she would be there. But whenever I saw her, instead of talking and joking with her like the other students did, I was so nervous about making a fool of myself that I would run away.

On the last evening of the term, the night before I was to leave, the school held a student-teacher dinner at a dumpling restaurant. After dinner, a few of us went to a teahouse to drink tea and play cards. My teacher was also there. While I was too shy to talk very much with her, she joked around with me in quite a jolly manner. A couple of times I even thought I caught her looking at me, and I smiled shyly back. It was kind of fun to be with her in a different kind of setting. Why, she actually seemed nice! When I remembered I'd be going back to the States soon and wouldn't see her anymore, I was so forlorn I felt like crying.

As the evening was ending and I walked away from the teahouse to catch a cab home, I heard a honk. It was my teacher driving a cute little Italian Vespa motor scooter.

"Which way do you live?" she smiled at me.

"In Mucha," I answered.

"Oh, that's on my way home. I can give you a ride."

She wanted to give me a ride? I couldn't fathom that this woman who had tormented me for an entire summer wanted to give me a ride home. Still, I reasoned to myself, she would do it for any student.

"S-sure…" I stammered, accepting. I hopped on the back of her scooter and grabbed the seat tightly.

She laughed. "You have to grab me," she said. "Otherwise you'll fall off. Don't be shy!"

I gingerly touched her hips. They felt hot beneath my trembling hands, and I felt myself get wet. As she headed toward Mucha, I was so overwhelmed that I was almost at the end of my wits. I had to do something about this. I had to. In a moment of uncharacteristic bravery, I decided I should tell her how I felt about her. If I didn't, I might regret it for the rest of my life. It's not that I wanted something to happen; rather, I thought I'd get a load off my chest if I said something.

When I got off the scooter in front of my house, I turned toward and blurted, "I have to tell you something."

She looked worried. "Oh no. I hope it's not about my teaching. I know I'm kind of tough, but…"

I cut her off.

"No. That's not it at all. Your teaching was fine. No, what I want to say is…I like you."

She stared at me. "You what?"

"I like you." I said.

"You know, I have a crush on you. And if you wonder why I acted so weird all summer, running away from you and generally being a freak, that's why."

She laughed nervously and stared at me. "I did wonder, actually, why you always ran away from me like a timid rabbit."

To my surprise she reached up and touched my long blond hair. "My sweet, timid rabbit," she said.

And that is how I found myself on her Vespa driving back into downtown Taipei. You see, I had a roommate, also a student at that school, and we didn't want our secret to be discovered.

"I know where we can go." she said.

"Where?" I asked.

"You'll see." She winked. She paused for a moment in her

driving to caress my nervous hand with her own cool and sur-
prisingly self-assured one.

She took me back to the school, where she unlocked the
door and led me by the hand to the director's office. The
director of the school had an office with soft carpet on the
floor—perfect for what we were about to do. I felt embold-
ened by my confession and the unthinkable events that were
now spinning out of it. I put my hands on her waist and leaned
over to kiss her. I expected her to be tentative, so I was surprised by her enthusiastic response. She boldly moved her
tongue between my lips and took my breath away. We kissed
for a while, and then her hands found my breasts and began
to stroke them slowly. The sensation was maddening, and I
ached to feel more of her. I slid out of my shirt and pulled off
my bra. She held her arms over her head and I removed her
shirt as well. She pulled me down onto the carpet, and I held
my chest above hers, rubbing my nipples against hers. It felt
so different from Steve's wiry chest hair, so soft and so good
that I could hardly bear it.

Impatiently I lifted her skirt and ran my hand along the outside of her underwear. Needless to say, they were soaked
through. I eased them down, and the next thing I knew, we
were naked and rolling around on the floor in each other's arms.
She straddled my belly, and I put my hands on her smooth ass
and slid her up so she was sitting on my chest with her girlish
pubis pressed up almost against my chin. I gently lifted her hips
and ran my tongue up and down the delicate crease of her
pussy, which hovered over my mouth. She sighed and moaned
as I worked the tip of my tongue between her turgid lips. She
moved rapidly, rubbing her pussy over my mouth and chin as I
struggled to keep up with her desire. I couldn't believe it. I simply couldn't believe it. Just yesterday this woman was giving me
a pop quiz. And now she was riding my mouth as if her life
depended on it.

When she came, her cries echoed throughout the office and
I held her shuddering body. After that it was my turn. My head
rolled back and forth as her nimble fingers delicately probed my
soft crevices and my legs opened to receive her.

We made love several times that night until the soft gray light of dawn entered through the office windows. We didn't say much to each other as she took me home on her Vespa so I could get ready to catch my plane back to America. I would never forget my teacher.

The Gamble

Bobbie Glick

There she is, stylish in tight jeans and T-shirt—and fully acces-sorized in that casual way only a true hipster can put together. Someone should write a guide. That flight attendant uniform she was wearing earlier had done nothing for her perfect figure. Not that it fooled me. I can undress a woman with my eyes, and I knew she was exquisite. Now I can't wait to get those hipster clothes off so my imagination will again be proved right. I'm always right. It pays to be when you play the corporate game, if you want to run with the big dogs—or, in my case, the big dykes.

She's walking over to my car, wide-smiling with full, glossy lips, and with each step seducing me with a prolonged sway of the hip to the left...right...left. How does she do it? Maybe she ought to write the guide. She is just that hot.

Oh, shit. What have I gotten myself into? I've never done any-thing like this before—these words skirt through my dizzy head before I manage to compose myself with just the sort of motiva-tional pep talk the situation calls for: *Relax, Bobbie. You're a fuck-ing high-profile litigator, loaded, well-dressed. And besides: (a) she told you the name of her hotel; (b) she heard you and nodded her acknowledgment when she was standing with those other flight attendants waiting for the shuttle* (as an attorney, I often think in outline form); *and (c) I rest my case.*

It had been a gamble when I'd told her, "I'm 30 minutes behind you. I'll meet you in front of your hotel," but I am used to gambles. And I had plenty of hard evidence on which to base my gamble. She had paid such lavish attention to me on the plane—it wasn't the typical first-class service when she put the dinner napkin on my lap and caressed my thigh to smooth it out, put her lips close to mine and said, "I really want to help you relax on this flight." We had over six hours of foreplay in an air-conditioned chamber hurtling at over 500 mph. This is really no gamble at all. Well, if you can call that napkin trick and a bit of flirtatious eye contact foreplay.

And here she is now, two strides away from me, still smiling. I wonder if she does this all the time. The hell with it; she's just too hot for me to get all nervous and ruin my chances. Besides, she wants to be with me. I can't believe it. But I make myself believe it by abolishing the predominant thought in my mind, which is that this is a scene from that old movie where the guy narrowly escapes the hangman's noose and the film takes you through the rope breaking, his fall into—and escape via—the river, then the woods, then right up to the point where the fellow sees his beautiful wife running to him, and at the last second, *snap!* his neck breaks and suddenly it's apparent he had never left that noose and that this was all just a man's last dying fantasy. That thought I dispel from my mind immediately.

She opens the door of my new silver Mercedes CL500 and seats herself in—of all places—the backseat. "Mmm, smells like new leather."

"Yes," I say. "Brand-new."

"Oh, so are you into leather?" she asks.

I respond—*très* suavely—that I am into anything she is.

She blows across the back of my neck. Wow.

I pause for a minute—do I take her to my house or to an anonymous hotel? *Don't be a fool! You can't take her home.* I remember an associate of mine telling me about a place that has deep Japanese tubs and luxurious service.

"It's been a long flight. How about a nice private bath?"

"Sounds wonderful," she responds.

I'm actually glad she sat where she did because I'm sure she'll notice my copy of Jonathan Franzen's *The Corrections* (pre-Oprah's Book Club sticker!) in the backseat. The great thing about this book is that everyone is impressed by the mere sight of it, and although I've never read it myself, I have pawed through the pages to make it look that way. Of course, she doesn't comment on the book, but I know she sees it and is awed by me.

We pull up to the valet and I grab my luggage. She has none. How do I handle this? It's all seeming rather lurid—and lurid is turning me on. So is her perfume. "Why don't you wait over there?" I tell her, and point to a couch in the cool, minimalist lobby. I soon have the key, and engaging in the same flirtatious eye contact—only more intense and without looking away—we ride the immaculate elevator up to our penthouse suite. She has the kind of dark brown eyes that never fail to make me wet. Mine are a pale, washed-out blue. Shark-eye blue, I like to think. Once we're inside the hotel room, I feel a bit shy—normal enough. I mask my shyness by going over to draw our bath, but to my slight embarrassment, the tub is already full of steaming water. There's a selection of fragrant mineral salts along the edge. I pour in some ylang ylang powder, a known aphrodisiac.

"Would you like me to order some sushi and champagne?" I ask her.

"Oh, my God, that sounds perfect."

We undress with our backs to each other, then slip into rich silk kimono robes. We walk over to the delicious, steaming tub, which is recessed into the floor and as deep as a Jacuzzi. We stand next to each other, and she tugs at my sash and my kimono slips open. I do the same to her, and as her kimono opens, I slip my hand around her small waist and pull her to me, pull her big breasts against my small firm ones. She could be a Victoria's Secret model. My God, I was right on that body! I lick around the inside of one corner of her lips. She shivers. I feel heady. As we kiss a passionate movie kiss, I slip the kimono off her shoulders. As it falls, I keep kissing her and wriggle out of mine. The soft silk runs over the small of my back and off my ass. It makes a small sound on the floor. Her mouth is sweet and wicked. I have to force myself to pull away. We stand naked next to the tub, gazing at each other's body—her hourglass figure and immaculate skin versus my lean runner's frame and freckled chest—before easing into the shock of hot water.

For a half second we sit apart, then she moves in as I close my eyes and enjoy the soothing minerals swirling over my skin. I feel her breath in my ear, then her delicate pointed tongue licking first the lobe—clicking my pearl earring against her teeth—then darting around my inner ear, sending chills down my back. What a sensation in the hot, hot water!

My ear is particularly sensitive—as her tongue glides in and over and around it—because it is still adjusting to the sharp changes in altitude during the flight. My nipples harden. My legs drift apart as her hand moves between them. Her fingers explore my cunt. I'm both eager and startled. Used to taking control of things, but curious to see what this freak does next. She does this: pulls away from my ear, takes a deep breath, dives under. Her hair splays out like seaweed between my legs. Her tongue laps at my clit. I put my head back—no one's ever gone down on me underwater before!—ready to come, but she runs out of air before I can, surfaces with a violent breath, flops out of the tub, and sprints giggling to the bed where she somersaults herself into a huge sprawl on the red silk duvet.

I want her bad now. I haul myself out of the tub and also run to the bed—but before I get there, she rolls off one side and crawls under it.

"You have to catch me," she says.

"Are you out of your mind?" I ask, thinking, *And what if she really is a lunatic?*

"Can't catch me, can't catch me," she chants.

"Oh, yeah?" I kneel on the cold black marble, reach my arm under the bed, and grab her ass hard. She squeals. I try to drag her out from under the bed by her ass, fail, grab her tit, play with the nipple, realize this game is getting her very heated up. Her eyes have a glazed look, and she's squirming around, giggling, but giggling sexily. We play this grab game for a while, for as long as I can put up with it, and I've got a raging clitty hard-on and she's getting sex-kitteny and sex-kittenier every second. When I pull her by the ankle, she's so sweaty and slippery she slides right out. I drag her up to her feet and she swoons into me. I turn her and throw her facedown on the bed with her legs hanging over the edge, grind my clit into the sweet crack of her ass, and work myself off.

She turns over as I stagger back, keeps her knees bent over the edge of the bed, and spreads those tantalizingly soft thighs. The movement spreads her pussy—just the faintest bit more open to expose her pink flesh, the nose of her clit. I fall to my knees and bury my tongue in her crotch. The hair is trimmed into the shape of a little heart—no lie—and while this doesn't do anything for my opinion of her intellect, it drives me crazy as a lover. I lick her luscious shaved lips till there's nothing left of that hot little pussy I haven't touched. Then I ease my three fingers in, toy with her clit with my thumb a bit, then push up into her G-for-glee spot. She's ready to go off now, so I take a chance and decide to play her out, lean my shoulder into one soft thigh as a way of pinning her, wiggle my fingers, finding good and deeper and better spots to press—and whenever I find one of those deep "best" spots, I give her a few licks to intensify the experience.

"Oh, come on, baby," she begs maybe two or three times before shouting, "Goddamn it! Suck me now! Harder! Or I'll get up off this bed, and so help me I'll…"

I do not want to know what she's going to do to me if I don't get her off now. So I suck and gently flick her clit. I hum and flick, then suck and flick, then pause and just suck the shit out of her. She blows her top—and I mean in a good way. Her orgasm splashes out onto my neck and trickles down between my breasts, but also up into my mouth. It's bitter, but I don't pull away until her hands—trying to pry me off her—are in danger of wrenching my neck.

Snap!

It's the sound of my briefcase closing. The plane is about to land, and while this is a hell of a hot scene and while the stewardess did whisper those words in my ear and has been making flirtatious eye contact with me throughout this flight, I'm in a monogamous relationship, and all electronic devices (which include the laptop I keep in my briefcase for the purpose of writing down little fantasies to entertain my girlfriend) must be shut down until the aircraft lands safely.

Lusting With Destiny

Mia Dominguez

I agreed to meet Sheryl for dinner after a long time of rejecting her numerous advances. Silly me, I thought it would be so easy to meet an attractive woman after my last breakup, so I put her off as long as I could in hopes that someone really awesome would catch my eye. But unfortunately, this was my fourth month without so much as a prospect of a fine woman in my near future. I guess it was destined that Sheryl and I would eventually go out with each other. She wasn't unattractive—she simply wasn't my type. I'm all for a nice soft-butch woman, but I don't like them to have that carbon-copy, old-school butch haircut. You know the one: long in back, cut over the ears, and too short on top. My butch needs to be stylish, sexy, and confident.

Sheryl didn't possess the attributes I seek in the woman of my dreams. Besides that dated haircut, there were numerous reasons she and I could never become serious lovers. I don't mean to sound shallow, but physical attraction is a good 80% of what holds my interest. Without an immediate attraction, I could never fall head over heels for a woman. I need the heat, the chemistry, and the passion ignited by my animalistic desires to feel that intimate carnal connection. I didn't feel anything resembling passion for Sheryl. But she stopped at nothing to change my mind about that. One of her favorite methods of going about this was to let me know what I was missing by suggesting how many other women found her irresistible.

"You know, there's this one girl at work who's constantly hinting that she's never kissed another woman before. Sometimes I feel like just walking up and obliging her. Just to shut her up, of course," Sheryl bragged to me one day.

"Why don't you oblige her, then?" I challenged her.

"I'm not interested in her. I'm only interested in you."

"Don't you think it'd be wise to be interested in someone who expressed an interest in you?"

"Aren't you the least bit interested in me?" she asked.

"For friendship only."

"I think if you went out with me, you'd see things in a different light. Why not see if there's anything there?"

Eventually, in an effort to put an end to this insanity once and for all, I agreed. "Fine. Let's go out to dinner Friday night. If nothing happens, we'll remain friends with no hard feelings. Agree?"

"You're on. It'll be a lot of fun. I promise you won't be sorry," Sheryl insisted.

I knew Sheryl would pull out all stops in an effort to sway my interest her way, but I also knew there was a snowball's chance in hell that my affections would ever grow into anything more than a comfortable friendship. When Friday night rolled around, I played it as safe as possible. Rather than allowing Sheryl to pick me up at home—meaning she'd also be taking me home at the end of the evening—I chose to meet her at our destination. I had no intentions of hooking up with Sheryl, although there has been a time or two when I have thrown caution to the wind while in an inebriated state. However, partaking in a tryst of the flesh simply to satisfy a need of the moment was not a place I wanted to visit with Sheryl. Certainly, if I gave her so much as a peek at a bare breast, there was no way I'd be able to turn her off again. Tonight I would be on my best behavior and carefully resist every weapon in her arsenal of seduction.

Generally, I don't consider myself a conservative woman. The Goddess blessed me with generous curves and bountiful cleavage, and it is only out of respect for her that I revel in my womanhood by accentuating these curves with formfitting, eye-popping femme fashions to make my beautiful butch admirers swoon to see more. But on the night in question I chose to keep myself under wraps, not wanting to emanate the slightest amount of sex appeal to Sheryl. The outfit I decided on was a long black suede skirt and black cashmere turtleneck sweater. It wasn't necessarily unsexy, but at least I was covered from head to toe. Like I said, I cannot blow sand in the Goddess's face. It is my innate need to garner as much admiration as I can.

That night, I walked into the French Market, a cute little bistro in West Hollywood geared toward our kind, and noticed Sheryl leaning against the bar.

"Hi there, Sheryl," I said. "How are you tonight?"

"Fine, Mimi. You look gorgeous this evening." She handed me a mixed bouquet of beautifully fragrant orchids and lilies. "These are for you." She kissed my cheek. "Thanks for showing up."

"Thanks so much for the flowers." I thought about what she said for a moment, and responded, "I told you that I'd show up, didn't I?"

"Yeah," Sheryl said, "but I just didn't think you'd follow through. This isn't the first time I've tried to plan something like this with you."

"Well, I'm here now, so let's get a table and have a wonderful meal."

The hostess led us to my favorite table, the one over by the marketplace, because I love to watch all of the handsome couples as they pass by. Sheryl and I ordered an appetizer and a carafe of a sweet blush chablis to begin our evening.

"Let's have a toast, shall we?" Sheryl said.

"Sure." I raised my glass. "To good friends," I offered, before she could construct a romantic, poetic verse.

"To good friends." Reluctantly, Sheryl sipped her wine.

Dinner was quiet for the most part until the wine began to take effect. It was only then that Sheryl had enough courage to confront me on my resistance to be anything more than friends.

"Why aren't you attracted to me?" she asked.

"I suppose you're not my type. It's nothing personal. I'm just not attracted to you," I stated matter-of-factly.

"Is there anything I could do to become your type?"

"I don't think so. I think that time has already passed. Anyway, you've become such a good friend, why would you want to spoil it by testing those waters?"

"Believe me, I wish I could just be your friend, but I can't get you out of my head."

"You know what it is?" I interjected. "It's that dynamic of

wanting what you can't have. You know there's no future for us, so you want it that much more. While in the meantime you're not pursuing other women who might want you in a desperate way."

"I'm not attracted to them," she said.

"You don't give yourself the opportunity to be attracted to them. You're always talking about all of these attractive women who come on to you, so why not respond to them? What do you have to lose?"

"Perhaps in time I will, but for now I'll enjoy my date with you," Sheryl sweetly whispered to me over the table.

Admittedly, I *was* thoroughly enjoying my dinner—not so much due to Sheryl but to the abundance of glances and smiles that came my way through the course of our evening. First there was the cute little butch who sat at the table across from us. She had a dinner companion but stole a glance in my direction whenever she could without being noticed. Then there was the attractive waitress who catered to my every need throughout dinner. Perhaps she was being flirtatious to garner a larger tip, but it made no difference to me. I was basking in the attention that was so generously given to me from these two—and an occasional passerby. So much so that I decided to take this animal magnetism that I seemed to radiate and put it to good use.

"Why don't we go to Encounters after dinner and have a drink or two?" I asked Sheryl. "I feel like listening to some music."

"That's a great idea." She seemed to grow enthusiastic with my suggestion of moving our date along to another place, but my intent with her remained the same. The wine put me in a mood for some serious flirting, and I knew that whenever I showed up at Encounters there'd always be someone to respond. I've never left Encounters feeling needy.

When Sheryl and I drove up to the club, a woman immediately caught my attention. As she was getting out of her car and I was slipping out of the passenger side of Sheryl's sports car, our eyes met. She smiled.

"Hi," I said.

"Hello there." She smiled again. "How are you?"

"I'm good. How about yourself?"

"Good." She locked up her truck.

"I guess I'll see you inside?"

"Sure," she said as she walked away.

I couldn't shake off the smile she left on my face, until Sheryl brought it to my attention.

"Geez, Mimi, I've never been able to make you smile like that," she said.

"Don't be upset, Sheryl. Not many people can."

"Please remember that you're out on a date with me."

"I know, and I will behave," I told her. "I won't do anything to hurt your feelings."

"Please don't."

I told Sheryl this because I was afraid she'd make a scene if I even suggested that I would respond to this woman's advances. Whenever Sheryl and I hit the clubs she was reluctant to allow me the opportunity to even visit the ladies' room alone for fear that another woman would try to seduce me. I decided that perhaps I could get this woman's attention enough to pass her my telephone number, but that would be the extent of my flirtation for tonight.

As I scanned the club to find my lone rangeress, I found her sitting alone at the bar, apparently looking for me. Then our eyes met. She smiled, and I smiled back. Sheryl and I got ourselves a table not far from the bar. Rather than wait for the waiter to come and take our order, I told Sheryl I'd go fetch us some drinks.

"Why don't you let me get our drinks?" Sheryl said. "I don't want you paying for anything tonight."

"Now, that's not fair," I told her. "You generously paid for dinner, so I'm going to get this round. As a matter of fact, I insist." Before Sheryl had the opportunity to argue the point, I was off the bar stool and on my way to the bar, where my parking-lot flirt sat. She turned to me, checking me out from head to toe.

"Who's that woman you're with? Your girlfriend?"

"No. Not at all. She's just a friend." I let out a bit of nervous laughter. "Are you waiting for someone?"

"Actually, I'm not certain what I'm doing here. I'm newly single and trying to get back into the swing of things."

"Oh, I'm sorry."

"For what?"

"For your breakup," I said.

"Don't be sorry about that. I'm not. It was a long time coming, and if I hadn't broken up with her, I wouldn't be talking to you right now."

I'd been speaking to her for a good five minutes until I realized I'd left Sheryl waiting for her drink.

"Look, I'm really sorry, but I kind of promised that woman I wouldn't leave her alone tonight. I don't want to be rude."

"I understand," she said, "but do you think we could speak again soon? I'd really like to get to know you."

"I'd also like to get to know you. If I get the opportunity, I'll come back and see you in a while—at least to give you my telephone number."

It took all the energy I had to focus on the conversation Sheryl corralled me into. Apparently, unwilling to forget our dinner conversation, she revisited the topic.

"So if I'm not your type, who is?" she asked.

"I don't want to answer that because I don't want to hurt your feelings."

"Is that woman you keep staring at your type?" Sheryl asked, knowing damn well she was in fact exactly the type of woman I could easily find myself taken with. But I didn't want to deliberately hurt Sheryl's feelings, although I felt I was actually the one suffering by keeping my distance from her for what seemed an eternity.

"Sheryl," I said, "I don't want to answer that because the answer will only result in hurt feelings." Just then I saw my magnificent butch rise from her bar stool and walk over to the ladies' room. "I'll be back in a minute, Sheryl. I've got to go to the restroom."

"Fine. I'll get us another drink."

"OK, whatever." I rushed to the ladies' room, hoping we'd be alone. I opened the door and there she stood, leaning against the sink.

"Hey, you," she smiled.

"Hi. I saw you come in here, and I really wanted to speak to you again. I'm sorry."

"Sorry for what?" she wondered.

"You must think I'm a jerk for not talking to you. I'm really sorry."

"You said she's not your girlfriend, so why should you apologize? If you weren't such a nice person, I'd have scooped you up and carried you home by now."

"Oh, really?" I was awestruck by her admission.

"I want your telephone number," she said.

"OK." I reached into my purse, rifling for a pen, when she stopped me. She took my hand.

"This might sound like blackmail, but I don't want your number right now."

"When do you want it, then?"

"At the end of the night. I want you to keep following me in here so I can get to know you better."

"Are you serious?" I asked.

"I'm totally serious. I don't want to take your number and then have to spend the remainder of my birthday watching the most beautiful girl here indulging someone besides myself."

"What do you want me to do?"

"Leave with me," she said.

"I can't."

"Then meet me in here again, without getting yourself in trouble, of course."

"You've got a deal, honey," I told her. "By the way, happy birthday."

"Thank you. Perhaps I can collect a kiss later?"

"I don't even know your name."

"Santana."

"As in Carlos Santana?"

"What can I say?" she laughed. "My hippie parents love good music."

"That's a great name."

"Thanks." She took my hand. "What's your name?"

"Mimi."

"Very cute," she said, then kissed my hand.

"I'd better go now. I'm sorry."

"I understand. But don't forget to meet me back here soon."

"I won't."

"Promise?"

"I promise." I looked up at Santana to meet her eyes, but before I knew what was happening, our lips were locked in a long, delicious kiss. Right then someone else entered the restroom and we immediately separated.

"What's the matter?" Santana asked.

"You made me dizzy," I laughed. "I'd really better go now." I gave her a quick kiss on the cheek. "I'll see you in a while?"

"Sure."

I returned to my table, watching with anxiety as other women approached Santana, attempting to pick her up. They were no prettier or sexier than myself; nevertheless I felt the green-eyed monster creeping up on me. I needed to see her again.

"Sheryl, I need to go to the ladies' room," I said. "I'll be back in a minute."

I rushed to the restroom, awaiting Santana's arrival. I counted …one…two…three, and before I reached four, Santana was in my arms. Her embrace was warm and welcoming.

"I missed you," I whispered in her ear.

"I missed you too. And don't worry about those other women. I'm not interested," she assured me. "It's not often that I meet someone that I'm so taken with."

I stuck my tongue out, touching her lips and tasting her sweet kisses. Forgetting where I was, I ran my hands through her thick black hair, forcing her to kiss me even harder and deeper. Santana had pinned me against the sink and was running her hands down the curves of my body.

"You feel so good, Mimi," she whispered as her hand brushed my breast. My first inclination was to take her hand, lead her outside, and take her home with me. But I couldn't do that to Sheryl. She was good to me and was, as difficult as it was to her, attempting to be my friend.

"We have to stop," I said. "I need to get back to my friend."

"Stay here just a minute longer." Santana reached down to feel the heat between my thighs. "I need you," she whispered as her hand roamed up my skirt.

I sighed as my thighs begged me to envelop her, then finally resisted. "I can't. I'm sorry, Santana. I have to go, and if I don't leave now, I'm never going to leave."

"Meet me back here soon?"

"Of course. I'll come back very soon." I fixed my skirt, smoothed a coat of lipstick onto my lips, and walked back to the table where Sheryl had been waiting, very impatiently.

"Do you think I'm an idiot?" Sheryl asked.

"Of course not. Why would you ask me that?"

"I see what's happening. Every time you're gone, she's gone. Don't make a fool out of me. Why don't you just leave with her if you want it that bad?"

"I'm not leaving because I told you I wouldn't."

"Don't do me any favors. I don't need your fucking pity." Sheryl rose from her seat and marched out of the bar. I followed her out.

"Sheryl, please don't leave. I'm so sorry. Please allow me to apologize?" I grabbed her hand before she could open her car door, and held it tight in mine.

"Sheryl, I'm so sorry."

"Don't be sorry," she said. "You don't want me. You can't help it." Tears rolled down her face. I felt helpless, and without giving it a second thought I pressed my lips against hers. Sheryl's kisses started softly and sweetly, then turned lustfully passionate. She grabbed my long auburn curls in her hands, keeping my head close to her. She held her body as close to mine as she could, rubbing it into me while her eager hands mapped the curve of my form.

"I want you," Sheryl whispered in my ear. "I want to make love to you." I opened my eyes to find Santana exiting the bar on the arm of another woman, and to my surprise I didn't give a damn. The passion Sheryl expressed to me was overwhelming, and my desire to feel her skin melt into mine couldn't be ignored.

"Let me make love to you, Mimi, just once. That's all I want," Sheryl breathed in my ear while desperately fondling my breasts and biting my hardened nipples over the sweater I'd worn to deter her.

I was so turned on, I could no longer resist her advances. "Make love to me, Sheryl," I demanded.

Without saying a word, she took my hand and we ran across the street to a motel. I waited for her in the lobby while she got our room, then I proceeded to fulfill her every desire. When I walked into the room, she gently pushed me to the bed, throwing herself on top of me. We kissed over and over again while she fumbled with my clothing.

"Take this off," Sheryl demanded.

"What do you want off?"

"Everything. I need it off now, baby. Please, you've teased me long enough."

No sooner had I removed my panties than Sheryl had her face buried deep within my thighs. My nectar flowed as she brought me to orgasm several times by plunging her tongue deep inside my pussy. My legs shivered and shook as she thrilled me more than I could ever imagine.

"Stop!" I screamed.

"Never. I don't know when you'll let me have you again. I'm not stopping until I'm ready."

Admittedly, I was turned on by Sheryl's aggressiveness, as I always am by the butches with whom I usually keep company.

"Take your clothes off," I told her.

"No," she said. "This is for me."

Sheryl didn't remove her clothes for the rest of the evening. Instead she presented me with some of the most incredible climaxes I'd ever experienced. Sheryl stayed on top of me while tempting every part of my body. She stroked my wet lips with her fingers, slowly working her way deep inside me, thrusting in and out, while I squirmed and pulsated on her expert fingers and she showered me with deep, eager kisses. As she worked her way back down to my wet pussy, I begged her again to take off the clothing that separated us like a suit of armor.

"I said no, Mimi," she told me. She held my arms down as I tried to slide the shirt off her back. "You're mine for tonight, so just be still and let me have my way."

I spread my legs for her to take me and taste as much as she wanted, until she tired. After she had her fill of me, we slept quietly in each other's arms, and when morning came, she drove me back to the restaurant where we'd met the night before. As I walked back to my car, I thought that maybe I could come to care for Sheryl on a deeper level, but that never happened. As Sheryl had asked for only one night with me, that remained the extent of what she'd ever ask of me, and we became closer friends than before.

The Busgirl

C.J. Evans

It was 1989 and I had just come out to my college roommates. I'd known I was bisexual since I was 16 or 17, but I'd never had the courage to act on my desires for women. My entire freshman year I was attracted to my English T.A., but she was straight (and kind of mean) and my crush was obsessive and futile. When my sophomore year rolled around and I was going to be moving into an apartment with three friends, I took them each aside separately and came out to them. Living as a closeted bisexual in the dorms my freshman year had been manageable, but I knew it would be rough to try to keep the secret from my new roommates. Fortunately, my friends were all open-minded (I probably wouldn't have told them if they weren't), and they were all cool when I came out to them. One of them, Kate, even checked out a book of lesbian erotica from the library and read it out loud with me. We were cracking up the entire time—a lot of it was so hackneyed and terribly written.

A few weeks later I saw an ad in the school paper about a dance that was being held by the Ten Percent Club, the campus gay and lesbian group, that Friday night. I asked Kate if she would go with me since I was nervous about going alone and didn't know any other gay people at school. Kate was straight, but as I said, my roommates were all pretty liberal, and she agreed to go with me.

"I'll split if any hot chicks hit on you," Kate smiled.

"Yeah, right. Like that's going to happen," I laughed.

The next day, Thursday, the day before the dance, I was running for the bus headed for campus, frantically trying to wave it down. I had a 7:50 A.M. anthropology class that I was chronically late for. Plus it was raining outside and I had a huge anthro project in my satchel. I finally caught up the bus at a red light and climbed inside. I was a complete wreck, trying to maneuver my way through the crowded bus with a cup of coffee, my umbrella, and my overflowing satchel. All of a sudden this grizzly guy turned around and jabbed me with his elbow, causing my entire project to spill out of my bag.

"Oh, sorry, lady," he said.

"Whatever," I snarled.

"Here, let me help you with that." I looked up and saw the prettiest blue eyes I'd ever seen on the sexiest woman I'd ever seen. She had short blond hair and a crooked smile and porcelain skin. A little on the butch side but slightly feminine. A tomboy, which to me is the sexiest kind of woman on earth.

"Thanks. Thanks a lot," I managed as she got my papers together and handed them to me.

"No problem. No problem at all." We were making some serious eye contact, but then she suddenly looked out the window and said, "Oh, it's my stop. See ya around…I hope."

Now, to this day I'm really bad at recognizing when someone's hitting on me. Usually, if I'm at a bar and some cute girl is staring at me, I think, *What? Do I have chili on my face or something?* But on this autumn day in 1989, I had actually been *checked out* by a girl. Man, did I ever hope I'd see her around again.

All day I thought about her, so much so that I was practically glowing. When I got home from class later that afternoon, I told Kate what had happened.

"See, you don't even need me," she said. "You can get all the girls you want by yourself."

"I need you for moral support!" I laughed. "Besides, what if she shows up at the dance tomorrow night?"

"How do you even know she's gay?"

"Oh, I know. Believe me, I know."

The next night I was so nervous I thought I was going to pee in my pants. But I didn't, of course. I got all dolled up in my best jeans, a black T-shirt, and my nicest pair of Doc Martens. I ran some gel through my shoulder-length brown hair, put on a little lipstick, and was ready to go.

"Meow!" Kate said as we headed out the door toward the student union, where the dance was being held. "Hello-o-o, Kitty!"

I cracked up and threw my arm around her, glad I had such a good pal.

When we got to the second floor of the student union, we paid our $2 cover and went inside. My eyes totally bugged out at the sight of so many gay people gathered together. The first thing I noticed was two gay men dressed in leather in the corner, one with his arm slung over the shoulders of the other. At one table a bunch of middle-aged butch women sat around totally cracking up and pointing at their clumsy friend trying to bust a move on the dance floor. Dozens of pink and white helium-filled balloons clung to the ceiling. The mood in the place was definitely celebratory, which put me in high spirits, even though I was nervous since I was attending my first official gay and lesbian event. Plus I was hoping I'd see the blond girl from the bus, so my adrenaline was pumping at full force.

After going up to the bar and getting a couple of bottles of water, Kate and I found a table near the dance floor and sat down and watched the scene before our eyes. The sound system was pounding out Sister Sledge.

"She's cute. What about her?" Kate asked, pointing to a girl on the dance floor.

"Too short," I said. "I wouldn't like being the 'big' one."

"What about that redhead in the corner?"

"Too pretentious looking. I can't go out with anyone whose earrings weigh more than she does."

"You're too picky," Kate said.

"Yeah, well, I have a right to be picky. I'm a freakin' sex kitten! Meow!" I keeled over laughing, which cracked Kate up too. In fact, we were laughing so hard, everyone around us must have been staring at us. And then the impossible happened: Right when I looked up, tears streaming out of my eyes, who was standing over me but the blond girl from the bus.

"I didn't know I was that funny-looking," she said, grinning from ear to ear.

"Oh…uh…hi," I said, trying to compose myself. "Kate, this is…um…I'm sorry, I didn't get your name."

"I'm Joanna." She reached to shake Kate's hand.

"I'm Carolyn," I told her.

I guess Kate could tell right away that this was the girl I'd told her about. It was probably pretty obvious by the way I was acting—like a huge dork. Plus I'd described Joanna physically in detail to Kate at least five times the previous day! Well, being such a good friend (or a tormentor), Kate immediately excused herself, saying she had to use the restroom. But I made some "Oh, my God, I can't believe you're doing this to me" eye contact with Kate before she left.

"Um…do you want to sit down?" I asked Joanna.

"Sure," she said, and she did. "Is this your first time at one of these dances?"

Man, were her eyes blue. I must have looked like I was freakin' hypnotized, the way I was just zoning out into them. Still, I had enough sense to answer her. "Is it that obvious?" I laughed.

"No, no, I didn't mean that," she grinned. "I just meant that I've never seen you here before."

"This is the campus Jews for Jesus dance, isn't it?"

Joanna and I busted up laughing, which was just the icebreaker we needed. I looked out onto the dance floor for a moment and saw Kate doing the funky chicken with two gay gays, which cracked me up even more. It looked like she was having fun, and now I had a little time to get to know Joanna better.

Joanna and I sat there talking for nearly an hour and a half—and Kate danced the entire time! All the dancing gay guys thought she was the belle of the ball, screaming, "Go, girl! Go, girl!" over and over as she undulated and shimmied across the dance floor.

I learned that Joanna was also a sophomore, that she was treasurer of the Ten Percent Club, and that she loved old movies and board games, just like me. In fact, we had a lot in common: We were both only children, daughters of preachers (why are so many preachers' kids gay, anyway?), and both rode green 10-speed Schwinns! She also told me she had just declared her major: art history. I told her I was still deciding between English and anthropology, but that I'd probably eventually do a double major, which would keep me in school for at least five years.

"You can't finish in four?" she asked.

"Well, I'm kind of slow," I laughed.

"I hope you're not slow with everything." Just then Joanna smiled and gave me a quick kiss on the cheek. A kiss so sweet and tender that I probably should have gone straight to hell for what it did to my loins: Immediately I was wet.

"No, not everything," I grinned.

Just then Kate ambled up to the table. She was sweaty but had a big smile on her face. "Hey, I'm going to this party at this guy Geoffrey's house," she said. "You guys wanna come? It's just down the street from our place on Wilson. He's really cool." She pointed to a cute blond guy on the dance floor grooving out to "Dancing Queen."

"Sounds good," Joanna said.

"Yeah, let's get out of here," I smiled.

So Joanna, Kate, and I headed out and walked the 15 minutes to Geoffrey's place, which, it turned out, was only two doors down from my apartment. I had a gay neighbor and didn't even know it! We went inside the upstairs apartment (it was a duplex), and the place was *packed* with gay men and lesbians, mostly college students but also a few older people.

"You guys friends of Geoffrey's?" a stunning, tall brunet asked us as we came in.

"Sorta," I said.

"Hi, I'm Sena, his roommate. He'll be here in a little bit. Grab a beer. The keg's in the corner."

We all grabbed a beer, then Kate—gay social butterfly that she now was—went over and started chatting up a couple of guys who looked like they might be straight. Maybe she'd get a date tonight too.

The place was so packed that we could hardly move, so Joanna and I went out onto the balcony in the back, which was for some strange reason empty. We looked out into the starry sky.

"So...you're really cute," Joanna said. "I noticed you right away on the bus. In fact, I noticed you when you were *running* for the bus."

"Oh, God, did you see *that*?" I laughed.

"Yeah, it was pretty funny."

"You're not just cute," I told her. "You're beautiful. And 'cute' doesn't get dates. 'Sexy' does." My whole life I'd been plagued by people calling me "cute". It was always, "Oh, Carolyn, you're so *cute*," never "gorgeous" or "sexy" or any of that. I guess cute is better than hideous, but it gets old after a while.

"I think you're absolutely breathtaking," Joanna said, and then she put down her beer and leaned in and kissed me—on the mouth this time. If there were a hundred stars in the sky that night, I wouldn't know it, because I saw thousands of them in front of my eyes once she pulled away. So *this* was kissing a girl. Right then I knew I'd never need to be with a guy again. This was it. Fuck bisexuality! I was a full-on *dyke*!

"That was nice," I said, fumbling for words, so instead of saying anything else, I kissed her back. This time it was more serious. Our tongues intertwined passionately; my entire body was aching for this. And *this* wouldn't do. I needed to sleep with this woman ASAP.

"Hey," I said, breaking the kiss, "I live two doors down. Wanna blow this place?"

"Good plan," Joanna said, grabbing my hand.

On our way out of the party, I waved to Kate, who was engrossed in conversation with a jocky-looking guy. She just winked as Joanna and I left and made the short walk to my apartment. Luckily, my other two roommates, Angela and Holly, were out for the evening, so we had the place to ourselves. I grabbed two beers from the fridge, and Joanna and I got comfortable on the couch.

"So you wanna finish where we left off?" I smiled.

I didn't even have to wait for an answer. Joanna pulled me to her and kissed me passionately. I put my hands on the back of her head; her short hair was fuzzy and tickled my fingers. I searched out her mouth with my tongue then nudged it playfully against her two front teeth, which had a small space between them. I bit her lower lip gently. Joanna trailed kisses down my face to my neck.

"Mind if I take this off?" She tugged at my T-shirt.

"Let's go into my room first," I said. "What if one of my roommates walks in?"

Joanna agreed, and we went into my room and shut the door behind us. She pressed me up against the door and kissed me again, this time a little more forcefully. "Let's take this off *now*," she said, and pulled my shirt over my head. I undid my black lacy bra and let it fall to the floor.

I turned on a small lamp by my bed and shut off the overhead light. We both got comfortable on my futon, me on my back and Joanna straddling me.

"Oh, baby, you are so beautiful," she said, kneading my breasts, and I was so glad to hear those words, especially coming from someone as hot as Joanna. My crotch was so wet, I thought I'd soak the futon.

Joanna scooched down and started sucking and biting my breasts, slurping on my nipples like they were candy, circling over and over with her tongue. She made her way down my torso with her warm, wet mouth until she got to my belt. In a couple of swift motions she undid the buckle. Her quickness and agility were turning me on more and more by the second. After I helped her take off my jeans, she went in for the kill, sucking my red-hot clit through my damp cotton panties. The sensation was exquisite but pure torture: I wanted that tongue right on my clit. So I pulled down my panties and let her have it.

Now, I'd had guys perform oral sex on me many times, but they never knew what the hell they were doing. I was always like, "Um, excuse me, are you going to be done soon? Your head is blocking *Nightline*." When Ted Koppel is more interesting than having your clit sucked, you know something's amiss. But with Joanna it was completely different. She knew just how to please me, sucking my entire clitoris into her full lips, tonguing under the hood, flicking fiercely then gently, then teasing it with little licks. When she put two fingers inside me and continued to eat me out like crazy, I thought I was going to burst. My pussy was sopping wet with slippery come.

"You taste so good," Joanna said, and she pulled her fingers out and brought them to my mouth. "Here, taste."

She was right. But I'd bet my entire checking account *she* tasted better.

Joanna put her fingers back inside and added a third, thrusting into me full force. She went back to tonguing my engorged clit, licking my entire vulva with her masterful tongue, around and around and around. My entire body started to shake as she brought me to the edge; chills flooded my skin as I cried out in release and ecstasy.

"That's it," I laughed. "Tomorrow I'm buying a monthly bus pass."

Joanna just laughed as she covered my face with kisses. We made love several times that night. And even though it was my first time with a woman, I knew how to please her—and brought her to orgasm several times—since I just did what I thought would make her feel good. And, as the saying goes, who knows a woman's body like another woman, right?

Joanna and I dated for the rest of our sophomore year, but then she transferred to a college with a better art history program. The program at our school had lost a lot of its best faculty members in the past few years, and its funding had been drastically reduced. (I was sure it was because of the new football stadium the college was building.) We tried to maintain a long-distance relationship, but we were now 900 miles apart, which took its toll on both of us, so we eventually broke up. But 13 years later we're still friends and even E-mail each other several times a week, updating each other on our love lives (we're both chronically single). Still, Joanna was one of the hottest—and definitely the most caring—lovers I've ever had in my life. And to this day, I'm mostly attracted to tomboyish blond women. Wonder why?

Oh, and by the way, my friend Kate ended up dating a tall, dark, and handsome lacrosse player she met at the party that night. They became "college sweethearts" (God, that phrase makes me cringe) and will have been married eight years this fall. Every chance I get, I remind her how my taking her out for a night of gay fun and frolic led to a lifetime of happiness for her!

One Weekend Morning

Helen M. Ethan

It is the morning of our seventh wedding anniversary. The sun is just up. The French doors have been left open all night, and the fresh, crisp air makes my bare skin shiver. Outside, the trees rustle and the brown-eyed calico mews softly—asking to be fed. I sit naked on Jenn's pliant stomach, my solid dancer's body in a groove all its own.

"You are so wet," says Jenn. "So wet."

"Mmm," I purr as I spread my knees apart, slide my wet clit to the border of her bush—her beautiful, crisp, red-curled bush—and work myself over it. The friction builds a nice warm sensation between my legs. I scoot up, dangle my left breast over her mouth. Lazily, as if accepting a roasted fig from a fan-wielding Egyptian slave girl, my lover parts her full warm lips, closes her blue Irish eyes. Her tongue flicks over my tender skin, fluttering, circling…

"Shouldn't I go feed the cat?" I ask.

"Uh, no." She takes a concentrated drag on my nipple.

"Before this turns into something?"

"This has turned into something." Her large hands hold the crests of my hips, the small of my back, lifting me, pushing me, guiding me.

"Ah…mmm," hums Jenn's tit-stuffed mouth.

"Oh, yeeeeah," I answer.

My clit careens over her mound of Venus, tickles itself on her hairs, rakes over her navel, and sparks against her pubic bone. My breast stretches up in her skillful teeth and my wet cunt slips up her belly. "God, your body's beautiful!" she mumbles from the side of her mouth. "So girly…and strong." Suddenly she reaches around my ass—a stretch, but she can just do it—enters my twat from behind.

"Oh!" I say.

It is the morning of our seventh wedding anniversary. The marriage of Mutt and Jeff—a short, flighty dancer and a tall, graceful redheaded pianist.

Jenn's pudgy, sweat-slicked belly is to me just like a cunt. "I'm fucking your cunt," I say. "Baby, what a sweet cunt you've got."

Jenn lets my nipple drop out of her mouth. Dark red. "You're the one with the sweet cunt," she answers, then goes back to her chewing and sucking, making sharp darts of pain travel through me. She wants me to look in the mirror after my shower today and to see a raspberry shadow half on my nipple, half on the skin of my breast, and to ride my little blue vintage Vespa to my contact-improv group and to feel a pang in my chest and to know the color of that pang, the color of Jenn's love.

Jenn relaxes and tries to yield, to let my clit—which is so swollen it bobs like a float in a sea of sweat and come—slide and move with impunity. Her forearm cradles and rocks my ass as she curls her wrist under to keep fucking me with her two, then three, then four fluttering fingers. She gives me a quite a ride.

Oh, yes, I know I can ride on those long fingers and that no matter how hard I buck, no matter how much of myself I forget, those fingers will carry me. I fuck down and up, my clit-line dragging a letter J forward and back, and as I drag back feeling that sublime friction building, as I rear back for the next plunge, I rear back onto those expert fingers—Jenn's loving, pianist's fingers—and a sharp pain rides through my breast and my heart at the same time and I hear my lover's moans and I breathe the fresh air and the fuck smell—and it is good.

"Oh, good G-g-god," My narrow, angular hips move in short stabs and, with cocked wrist, Jenn fights to meet those stabs.

"Honey, yeah," she says. "Honey...."

"OK, OK, OK..." I call out. "Oh, bull's-eye! Honey, oh, OK, OK...O-o-oh! O-o-oh!" Jenn pushes all the way in and holds on for dear life as I gush over her in wet spasms.

Then I am gone for a while. Busy ripping my sore breast from Jenn's mouth, busy slumping over, busy shaking my head like I've just been spit out of a time machine, busy heaving my chest, busy blinking wet eyes, busy half-smiling, busy contracting and relaxing my cunt around Jenn's fingers, busy being so very, very unconscious.

Jenn strokes my hair.

A sound drifts in through the French doors; the feral cat gives a plaintive cry.

It is the morning of our seventh wedding anniversary. When I come back to earth I look my freckle-faced honey in the eye and say, "Baby, now it's your turn."

Ruthie the Riveter

Melissa Robinson

My parents sent me off to Vassar my freshman year with best wishes for a fulfilling college life and a modest monthly allowance. Unfortunately, it was too modest. In an effort to fit in with my dorm mates, beautiful dark-haired girls from New York City, I blew through all my money my first week there. These girls wore stylish clothes, all black of course, smoked cigarettes like they were going out of style, and drank gin and tonics in the evenings.

The first thing I spent my money on was a new wardrobe. Jane, my roommate, sniffed at my acid-washed jeans and white sneakers and took me shopping. "You're in college now," she instructed me. "You need a new, sophisticated look. Don't you think? Ooh, yeah. Those black boots look much better than those dorky sneakers." And of course I soon took up smoking, which was also expensive. So was the beer and pizza we ordered when we didn't feel like going to the All Campus Dining Center, or ACDC as the students called it. To make a long story short, when I went to the ATM late one Friday afternoon to withdraw money for the weekend, I learned I had only $17 left in my account. Thus, the following Monday, I found myself at the student employment office looking for a part-time job.

"Hmm, let's see…" The woman behind the desk touched her finger to her tongue and ran it along a list in front of her. "Well, unfortunately we don't have much left in the way of jobs. It's a little late. Usually it's best to apply for these jobs early in the summer. Oh wait…here's one for manager of the men's lacrosse team." She looked up at me. I swallowed. I definitely didn't want to chase balls for a bunch of jock guys. My cool new friends despised sports. But then again, I was desperate for money…

"Or…can you sew?" she asked me. Sew? I could sew buttons on my shirts and patches on my jeans, but I didn't think that counted. I didn't know how to operate a sewing machine or anything. Still, a sewing job sounded much better than being a lacrosse team gofer. "Sure," I lied. "Oh, goody!" The women said brightly. "That's perfect because the drama department needs an assistant in the costume shop. Can you start Thursday afternoon? You'll be paid $7 an hour, on the last day of each month." I filled out some forms, got directions to the costume shop, and headed back to my dorm, feeling a little glum at the idea of working but also excited that I'd be earning some more spending money.

That night at dinner I found out something about my new friends. They were all bisexual! Or at least they claimed to be. We were sitting around eating, smoking, and drinking coffee when suddenly Logan Foster looked up and giggled. She put her hand to her mouth. "Don't look now, but guess who just walked in."

"Who?" Jane leaned forward eagerly, her cigarette dispatching a chunk of ash into my cola.

"Ruthie!" hissed Logan.

Logan, Jane, and Cory Moscowitz all looked down and studied their trays. I, not having a clue what was going on, looked in the direction of the door.

Whoa! A fairly tall, heavyset woman carrying a heavily laden tray was making her way to a table of people across the room. She wore a T-shirt with the sleeves torn off, and her freckled biceps, as big as ham hocks, sported what looked to be some homemade tattoos. Her hair was sandy blond. It was shaved at the sides, and the rest just sat on her head like a puff of cotton. Her jeans were rolled up to reveal worn combat boots. Her big gut hung over the edge of her pants, barely revealing a…tool belt! "Hey, frig that shit!" she bellowed to her friends in a rasping voice, then dropped her tray and sat down.

"Who *is* that?" I asked.

"Oh, that's Ruth Norman," whispered Jane. "But everyone calls her Ruthie. She's the campus lesbian."

"Lesbian?" I asked.

"Well, duh!" said Cory. "Look at her. She's OK if you like 'em really butch."

Jane shot her an incredulous look. "But she's not my type," Cory quickly added.

"Your type?" I asked weakly, totally confused.

"Yeah." Cory continued unfazed. "I like pretty girls with long hair. And I like girls who look like girls. Not like *that* thing." She giggled and pointed her chin toward Ruthie.

"I didn't know you were—" I started.

"Oh, I'm not lesbian. I swing both ways," Cory quickly interrupted. "Don't you?"

"Me?" I said. "Uh...no. I don't know, I mean..." I looked at Jane for help.

"Don't be silly, Melissa." Jane took a long drag of her cigarette and looked at me coolly. "It's very common, you know."

"Are you?" I asked in surprise. I didn't know if I felt comfortable with a roommate like, well you know, like *that*.

"Well...yeah!" Jane looked at me like I was crazy. "I mean, I prefer guys, but sometimes it's fun to make out with a girl. You know..."

"Yeah," Logan chimed in. "Don't knock it till you try it!"

"Say," Cory giggled. "Let's set Melissa up with Ruthie. Ruthie can break her in."

I looked over at Ruthie, who was shoveling down some mashed potatoes and gesticulating wildly, laughing with her mouth full. She pounded the table. I quickly looked away.

On Thursday, after my last class ended, I headed over to the costume shop to start my new job. I was still a little troubled about what my friends had revealed to me, but during the week they acted so normal and were so nice that I just put it all out of my head. And Jane even had a date with a guy on Saturday night. Still, I didn't know whether to believe them. They were all so attractive and stylish. Not like Ruthie. *Woof.* I shuddered just thinking about those freckled arms and that crazy tool belt.

When I got to the costume shop a meek looking woman in a corduroy jumper and turtleneck was frantically running a piece of turquoise cloth through the sewing machine. "Oh! Are you the new assistant?" she said, standing up expectantly. "I'm

Holly Peterson. Thank God you're here. *A Midsummer Night's Dream* is going up in 10 days, and we are *so* behind on the costuming. Can you finish piecing Titania's gown? And then feather the bottom and add some simple tunic sleeves. I have to leave for a bit. I'll be back in an hour to give you another assignment." Piece Titania's gown? Feather the bottom? Simple tunic sleeves? I had no idea what she meant. "Um…what do you mean by feather?" I muttered. Holly looked cross. "What? Oh, jeez. They always send me over someone who doesn't know what the hell they're doing." She sighed theatrically. "Look, can you sew buttons?" I nodded with relief. "OK, then put these buttons on Bottom's shirt. I'm gonna have to have Ruth train you. She's on her way over now."

Holly threw a white shirt at me and left. I had been sewing buttons for 10 minutes when I heard a noise. I looked up. It was Ruthie, the woman my friends were laughing at the other night at dinner! My stomach felt kind of funny. Ruthie looked at me but didn't say anything. "Hi," I said shyly. "Um…I'm Melissa, the new assistant. Holly says you can teach me some sewing techniques." Ruthie, without introducing herself, rasped rudely, "I wish they would hire someone who knows how to sew." I felt humiliated my ears burned scarlet. Now I was wishing I'd taken the job with the lacrosse team. At least I knew how to pick up balls and fill water bottles. But heck, here I was. I needed money and it was too late now. Ruthie came over with Titania's gown. "Awright, first I'm gonna teach you how to do piecework." She bent over me, and I smelled a combination of perspiration and men's cologne. The smell was repulsive but carried a deep tanginess that much to my surprise and disturbance made me wet.

"OK…now you cut along this line here and then add an extra stitch…no! Frig that shit! That isn't how you do it….here." Ruthie took some pins out of the fabric and put them in her mouth, then expertly cut, stitched, and snipped. "Voilà!" She smiled for the first time, holding up the gown. Her biceps shook. "OK, now you try again."

We spent the whole afternoon working on that dress. By the time I left, I had the hang of it. It felt strange to be sitting so close to someone who I knew was a lesbian. I had never met a woman who looked like Ruthie, with those ripped T-shirts and that tool belt. I left feeling confused.

I continued to assist in the costume shop during the next 10 days. Ruthie sometimes came in to help. She pretty much ignored me, laughing and talking over my head to Holly about various drama-related subjects I knew nothing about. Holly taught me a lot of stuff about sewing, though. Once in a while, if Holly was busy, Ruthie would show me how to do something. Each time I smelled that earthy combination of Ruthie's sweat and cheap men's cologne, my vagina throbbed and gushed. I wished I could have talked to Jane about it, but every time I approached her, I remembered how they had joked about having Ruthie "break me in." I thought it best to let it pass.

The night *A Midsummer Night's Dream* opened, I was required to hang out backstage to help out with the costumes. Holly had stationed me in front of a sewing machine in a large closet full of old costumes just off the stage. Periodically she'd throw a shirt or tunic toward me and hiss, "I need you to fix this in a hurry." Halfway into the final act, I had my back to the door, rummaging through a box of material when the room went black and I heard the door shut. I was about to scream but felt a hand clamp over my mouth and smelled a tangy cologne odor that made my pussy wet. "I'm here to keep our appointment," a voice rattled. It was Ruthie!

"Appointment?" I struggled to ask, but her hand was clamped over my mouth. "Now lean against the wall. That's right, little girl. You're a good girl even if you can't sew." Ruthie's meaty paws were rubbing my breasts through their shirt. It was difficult to describe the mixture of disgust and arousal that I felt. Ruthie was quite overweight. She dressed sloppily and spoke loudly. I found her woolly blond hair and her huge shaking arms very unattractive. Most important, she was a woman. Yet when I smelled that atrocious cologne, my cunt became hot and wet and my clit throbbed with longing. What the hell was going on? I didn't really have time to think about it, though, because her hands were now expertly unfastening the front of my jeans. "Frig that shit...you really want it, don't you little girl?" The fat pad of her forefinger was circling around inside my soaked underwear. I gasped. "Don't you?" She vibrated her finger rapidly over my wet pussy and then suddenly withdrew it.

"Yes…" I whined.

"Say it louder, little girl. Tell me what you want." Ruthie had me pressed to the wall.

"Yes…I want it," I gasped. "I want you to fuck me. Finish me off." Christ! What was I saying? Is this what I wanted? A super-butch woman to fuck me in the costume closet backstage during the opening night of *A Midsummer Night's Dream*? But I guess it was, because I heard myself urging her on. "Yes, fuck me, Ruthie. Fuck me." I spread my legs wider to give her better access as she rubbed and poked me from behind.

Fortunately, just as I loudly climaxed, the play ended. I was mercifully drowned out by the clapping and cheering. As I sweated and shook, my pants around my ankles, Ruthie whispered, "I thought maybe you were joking when you asked me to meet you here. But I guess you were serious, weren't you? See ya around!" Then she left, closing the door behind her.

By the time Holly returned after the final credits, I had dressed and composed myself. But I was disturbed. What had Ruthie meant? Then it dawned on me! *Those assholes!* I screamed silently to myself. When I got back to our dorm room, Jane, Cory, and Logan were lounging around smoking cigarettes, drinking wine, and listening to Billie Holiday. When they saw me, they started giggling. "How was opening night?" Logan asked innocently.

I lit into to them. "You know how it was!" I shouted. "You wrote a note to Ruthie, didn't you? Didn't you?" I was walking around the room, picking up things and putting them down. Their gales of laughter affirmed that I was the butt of a cruel joke.

I left the room and basically refused to talk to any of them for the next month. And I was sure that they had all been putting me on that night in the cafeteria and were straight as pins. But I wasn't so sure about myself. Ruthie had awakened something in me, so it was hard to stay mad at Jane for long.

Caught

Zonna

I climbed into the car and Karen drove. She was being very mysterious and wouldn't tell me a thing about her evil plans. The suspense was killing me, but I knew better than to ask. All I could possibly accomplish by badgering her would be to piss her off. Then I'd *never* know, because she'd just turn the car around and drop me home without thinking twice about it. I knew from previous experiences with my cryptic companion that I was in for a good time as long as I managed to play it cool. She had yet to disappoint me.

Aside from her initial greeting, she didn't say a word. She did kiss me and run her hands under my shirt, briefly, just to check. I had followed her intriguing instructions to the letter: I was wearing only a pair of sweatpants and a ratty T-shirt, nothing underneath. Now and then she rubbed my pussy a little through the thick cotton with one hand while she steered with the other. I felt myself getting aroused as I wondered what she had in store for me. I was pretty sure it was going to be more than just some cheap-thrill car sex. Been there, done that. Karen was not one to repeat herself.

We drove in silence for about 45 minutes. She wouldn't even put the radio on. I knew she wanted me to sit there and stew. Karen could be kind of cruel and demanding at times, but I had to admit, I liked it. She was by far the most creative lover I'd ever had, or rather, who'd ever had me. I caught a glimpse of her when the moon shone in at an angle, and she had this mischievous grin threatening to crack her face in half. Nervous, but in a good way, I glanced over my shoulder and saw a gym bag in the backseat. I felt a lump form in my throat.

"What's in the bag?" I asked, trying to sound casual.

She answered by pinching my nipple hard till I yelped. I got the message.

We turned off the highway and headed down a bumpy little dirt road I didn't recognize. Leave it to Karen to find some wonderful new playground to explore. She parked between two tall trees and shut off the engine. She reached into the backseat and took something from the bag.

"Turn around." Karen tried to keep her voice level, but I could sense her excitement.

I did as told. Soon a blindfold was secured, and my world was enveloped in a velvety darkness deeper than the night.

She led me from the car, moving a bit too fast, causing me to stumble. It was very unsettling, walking in an unfamiliar place without being able to see where I was going, and I remember feeling like I was about to smack my head into a tree or fall on my face at any minute. I was helpless, and I had to put all my trust in Karen's ability to steer me safely through whatever obstacles lay in my path. I was sure this was all part of her plan, though, so I just held her hand and hoped for the best. The ground was uneven, and I heard leaves and twigs crunching under my feet. I smelled the strong, sharp scent of pine.

After a good 10 minutes, we stopped walking. Karen let go of my hand, and I stood very still, afraid to move. I heard her unzip the gym bag.

"Hold out your arms."

I felt nylon rope twist tight around my left wrist; then my arm being stretched as she tied the other end to what I guessed was a tree. Soon I was anchored, unable to move more than half an inch in either direction.

I heard her walk away. Where was she going? I strained my ears for a clue. My nose was itchy, and I wished I could scratch it. Time passed. I felt a moment of panic when I thought she'd left me, but then I heard her footsteps. Her breath on my face was a sweet relief. She kissed me hard on the mouth. Then she hooked one of the bigger holes in my T-shirt with her fingers and ripped it off.

The breeze on my bare chest was delicious.

Karen took a nipple in her mouth and sucked on it, sensually.

I felt the tingle all the way down to my toes. She bit me playfully. While her lips and teeth worked my left breast, she squeezed my right one with her other hand. Soon both my nipples were stiff. Every time the wind blew over them, it sent chills down my spine. This was getting good.

Suddenly I heard a rustling sound about 15 or 20 yards away, then voices.

"Someone's coming," I hissed. "Let me down."

"It's just some townies—probably in the woods to get stoned. They won't even know we're here." Karen ran her tongue over my ear, ignoring my request.

"That's easy for you to say—you've still got your shirt on. Come on, Karen, cut the ropes."

"Just relax and enjoy it."

"How can I relax? What if we get caught?"

Karen stuffed what was left of the T-shirt in my mouth, putting an end to my protests.

I tried to spit it out, but I couldn't. I was powerless as she continued to play with my tits mercilessly, making me hotter by the second. I shook my head violently back and forth as her hand ventured lower, pulling the cord on my sweatpants, loosening them. I felt her begin to slowly slide my pants down. My heart was beating faster now. I heard laughter in the distance. I struggled, but it was pointless. This was going to happen, no matter what.

She pulled my sneakers off and grabbed my ankle. I felt my legs being spread wide apart as she tied each one to a tree. Oh, God, she was going to take her time. A cool wind ruffled my pubic hair. I could just imagine what a sight I'd be if someone decided to wander over this way: completely naked, tied between two trees, and spread wide open for anyone to see. The image alone made me wet.

It was starting to get chilly now. I felt the heat from her body as she came closer, teasing me. Her hands were on my breasts again, then tracing a torturous, tickling trail down my sides. I couldn't move to wriggle out of the way, and the sensation was excruciating. She followed with her tongue, licking from my armpits down to my hips, around my stomach, then down the crack of my ass. She traveled that route again and again, licking me every place except where it counted.

Just when I thought I couldn't take any more, Karen showed some mercy and turned her attention to my trembling cunt. She tangled her fingers in my hair, which was soaked with my juices from all her teasing. She opened my folds and rubbed soft circles around my clit, causing it to swell. I tried to push up against her, but I had no leverage.

She chuckled. "Calm down. It's no use trying to rush me. This is gonna take as long as it takes."

She kept taunting me: touching me, then not touching me; pressing hard against my clit, then taking her hand away altogether.

I was dying. My muscles strained against the ropes, but she was right—it was no use. Karen was completely in control of my pleasure. I could do nothing except hang there while my pussy ached with desire.

As she rubbed alongside my clit, but not directly on it, I felt it twitching, begging for her to touch it. I moaned behind my gag as first one, then two of her fingers worked their way deeper inside me. I was so wet it wasn't long before her whole fist was in there, pumping slow and steady.

She filled me up. It felt so good that a part of me never wanted her to stop. But I couldn't help being conscious of the voices. *There must be a whole bunch of them out there*, I thought. *How many? Four, five? More than that? How far away? A few yards? Over a hill? Just beyond the trees?* I couldn't tell for sure. Sometimes they sounded far away; other times they sounded too close for comfort. I wished Karen would let me come, but she was setting the pace, and she was in no hurry. I wondered how long we could go on before we were discovered.

From out of nowhere, her free hand landed with a sharp smack on my ass. Then another one.

"Come on," she growled, "let me hear how good it feels."

She struck me again and again, this time with what felt like a long twig or a switch. It left a nice, burning sting on my ass and thighs. And all the while she pounded her fist in and out of my cunt relentlessly.

"Come on, bitch—let me hear it!"

Karen's voice was way too loud. *Shut up,* I wanted to cry. What was she doing? Wouldn't they hear? She was crazy. All at once it occurred to me that she wanted them to find us. She had set the whole thing up in the hope that we'd be caught. As soon as I realized this, I felt my orgasm approach like a storm.

"What's going on here? Oh, my God! Hey, everybody—look! There's a naked girl over here!"

The voice sounded only a few feet away. My heart froze. I came so hard I felt my cunt spasm around Karen's fist. I heard her groan in appreciation of the intensity of my climax. I didn't hear anything from our audience. I assumed they were probably too freaked out to comment.

When she finally cut me down, I pulled out the gag and yanked the blindfold from my eyes. I scrambled to find my sweatpants and cover up as best I could.

Karen just stood there with a strange smile on her face.

"Help me!" I scolded. My legs still felt weak and shaky, and I couldn't find my left sneaker anywhere.

"Help you what?"

I looked around. We were alone.

"Oh, my God, they went to call the cops!" I didn't know where to run first.

Karen started laughing.

"What's wrong with you?" I was so pissed. I was all for a little fun, but this was too much. Maybe she didn't care if her name turned up in the local papers, but I certainly did.

She turned around and disappeared behind a tree.

"Where are you going?" I hopped after her, trying to wrap my tattered T-shirt around myself.

She bent down and retrieved a small black box.

"What the hell is that?"

Her hand moved. I heard a click and then the sound of a tape rewinding. She pressed another button and smiled a wicked smile in the moonlight. Leaves rustled in the palm of her hand and an excited voice said, "What's going on here?"

All I can say is, it's a good thing Karen runs faster than I do!

Sex for a Cigarette

Caitlin S. Curran

"Look," she said again in her little Tinker Bell voice. She sounded completely, utterly desperate. "I will give you all this," and she pulled apart the ends of her opened blouse again, revealing to my astonished eyes a naughty nothing underneath, "just for one lousy, small, stinky little cigarette. You shouldn't smoke anyway, you know," she finished in a pragmatic tone, closing the silky top that was the same lavender-blue color as her eyes and giving me a soulful stare. "Well?"

Well, holy shit.

Earlier that day at the office, my coworker Maria had urged me to come to her party. Maria's always trying to set me up with reliable, earnest women, because she thinks my willful ways (her phrase; I prefer to say "adventurous spirit") are going to be my downfall. I'd showered, dressed up in my best jeans and white button-down shirt and snazzy black cowboy boots, and melted into a corner of the garden almost as soon as I'd arrived, to nurse my beer and watch the goings-on around me to see if anything would make this a noteworthy evening. Maria had finally gotten me to go by begging, "Come on, Caitlin. You never know what might happen."

Well, not this, that's for sure. Maybe the night was going to be interesting. As I stood talking with this woman, I saw Maria from across her backyard smiling.

"So?" asked my shameless propositioner, casting a covetous glance at the pack straining against the front pocket of my shirt. I've had some interesting times living in Los Angeles, and this was definitely intriguing, especially because I could tell Tinker Bell was not drunk. When I paused, she went on, "My friends know I've quit, and they're all here watching me, but there are some people smoking, and I just can't stand it anymore." An even more frantic note was creeping into her voice. "It's been three months, and a friend of mine told me that's a prime time to relapse. You're my last chance," she finished wistfully, giving me a hopeful look.

"Hmm," I replied, still eyeing her. My friends always say I'm up for just about anything. I was the first—sometimes only—one in our group to parachute, trek in Nepal, swim with sharks, and have sex with a movie star, among some of my rowdier experiences. This, I decided, would be a piece of cake: Just call the bluff.

"Are you any good? It's my last cigarette." I kept my voice light and teasing so she could back out if she wanted. But I also gave her my best smoldering look, which I'd learned from that movie star during our wild one-night stand.

Now it was Tink's turn to stare. I noticed about five silver studs ranged along one ear, and maybe seven in the other. She shook herself a little, threw back her shoulders, and said in a firm voice, "I'm really good. You won't regret it."

"Then," I said nonchalantly, "you get the cigarette after. Not before. Just so I can be sure."

Her jaw dropped. So did her hands, which let her blouse flap open again in the gentle summer evening breeze. Of course my eyes went right to her chest, just to make sure she really had nothing on underneath, and of course there they were again: medium-size, pert, and with fairly big, dark nipples. I had to blink to make sure this wasn't an illusion. I knew I certainly wasn't drunk; I'd arrived only 20 minutes ago.

"OK," she said in that little voice, and she sounded pretty sure of herself.

So that's how I ended up following Tinker Bell, who had just offered me sex for a cigarette, even farther back into Maria's huge garden. Maria's lover was some bigwig at a movie studio, and they lived in style. As Tink propelled me across the lawn and into the willows gracefully listing about in the background, we passed a small pond complete with ducks, a fenced-off garden with vegetables and flowers making squat little dark shapes in the night, and finally a gazebo situated beside a small, cheerfully running waterfall. What with Tinker Bell, her proposition (which I seemed to be accepting), and the fabulous backyard, I wondered if I had suddenly landed in Disneyland.

Tink started to climb the few stairs up to the wooden structure, me on her heels, when she stopped and turned around. Because she was a few steps above me, we were at eye level.

"Will you kiss someone you've just met who made you an offer like I just did?" she asked, sounding very serious. I could see her eyes, just barely, in the light that filtered through the willows from the big house. They were unreadable, but her lips were lifted in a little smile.

"Sure, darlin'," I drawled in my best cowgirl voice, and I reached out for her and pulled her body toward mine. The second I felt her bare breasts against me, I was a goner. It had been another oddball exploit up till now, but damn—was she hot. Small, probably only 5'4", and compact, with lots of muscle. Her light hair was short and sculpted to her head; her multiple piercings pressed against my cheek when she turned her face to nibble at my ear, and her hands got busy on my back and then my ass. And it was not novice fumbling or a quickie grope so she could get to what she really wanted: that cancer stick. Nope, Tink knew what she was doing, and mmm, did she do it good.

We stood out there on the steps kissing and sucking and biting lightly at each other for a few minutes, me beginning to get slick between my legs, her beginning to make this little sound in her throat that I hoped meant she was getting turned on.

"Let's go inside," she said, and the tiny voice had gotten husky. Aha—she was aroused. Either that or an actress, but I was pretty adept at spotting fakers, and she seemed real enough.

We went inside the gazebo and Tink immediately pushed me down onto the bench that circled around the walls. She meant business, and I was her favorite product at the moment. She stepped over my outstretched legs, straddling me, and squeezed her knees together, forcing my thighs to press against each other—now, wasn't that a pleasant sensation. My nub was beginning to throb very faintly, and I started to squeeze my own thighs to keep up the rhythm.

"Mmm, you really want that cigarette, don't you?" I said in

this little purr that I'd also learned from the movie star. I reached out a hand and stroked her still exposed breasts. She jumped at the touch, then leaned into it. A sliver of light showed her tongue running over her slightly open lips, and damn if I didn't get a gush of damp warmth that I could feel trickle down my thighs.

"I do want that cigarette," Tink said, her voice breathy. "But to be honest, I also want you. I liked your boots the second you walked in the door."

"Really," I said. My hands were busy with her belt buckle.

"Yeah," she whispered. "I confess to having a thing for cowgirls. I hang out at the L.A. Equestrian Center just to watch them ride around in those formfitting Wranglers."

"Huh," I said, freeing the buckle and pulling her pants down all in one motion, which made her inhale sharply. She didn't back away, though, so I gently tugged down her panties too, which were flimsy and silky, just like what I imagined a Tinker Bell would wear. "And here I thought you were from Disneyland."

"What?"

But I shushed her by leaning forward to flick my tongue over those dark nipples, then to take one into my mouth and roll it about and suck on it and feel it get taut, stiffening quickly under my hungry bite. I rubbed the other one with my fingers, and she moaned, and she didn't sound at all like Tinker Bell anymore. Liking the noise she was making and taking it as a good sign— and anyway, she was the one seducing me—I started licking my way down her breastbone, pausing to slurp my tongue on each breast, getting a satisfied groan in response.

"You know what you're doing," she said raggedly, and I paused long enough to reply, "Funny, I thought the same thing about you," before getting back to work.

After a few minutes of licking her breasts and then her belly and darting my tongue in and out of her belly button, and with her still squeezing my thighs together, I was getting really amped and ready for a more action. I circled my hands around her hips and then her ass, which was small but firm. She stiffened for a moment, and I stopped until I realized she had arched her back a little and was breathing faster. She liked it. So I ran one finger down her crack and up again, then down, then up, until she had stopped squeezing my legs and was concentrating on her own pleasure.

That was more like it. She wanted the damn cigarette, so I might as well be the one calling the shots. What I was doing to her made me feel hot and bothered too, and I must admit I enjoy being in control.

I then put one of my fingers in her mouth and said softly, "Suck on it." She did, slowly and with a lot of juice, eyes still open and looking right at me. She could take as good as she gave. Then I carefully removed my finger, and she grazed it with her teeth as I pulled it away, which sent a shiver right down to my crotch and made more wetness pulse out of me. With my other hand, I pushed her back a little. Then, so it wouldn't dry out, I put the wet finger down between her legs, through the kinky little hairs, and right into her hot, waiting cunt.

"Oh, fuck," she muttered in a low voice, and I paused again to assess. She reached down and grabbed my chin, hard, and said clearly, looking right at me, "I mean, fuck me. Please. With your finger. Or as many of them as you want."

"Sure," I said, amused but feeling short of breath myself. I pushed my finger in as far as it would go, which wasn't difficult—she was sopping wet, so soaked I could feel her dripping onto my hand. I drew in a breath, quickly, and heard her sort of laugh and moan at the same time.

"I know," she said, voice still ragged. "I told you I have a thing for cowgirls."

"Especially ones with cigarettes?" I asked, and without waiting for a reply I jammed my finger back and forth, then added another finger, then three, then eventually my whole fist. I never would have thought she could take it, she was so small, but her cunt just opened up for me, it was absolutely soaked and just huge. It enveloped my hand knuckle by knuckle, and Tink just rocked on the end of it, groaning in that small voice that seemed deeper, rougher, when I was touching her. She was slippery inside, and held my fist tightly, the muscles constricting around my fist as I worked inside her. I flexed my fingers, and this brought a sort of ripple in her vaginal walls and a tumbling cry from her lips, so I did that for a while, enjoying both the feel and the sounds.

"Oh, yeah," she murmured, and those simple words were said so passionately—so caught up in the moment—that I felt a tightening flare along my limbs and knew that she was about to tip over the edge.

When Tink came, with a flood that cascaded down my arm, a spasm that firmly grasped my hand, and a rising shriek that was entirely awesome coming from such a small body, I rode it with her. The feel of my hand inside her, wet and slippery, rushed straight to my own cunt, and I almost came while she was still involved in her own rushing freight train of pleasure. But I was more invested in her at the moment, so I let it go—for the time being.

We stayed like that for a long time while I let her relax enough so I could pull my hand out of her. She sort of collapsed over me, still on my legs, and just stayed there until her breathing quieted. She was heavy against me, and very comfortable.

She finally said, without bothering to lift her head from my shoulder, "See, I knew there was a reason I liked cowgirls. Though there aren't many of you in L.A."

"We're a rarity around here," I agreed. After a beat, I said, "Don't you want that cigarette?"

"Oh," she said. She sounded surprised. "Well—sure."

Hmm. That was suspicious. "You were jonesin' for one earlier," I said warily.

She lifted her head up and looked at me for a long moment. Then she took a deep breath and said, "I just thought you were—well, I really wanted to touch you."

Another shiver down my spine when she admitted that. "Oh, yeah?" I said encouragingly.

"Yup," she said in this cute cowgirl drawl. "The cigarette story was just a front to get you to come back here with me. I've never done this sort of thing before," she added shyly, putting her face in my shoulder again.

Really. "Well," I said, running my fingers down her back and to her ass, which made her jump. "Seems I've still got all my clothes on. And seems I didn't have quite the experience you just did. Do you think you'd—?"

I could feel her smile against my shoulder, and then she

gently bit me through my top. "I think I might be able to help you out there," she said, reaching her hands down to pull my shirt out of my Wranglers.

"Thanks, Tink," I said.

"Who?"

"Never mind. I'll tell you later. Just don't stop," I said. "Please."

Yep, sure was going to be an interesting night after all.

Shave and a Haircut

Isabelle Lazar

I am a hairy beast. Forgive me if my language startles you, but I believe in being blunt. No beating around the bush, so to speak. If this bothers you, I suggest you stop reading now. Go back to your crocheting, your backgammon matches, your vanilla sex. This isn't for the faint of heart. I believe in saying it like it is. And how it is is hairy. Very hairy. Greek roots, you see. Grandma was an Amazon—over six feet tall, and this was in the 1900s—post-suffragist and just a hair, uh, short of feminist. You'll have to forgive me again; you see, the hair references have become a mainstay of my verbal diet, a beacon in the vast sea of definition that is myself. As a youngster, growing breasts faster than the other girls in school and a mustache faster than the boys, I've had to have a sense of humor about it. Not like anyone messed with me, 'cause I happened to be a head taller than everyone else too, but being known as the female Andre the Giant didn't exactly ingratiate me with the in crowd.

Which was fine. In fact, none of this would be a problem if it weren't for one thing: I'm a femme. Not just a femme but a high femme—lipstick, heels, garters, the works. This is where my sense of humor really pays off because, you see, I find that I'm God's little joke. He gave me all the tools and none of the skills or gumption to use them. Had I been butch, I would have it made. Heck, I could pass as a guy, or at least try. Living in the Midwest as I do, I would fit right in with what we call the husky contingency of the well-bred man, because in addition to *not* being follically challenged I also weigh a healthy 180, a load carried not too lightly on my 5-foot-7 frame. I'm what you'd call zaftig, and I look good in red, but that's another story.

Now, given my predicament, I'm not at all unfamiliar with

the inside of a waxing salon. A third of my income goes to one in particular, a high-class joint in the affluent suburb of Lake Forest. My assailant's name there is Lou, though it could be Lulu, and sometimes even Louise, depending on who *you* are talking to her, not who *she* is answering you back, because Lou never changes. She's like the intractable Rock of Gibraltar, just as solid, and stone.

She deals with the high-class persnickety broads that come through her torture chamber on the way to the Bahamas, the Hamptons, the Poconos in much the same way she changes the spark plugs on her '67 Chevy when she gets home: steadily, carefully, powerfully. That's what keeps them coming back, you see, 'cause they think one of these days they're going to crack her. I know that's why I come.

Now a Lou experience is something to behold. I gear up for it two weeks in advance. Considering I come here once a month, it doesn't leave much of a reprieve from thoughts of her, which is all right by me. Lou's technique is merciless. One feels positively violated when she leaves her, at least that's what the straight chicks tell me. I have my own opinions of the sessions. Now bear in mind, I am a hairy beast, I've already told you that. Lou concurs and blocks out an hour for me each time. The type of waxing I get is called a Brazilian wax—that's everything, boys and girls, every last hair.

The experience is not for the demure. The only privacy I'm allotted is when I first arrive. Lou allows me to undress in silent contemplation of how she is about to ravage my body. Until Lou enters and begins working on me, the room in decisively chilly. I've often suggested she make the atmosphere a bit more intimate, like maybe mood lighting as opposed to fluorescents. Lou dismissed that with a wave of her muscular arm. Mood lighting would mean she couldn't see what she was doing, and that would never do. Perfection is what she strives for and perfection is what she achieves, especially when she brings out the magnifying glass and tweezers. Louise, you see, also does eyebrows. In fact, there is no area on the body that is not under her jurisdiction if it contains even a hint of hair. In my case, that hint hits you over the head like an iron frying pan. I have to limit myself to one section of my body at a time, otherwise I'd be there all week, folks, and someone has to work to afford all this pampering.

Today it's bikini wax. I'm on my way to Greece to see the relatives. It's summer; my legs, thighs, buttocks will be exposed, especially when we go to the nude beaches of Mykonos: paradise and super paradise.

I contemplate this as I peel the G-string off my ample derrière and lie back on the butcher paper lining Lou's table. I saw her having a smoke outside when I came in. She nodded to me once, not smiling. I begin to shiver a little from the cold and anticipation, the silky black hairs on my thighs rising above the goose bumps. I've let my pubic hairs grow for a month in anticipation of this visit, so I feel at least partially clothed there. I try to calm my nerves by stroking the thin black line of hair that edges down from my belly button to my crotch. On a guy it's considered sexy. Protruding out of my garter belt, I consider it obscene, and I rip it off once a month after I torture it in hot wax. Or Lou does.

She comes in all business. First she washes the smoke off her hands, running them under scalding water so as not to shock my skin with the cold when she touches it. She's very sensitive that way. As she rubs cream over her hands, she fires up the kiln under the hot wax. The hairs on my body know what's coming and try to play dead. It doesn't work. She sees them. She sees everything, in fact, her eagle eyes able to take it all in at once. She looks at my nakedness and seemingly looks past it. If she didn't, I'd drown in a sea of shame, I think.

She walks over to me and habitually removes my hands from my belly and places them at my sides.

"Now, are you going to be a good girl, or do I have to strap you down?" she asks. Only her eyes are smiling. This is a ritual we do every time.

"I'll be good," I whisper. She makes a show of not believing me by not releasing me from her stare. She holds on to one of my arms as she reaches back for the tongue depressor that protrudes out of the molten lava of wax. Her gaze still penetrating, she slathers the hot goo unceremoniously on my abdomen. Now I'm caught, like a fly in a spider's web, sticky, immobilized, able only to helplessly witness my own undoing. She gingerly lays a strap of cloth atop the wax and presses in the corners. I close my eyes and brace myself. The first one is the worst, I think. After that it is all downhill. I can hear her chuckling at my cowardice. It unnerves me, as Lou knows it will. Just as my eyes fly open in indignation, my mouth circling around a curse I'm about to hurl at her, she yanks the strip. *Hhhhrrrrchchch!* The first gallon of blood hits my clit. I squirm helplessly in my spindly prison.

"Don't move," she growls menacingly. I lie still, straining only with my nipples which, thankfully, are covered. I'm not doing my chest until the next visit.

From here on, the waxing comes in quick successions. My body is no longer my own, and that's all the foreplay I'm going to get. Now is when Lou is at her best, when she's concentrated. She lays a strip along my mound. Two seconds of heavy petting the fabric and *Hhhhrrrrchchch!* I look, from the outside, like a 12-year-old girl, baby-smooth skin, not even peach fuzz. Now my bikini line. This is quick. *Hhhhrrrrchchch! Hhhhrrrrchchch!*

She starts on my thighs. This takes a while. My legs are burning from the continuous lashes. The heat travels to my cunt and thumps a rhythmic beat in tune with Lou's whipping. She waxes all the way down my legs. The front (and the easiest part) is done. *Hhhhhrrrrrrrrchchchch!*

Lou places her massive hands on my legs and presses my knees into my chest. Then she splits me like a ripe peach, positioning my heels next to my butt. I feel myself starting to tingle from my blue clit, which is protruding high enough for me to see its scarlet tip—lying down. Lou remains stoic, though her eye muscles start crinkle again. No one can be that stone.

She smears the wax on the outside of my inner lips. *Hhhhrrrrchchch! Hhhhrrrrchchch!* Now comes the acrobatic portion of our show. Ever change a baby? Know how high you have to lift their legs in order to get the diaper out from under them? That's what Lou expects of me.

"Alley-oop," she says and smacks me playfully on my butt cheek. I roll my hands into tight little fists and secure them under my lower back, then lift my legs into a high V. I whimper quietly, holding in my orgasm.

Mercifully, Lou is quick. The wax glides over my externally numb organs and is removed from the area that connects my rump to my cunt. Lou wipes light perspiration from her brow, now.

"OK, toots, flip over for me. Half way there," she says. I grunt my laughter.

Maybe you are, but I'm almost done, myself, I think. I lower my legs and turn on my stomach, panting slightly.

Lou is less gentle with my ass. Well, I can't really blame her. That's a lot of territory to cover. We work in partnership on this. I rotate slightly giving her maximum access, and she in turn speeds up her pace. She unrolls the longer strips of fabric and starts peeling off the hairs from the top of my ass to the back of my knees in one fell swoop. *Hhhhrrrrchchch! Hhhhrrrrchchch! Hhhhrrrrchchch!*

That task completed, there remains only one thin strip of hair that clings to my flesh for dear life. It is in the place where the sun seldom, if ever, shines. But Lou's magnifying glass is indiscriminate. There is only one way to get to the thin patch of skin hidden deep in the fold of my ass. Lou taps me lightly and I know it's time. I rise up on all fours and wait, like the bad girl I am. I know this is not the position she wants, just as completely as I know she's going to bend me to her will. This is the part I wait for with near-suffocating anticipation all hour long.

"Tsk, tsk, tsk." Lou walks around the table until she's right behind me. "How many times do we need to go through this?" I don't answer—the question is rhetorical anyway. She places her palms between my knees and spreads them wider. Too wide for what is necessary. I struggle to keep my balance. If I were to uncoil my limbs I'd be doing the Chinese splits. With a heavy click of her heels she walks back to the side of the table and forces my head down on my arms.

"Kiss the table for me, sweets," she murmurs, and I obey. Then with a final, smoothing stroke she rolls me into my haunches. My genitals are spread open for her like a Thanksgiving feast at the HomeTown Buffet, with my ample bottom rounding out the edges. She walks back around and takes a position behind me. I hear her stifle a moan. Then she whispers the words I've been longing to hear:

"Did you want the works today, sweets?"

"Y-yes," I whimper, hot, shameful tears stinging my eyes. I hear the familiar thwack of her latex glove as it closes around her wrist. I hear her opening the special ceramic jar, the one filled with petroleum jelly. Its presence is fairly innocuous to the average customer, but not to me, for I know what comes next.

My heart beats in my ears. My body opens to her willingly. At the exact moment of insertion, I come. This will be the first of many, and I brace myself for Lou's onslaught. She pounds me steadily with the smooth in and out of two-finger agility.

"You're open today," she says and inserts a third. I feel myself wanting to clamp down around her but not today. I can go all the way today, and I begin to push open against her invading digits.

"More?" she says a bit surprised.

"Yes, please," I groan. She inserts a fourth. I can tell she's staring to sweat. I can hear it in her shallow breaths. "All the way, Lou, all the way. Please…" I rock back and forth meeting her hand half way between my heart and oblivion.

Suddenly there is utter silence. Lou retracts all the fingers. I am held in suspended animation for what seems like eternity. Then with a piercing blow she's back, her hand rolled into a tight fist inside me. Slick with my juices and added jelly, she pumps me mercilessly. The fly has but a few last breaths to take before the blood is drained irretrievably from her body. Deeper and deeper I will her, losing all conscious hold on reality. As I near climax I smack the table with the force of my orgasm, choking back a scream, as my swollen cunt takes the last pounding strokes of Lou's forearm. I collapse head first back on to the table, holding her prisoner inside me.

Years go by. Seasons change. The ozone gets replenished through the combined efforts of orgasmic lesbians everywhere. H.G. Wells's time machine lands and it's a much finer place than anyone ever imagined. Flights to Neptune are routine. In fact Lou and I are planning to buy a home there—the real estate is prime now…

Slowly Lou disentangles herself from me, and I collapse like a deflated balloon.

"Ah-ah-ah. We're not quite through there, deary," she rasps, trying for composure that I know she lost somewhere around the rings of Saturn.

"Oh Lou, can't you just let me rest?" I whine.

"Can't, toots, got another client in 10 minutes. Saddle up for me, baby. I just have that cute asshole of yours to take."

With great effort I rise upon all fours again and shamelessly shove my ass in her face. She chuckles.

"OK by me, babe, any way you want it." The wax feels heavy and thick on the thin membrane surrounding my anus. The cloth assuages the heat. I start to brace myself but too late. *Hhhhrrrrchchch!* Before I even know it, it's all over and Louise is rubbing my squeaky clean little parts with baby oil. She gives me one last smack on the rump to let me know she's done.

I lie back on my elbow and turn to look at her, letting my legs fall open. Lou takes the cigarettes out of her breast pocket and hits the back on the butt several times, her gaze never wavering.

"You're an artist, Lou. Michelangelo can't hold a candle to you. You have hands of gold," I say.

"They're made better by the canvas on which they work," she says humbly.

"I can provide you with an endless supply of raw material, if you're game," I offer. Lou shakes her head.

"My art is a hologram. It doesn't exist outside these walls."

"Tell me why again, Lou. I forget."

Lou examines her fingernails then begins quietly without looking up. "Because when you come here, I'm someone special. But out there," she points to the door, "it's just me. And I don't know if me is what you or anyone else wants." I start to protest, but she quiets me with her hand. "This is a safe place for me. And it's how I like it."

I frown slightly. "I guess I knew that." Oh, well. "See you when I get back? Schedule me for an hour."

"After two months in Greece? I'll clear the afternoon." She winks and leaves me to dress.

The Latex Virgin and the Frisky Femme

Rachel Kramer Bussel

I met Amelia at a writing conference, and from the first time I saw her, I was attracted to her. I got a little jolt from standing next to her, like all of a sudden she was the only woman in the room. The funny thing is, I'd known her through E-mail but hadn't known she'd be at the conference. The way she looked in real life and the way I'd imagined her were completely opposite. When my friend told me she'd be at the conference, I shrugged, not really caring one way or the other if we met up. For some reason that I can't fathom now, I was picturing a frumpy, rather dour woman in her 40s with whom I'd make pleasantries. Boy, was I wrong! She turned out to be a lively, fun girl in her late 20s, full of gossip and mischief and stories, whom I wanted to talk to and get to know better. I enjoyed hearing her tales of dyke life in the South and was glad for the presence of some younger people at the conference.

Amelia got along really well with my friends and me, and we ended up going out for dinner that night. I sat across from her and got to watch her without it being too obvious. She was animated and fun and cool, and I knew that I was starting to get a crush on her. We talked and laughed about pets, breakups, sunburns, and computers, among other subjects. We wound up talking about S/M, sharing stories of different kinds of fetishes. My friends were planning to go to an S/M party the next night, and I invited Amelia along.

The following night, as we got ready for the party—four femmes crowding the mirror in an effort to perfect our hair and makeup—I was excited but also a little nervous. For my friends, this kind of party was old hat, something they did all the time. I'd been to a few play parties but in no way considered myself an expert. The play parties I'd been to at home were pretty similar to one another, with familiar faces and locations, but this would be a different crowd. I didn't really know what to expect and was a little nervous that everyone would look down on me for being such a novice or would think that Amelia and I were intruders into their special arena or something.

Also, I didn't have anything appropriate to wear, which isn't a good thing if you're going to a play party. Luckily, my friends had brought trunkfuls of kinky paraphernalia: toys like paddles and whips, and slinky, rubbery clothes galore, enough for Amelia and me to borrow outfits. Our crammed hotel room was filled to the brim with our many belongings, and the fetish clothes made a pretty picture hanging on the rack. I imagined the hotel didn't normally have guests like us.

After perusing our fashion options, Amelia chose a long, skintight latex dress, the red color matching the streaks in her hair and the dress molding itself beautifully to her body. It was fun to hear her squeal in delight as she applied baby powder to get the dress on. The dress's shape clung to her curves and made her look like a mermaid. We all admired her new look, especially me. I put on my own very short black skirt, and then, at the urgings of my friends, got squeezed into a corset that made my already fairly large breasts look enormous! I felt a bit ridiculous in the getup, with my tits feeling like they'd pop out at any moment, but everyone assured me I looked great. I definitely felt like a new person, with most of my legs and chest exposed, and it felt fun to dress up and be daring.

Off we went, piling into the car to head out to the suburbs. I learned that a well-known dominatrix would also be attending, which sent another shiver up my spine. Would we be welcomed or considered nuisances? I figured we'd find out. When we drove up, I did a double take as we parked on the street in a completely residential area. This is where the play party was being held? All along the street the big suburban houses were quiet and tranquil, cars parked in the driveways and lights on in the living rooms. Where were the dark dungeons I was used to in New York, with anonymous storefronts that we had to be buzzed into? The setting of this kinky soiree made me laugh.

We made quite a sight, tiptoeing toward the door, careful not to draw too much attention to our slick, shiny outfits and very unsuburban look. When we got to the door, the owner of the house greeted us warmly, and we presented ourselves to the assembled guests. It felt a bit like being at a ball.

From the time we were getting dressed that night, I knew that I wanted to sleep with Amelia. Well, I probably wanted to even sooner than that, but when I saw her in that dress, and heard how excited she was about going to the party, it made me even more smitten. The truth is, I didn't really think it would happen, but lust was definitely lurching through my body. That helped distract me from being nervous at the party, or maybe just made me more nervous about Amelia than what others at the party would think. I had resolved that even though I didn't know precisely how I would make my move, I would find a way to show her how I felt. Usually I hold back, afraid that the other person will throw my desire straight back at me, but I told myself that I would never know unless I tried. And being at the party made me think there was more of a chance of something happening than if we'd gone bowling. The whole setting made my lust for her seem even more urgent—like with sex surrounding us, it would somehow magically touch us as well.

We were introduced to the other party guests, who admired our outfits and seemed happy to have us there. We then got a tour of the house, which was quite enlightening. The downstairs seemed like any living room in America, with plush carpeting, comfy couches, and trays of food to nosh on. The only thing differentiating this from other parties I'd been to were that the guests were attired in leather and piercings and I could almost see the dirty thoughts flashing through their minds as they contemplated the night's festivities. There was also a little room downstairs that had sodas and beers as well as a hallway and bathroom and a door leading outside.

Upstairs, however, was a different story. There's where the house transformed itself into full dungeon mode. The first room we saw was fitted with all sorts of kinky accoutrements. Hanging on the wall were various paddles and whips. When we walked in, a detailed rope-bondage scene was going on. As we walked through the hallway, we also saw a stark white medical room. Another room had mirrored walls and a cage under the bed, where a woman was being tormented mercilessly as she vainly tried to escape. The last room I saw really blew me away. There was a crib and big bottle and diapers and other baby parapher-nalia, but also telltale whips and paddles. That room, with its pink innocence and kinky underside, fascinated but also unnerved me. This was definitely not something I'd seen in my local dungeons.

We looked around for a while, then headed downstairs. I started talking to some people, and then out of the corner of my eye saw that Amelia was heading upstairs with Lisa, the woman who owned the house. I wanted to attach myself to them and tag along, but I just sat there and watched them walk away. I figured that probably when Lisa showed Amelia around, they might get to a little more than just a tour. But I decided to be patient.

About half an hour later, Amelia came back downstairs. Everyone else was upstairs or outside, and we talked and giggled and took pictures of ourselves in our sexy outfits. Then we went to replenish our beers in the little soda room. We talked and drank, and I started to get a nice buzz, which helped alleviate my nervousness.

Amelia was in the bathroom, and I was standing in the hall-way waiting for her. I knew that if there was ever a good time to act, this was it. When she came out and began fixing her make-up in front of the mirror, I knew I just had to touch her, even if she rebuffed me. I reached my hand under the latex clinging to her back, leaned against her, and touched her skin. It was warm and felt forbidden, like I was crossing a line that maybe I shouldn't be, that maybe I would regret. But she didn't move or push me away. I liked the feel of her warm skin and the cool latex, with my hand snug in between them. I pulled the shiny, slippery red latex back and let go; the slap it made against her back sounded wonderful, like the fabric was suddenly an instru-ment. I looked down at her back and wanted to kiss her there, but instead we just kept talking with my hand against her back, as I enjoyed the feel of her.

It's a bit of a blur how we ended up by the couch, knocking

over a beer and lifting each other's skirts, but that's what happened. After I started touching her back, I kind of tuned out what she was saying. We moved back over the couch, this time standing near each other but not touching, sipping our beers and talking. I was staring at her really intently, wanting to soak in her features and somehow prolong our short time together. I know we were standing by the couch, with her leaning against it. We were continuing our earlier discussion about personal bankruptcy when suddenly I couldn't stand it anymore. I pulled her to me, my hand on her latex-clad hip, and kissed her.

After that we moved quickly, fumbling and tumbling against each other. I liked how easily her dress slid open, the wide bottom easily opening and sliding up over her hips. She didn't have any panties on, so once I lifted her skirt, her pussy was right there, inviting me to touch it. When I slid my fingers inside her, I felt really powerful and happy, like that's where I belonged right at that moment. After my evening of plotting exactly how to get into this position, I felt I'd achieved some big goal, to be pressed up against this chic, stylish woman, my fingers moving inside her and hearing her breath catch.

We were kissing and touching and laughing, our eyes closed as we pushed aside our clothes. We turned over and one of our beers went splashing across the floor, but we were too busy right then to clean it up. She reached under my skirt and upon finding my panties told me that I was "cheating" by wearing them. "You know what I love about girls with long hair?" she asked in a very sexy, deep voice. "I like to pull on it." And she did, pulling my dark brown hair back and kissing my neck. We heard people enter and leave the house, passing by us, but we didn't care. She undid the zipper of my corset, tossed it aside and sucked on my nipples. She fingered me too, with an aggressiveness that made me smile. I slid against her fingers as we tangled our bodies on the couch, me lying on top of her.

It was all breathless and fast and definitely fueled by our beer drinking. I felt naughty, even though we weren't breaking any rules; in fact, we'd probably be breaking some rule if we hadn't gotten it on. Despite our setting, I felt sexy and warm and happy to be fucking Amelia on a small couch in a corner of that almost-room. All in all, we were probably only on that couch, naked and eager and panting, for about 15 minutes, but those 15 minutes stand out in a prolonged special glow from that long night.

At the end of our rumble and tumble, we laughed and leaned against each other, pulling on our clothes. I was trying to be extra careful with the borrowed corset, and in my care, I ended up pulling the zipper right off. Oops! I borrowed one of Amelia's shirts, and we went to find out friends. They were in the middle of some of their own action, but paused to take notice of us. "What happened to your corset?" Donna asked.

"Oh, um, the zipper came off when I was putting it back on," I said.

"Why was it off?" she probed.

"Well, um, we were kind of fooling around," I said, blushing.

My friends looked at us inquiringly. "What happened, did she fist you? Did she do you?" Cat asked Amelia.

"I've definitely been 'done,' " Amelia said coyly.

We stayed for a few more hours, and then in the wee hours of the night we all piled into the car and went back to our hotel. I grabbed my things and went to Amelia's hotel room. I slept dreamlessly next to her, waking up against her unfamiliar body, feeling like the night itself had been a dream. My friends started calling me "Big Pig" as a result of our tryst, which is pretty funny considering that was the first time I'd really just picked someone up like that. I did see her later during the weekend and kept feeling like everyone around us could tell just by looking at us what we'd been up to at the party.

Amelia and I are friends now and still keep in touch. Whenever I'm feeling lonely or that my life is the epitome of dullness, I think back to that weekend and remember what a wild time we had.

Bossy Girl

CeCe Ross

I hung up the phone in a state of shock. She had dialed the code to my building and was right outside on the front steps. She was tall but not too tall—about 5 foot 9—and slim. Her navy bib overalls were so dark they almost looked black. Her tank top was so spare I could barely tell she had anything on under there. And her smile was so warm it just killed me. She held a pink Hello Kitty backpack—the strap draped over her relaxed fingers—and it dangled and twisted back and forth beside her knee like a Christmas ornament.

"Hey," I said and stepped right past her. "Follow me. Saved you a parking spot on the street."

"Oh, that's OK. I found one right out front." She swung her long, sculpted bare arm in the direction of a dusty but very cool blue '78 Camaro; then, in slow-motion, she seemed to glide toward me, and I saw in wonder the light dancing over her brown pixie haircut, saw her tongue move over her thin pink upper lip, saw her black eyes sparkle, and I had no choice…I ran right past her.

With about 10 feet safely established between us, I shouted, "I'm just gonna move my car into the garage. Go ahead on upstairs. It's apartment 207. The door's wide open."

As a former college track star, I was flying down that sidewalk before you could even say "lesbian sex with a white girl."

Ouch, I thought on the way to my car, which was parked at least a block away around the corner. *You saved her a spot, but she found one right out front. How cool is that?* After pulling my Volkswagen four-door into the parking garage under my building, I did a quick face-check in that little mirror they put on the back of the sun visor—a little AQ (Attractiveness Quotient) test: Face good. Hair tight. "Hey, good-lookin'!" I winked at my reflection just to psych myself up, but it was true. I am blessed with smooth, blemish-free skin, high cheekbones, and a bright smile. On top of that, I've kept up my curvy but fit figure. OK, maybe I'm not as fit as when I was on the sprinting relay team for my university, but still, not too many women had my body at age 30. Heck, if I was a lesbian, I'd want to sleep with myself.

If I was a lesbian. Ha, ha.

I was soon going to find out.

We met at a bar in West Hollywood called the Palms. I was there on the pretense of doing "research" in order to be more comfortable with an old sorority sister who'd just come out of the closet and moved to S.F. in a U-Haul with her girlfriend. At the time, I believed my own caca, but in the course of an evening this tall, tomboyish Italian woman had charmed me. I could not ignore how my pussy thrummed when I looked at her, so I gave her my number and we hung out a few times, me still pretending to be straight and asking her all kinds of crazy questions like, "Were you always a tomboy?" and "What do you think made you want to sleep with women?" One day she stopped answering my calls and found excuses not to see me—in short, I got ditched. I couldn't blame her. Who wouldn't be sick and tired of all those mixed messages? Three months later, in the middle of yet another sweaty, sleepless night, I called her and confessed, "I have strange feelings for you."

"Well, then, why don't you just come on over?" she told me.

It was 2 o'clock in the morning, and I didn't think I could handle that, so I babbled out, "I'd be a lot more comfortable if you came to my place."

"See you tomorrow around six, then," she said and just hung up on my freaked-out ass.

When I returned to my apartment from the parking garage, the door was still wide open. She'd kicked off her sneakers— white sports socks still on—and made herself comfortable on my sleek chrome-and-black-leather sofa. She was adorable and terrifying—and all she was doing was leafing through my copy of *Sports Illustrated for Women*.

She looked up when I came in. "Does the fact that you sub-scribe to this magazine give you any clues about yourself?" she asked.

"Very funny," I said, and—for better or for worse—closed the door behind me. "You could cut me some slack, you know. I'm very uncomfortable with all this."

"Rite of passage, baby. Gotta walk over the hot coals," she said, referring I guess to how I strung her along for weeks, pre-tending not to have feelings for her. Now she intended to make me work.

"Are you hungry? Want something to drink?" I said.

"No, thanks," she said. "That's not what I came for."

She was definitely not going to make this easy. I was freaked. Very freaked. She was on one end of the sofa. I sat on the other end...of the love seat. She made eye contact. I looked away and tried to swallow. (Anyway, since when did swallowing get so hard? I had thought that shit was a reflex.) She moved to the other end of the sofa to get close to me. I hopped up and ran into the kitchen. "Think I'll tidy up," I said in a high-pitched voice, banging around in the dishwasher. For the umpteenth time that day, I wiped down my immaculate Formica. Yes, I was making an ass out of myself. But damn.

She stood up, hands hidden in the pockets of her overalls, and sauntered stealthily toward the kitchen.

I scooted out of the kitchen and into my room. Frantic, I looked around for something to clean and saw my coat hanging over the doorknob on the inside of the door. As I went to it, she was right behind me. Like a panther, she had stalked me into the bedroom.

"Where are you going?" she asked.

"To hang up my coat," I said.

"No, you're not." She closed the bedroom door and cornered me against the wall.

I clutched the collar of my coat with both hands. She had a look in her eyes that made me gulp. I was immobilized.

"I really need to hang up my coat. For real...so can I just...?"

"No."

I blinked at her. Her dark eyes held a terrifying tenderness. I tried to move, but she had me pinned. I felt warm. My breathing quickened. I thought, *She is loving every minute of this,* and could feel the heat coming off her as she moved in close to kiss me on the cheek. She scooped me up in strong, confident arms and carried me over to the bed. She pressed my shoulders to the mattress. I still had the damn coat in my hands. Her long body stretched out over mine, and she slowly…sank…down as if to let me enjoy her by degrees. *What arrogance.* She kissed the corners of my mouth, then circled my lips, appreciating their fullness. Her tongue plunged inside my mouth, taking it over; then she pulled back, stared into my eyes and leaned in again to brush her lips across mine.

"Now you can hang up your coat."

"Now I don't want to."

We took a bath in my clawfoot tub, kissing our nipples together, then pressing and sliding our lathered-up tits against each other. I had never bathed with another woman—let alone a white woman—and, though I never thought of myself as racially naive, found myself exclaiming, "You're so pink!"

Buzz kill.

"Well, what did you expect?" she replied.

"I didn't expect you to look like a lobster."

It was a statement I regretted, because there was a bit of distance between us after that point. But by the time the two of us slid between the sheets we had gotten well over it—and I actually think it broke the ice some because we then felt free to murmur various silly things to each other, like when she told me I had a "berry mouth" like Horace Grant of the Chicago Bulls (which definitely made up for my "lobster" comment).

I wanted to please her so much, and I ran my fingers along her waist and tentatively kissed her breast. It was pale and full and had a small red mole near the nipple.

"Yes, harder," I heard.

OK, bossy, I thought. So she knew what she wanted and wasn't afraid to ask. I liked that.

"Make me feel it," she said.

I put a mad vacuum-suction on that nipple and, believe me, it was just what the doctor ordered. She moaned and clawed my shoulders. "Roll over," I whispered. When she did, I worked my tongue down the nape of her neck, along her long moist back, then kissed and licked her bottom as if it were a giant all-day sucker. Her nipples were tight and sassy—they felt *so good* pinched between my fingers.

She was spread-eagle on her belly when I entered her luscious pink pussy with my right hand and held her hips tightly with my left. I think my aggression surprised her, because her lower back muscles tensed. But once I eased up some she relaxed and adjusted her elbows to help raise her ass and give her leverage to push back against my thrusts. She moved back and forth in a rhythmic motion, her face buried into the pillow she was chewing on. As I fucked her, I ran the fingers of my left hand through her short brown hair, and I nipped her back and ass. Then I found a real hot spot. It drove her wild, and she growled and swiveled her hips. When she came it was like a handful of paradise—hot, wet, and wrenching.

I was covered in a thin layer of sweat. I fell with my face on her smooth, buoyant ass feeling her contract around my fingers, the spasms growing fainter and farther apart.

She slowly pulled away and leaned over the side of the bed.

Zip. She was opening her backpack.

"What are you getting?" I asked.

"You'll see."

Click. The sound excited me.

"Lie back," she said. Her face was flushed like a rose.

"O-o-oh, mmm," I moaned. What is that? I like it." The slippery cool gel sent a chill up my spine and put a deep arch in my back. Her thumb was the first to disappear, and the other digits soon followed, slipping in and out, massaging—I had never experienced anything like this. I felt open and full. I felt...like a cloud.

"I'm in up to my wrist," she murmured. "You feel so good."

Damn, this girl had talent.

"Oh, this feels nice."

"Yes, it does." Her voice was low and pleasing.

My body shook. I had just begun to explode when she suddenly—but painstakingly—eased her hand out. I wanted to cry.

My cunt made a sound. Then, doing the splits, she eased right down into this crazy clit-in-cunt position. She found my rhythm and a series of exotic moans rolled out of her. Sure hands gripped my legs. Her pelvis shifted and rocked as she ground her wet lips against mine. My clit throbbed, each throb like a drumbeat filling my head, slow, building, loud, louder...

"This is it, babe. Oh, yes! Oh, yes! *O-o-oh! Y-e-e-es!*"

We lay in each other's arms, silent, our breathing synchronized. Without saying a word, we both knew this was the beginning of something real.

Finally the silence was broken. "Andi?"

"Yes?"

"That was incredible, babe."

"Yes, it really was," she said. "And it gets better."

Flea Market Find

Jenn Hwang

Last year I was working a booth at a flea market in Los Angeles, something I do every few weeks to bring in some extra cash. I go to thrift stores just outside of L.A. where I can buy collectibles and vintage clothing for next to nothing, load them into my mint 1965 Ford pickup, then haul them back to La-La Land, where I can totally jack up the price and sell them to unsuspecting "antiquers." It sounds cruel, I know, but I'm a record store manager struggling to make ends meet. Plus it's hard work driving around for hours and hours looking for cheap finds and rooting around in dozens of crappy thrift stores. So I figure I deserve the cash I bring in from my merchandise—which is always high quality.

Just two months before, I'd split up with my boyfriend of three years, Brian. Mostly it was because the sex was bad and not nearly as frequent as I would have liked. I'm pretty much a sexual animal and like sex to be down and dirty but not quick—which was Brian's M.O. He was in and out so fast you'd think I was a Taco Bell drive-through. And I was probably just too aggressive for him. One time I ordered a strap-on dildo online, and when I got it in the mail, I suggested I screw him with it that night. He was into it at first, or so he said, but right before I was about to enter him, he backed out, saying it was too weird for him, it would make him a fag, etc. If you can't stand the heat, get out of the kitchen, I always say. So I didn't miss him that much. But I did miss having sex.

It was a hot summer Saturday afternoon, nearing 3 P.M., and business was slow, so I started packing up my stuff. I'd already brought in 325 bucks that day, so I was ready to split and head for the beach to catch a few waves (I've been an avid surfer since high school). Just as I was packing up the last few things, two striking women approached my table.

"Hey, how much for this cool '50s lamp shade?" one of them asked. My God, she was almost six feet tall and had long, silky brown hair past her shoulders. Her black T-shirt read MOTHER in silver lettering.

"I'll give it to you for 30," I said.

"Thirty bucks? You're kidding," her friend, a gorgeous petite brunet, said. "I could get this at Goodwill for a dollar."

"Then drive out to the Goodwill in Chino and see if they have another one for a dollar," I told her. "That's what I paid." I laughed, since I was just teasing them. I'd actually bought the shade on eBay for $12 (plus shipping).

"Well, I never!" the tall one said, laughing. "OK, how about 20?"

"Twenty-two and you've got a deal."

She pulled out a twenty and two ones and handed them to me, but as she did, she squeezed my hand meaningfully. "I like your style," she said. Then she turned to her friend and added, "This one's a keeper."

"And I like your shirt," I told her. "Are you really a mom?"

She turned around and showed me the back. More silver letters spelled out FUCKER. This time the joke was on me.

"Now I really like it!" I said.

Even though I'd only ever dated men, lately I'd been increasingly interested in the possibility of sexual exploration with another woman. Maybe it was from finally getting out of my half-baked relationship with Brian, maybe it was from living in L.A. where pretty much anything goes, maybe it was from watching too many episodes of *Jerry Springer,* or maybe it was just because I'm a horny bitch willing to try anything once. One thing was certain, though: This tall chick was H-O-T. Her frame was thick but not fat, she had curves in all the right places, and she had sort of an "alternative" edge about her; she looked like your typical rock-and-roll L.A. *guy,* but with a lot more class and the silkiest, shiniest hair I'd ever seen in my life, outside of shampoo commercials. She was a rock-and-roll Amazon to die for.

I packed her lamp shade into a box with some tissue paper

(I always treat my customers well), but when she wasn't looking, I took one of my business cards and brazenly scrawled on
the back, "Call me. I promise I won't disappoint." Now, I never
would have done this if I'd had the slightest inkling that this
girl was straight. But both of these chicks were sending out
major dyke vibes, so I figured I had her pegged as a lesbian—
or at the very least bisexual, especially since half the women I
knew in Los Angeles had slept with a woman at some point or
another.

"Thanks for the great deal," the tall chick said. "I'll have to
come back when all your stuff's not packed up."

"You do that," I smiled. "I promise I won't disappoint."

A few days passed, and I was at work at the record store
checking my voice mail on my lunch break. Message 1: "Jenn, it's
Mom. Your dad's trying to fix the vacuum cleaner again. He's got
dirt and lint all over my linoleum! Call me!" Message 2: This is
The Gas Company (the gas company in L.A. is *actually* called
"The Gas Company"—how original). Please call us to make payment arrangements." (Like I'm going to waste a check to send
them $6 a month, which is the usual amount of my bill. I prefer
to let it build up for a while, then send them the payment.
Please.) Message three: Hi...um...this is May, the woman who
bought the retro lamp shade from you on Saturday? I got your
note. If you wanna go out Saturday night, I'm game." And then
she left her number.

Yeah, I was game, all right. I played it cool, though, and waited until I got home from work to call her back.

"Yeah, May, this is Jenn...from the flea market," I said when
she answered the phone.

"Hey, thanks for calling me back."

"So you wanna go out Saturday?"

"Sure," she said. "I'd love to. By the way, that shade looks
great on my lamp."

"Another satisfied customer of Jenn Hwang," I laughed.

"So do you want to go to a movie or something?" Her voice
was much more timid than it had been Saturday afternoon.

"A movie?" I asked, and then I took a more serious and direct
tone. "Listen, let's just cut to the chase. I know what I want. Do

you know what you want? Why don't you just come over to my place around 8 on Saturday night? I live in Silver Lake, near the reservoir. Know where that is?"

She said she did, and then I gave her directions to my place. She told me she lived in West Hollywood, which is gay central in Los Angeles. Figured. "This is kind of crazy," she said. "I mean, you could be a serial killer or something."

"A serial killer who sells bad velvet paintings and windup toys?"

May laughed. "All right, all right. I'll be there at 8. But only because you're fucking hot."

Now, *this* was the woman I'd met at the flea market. "And wear that MOTHER/FUCKER T-shirt," I told her, "so I can see if there's any truth in advertising."

Over the next few days all I could think about was Saturday night. In my head I kept replaying various sexual scenarios that I'd hopefully engage in with May: We'd do it on my kitchen floor, in my bathtub, up against the wall, etc. I even went to the mall to buy something sexy to wear: black leather pants and a tight black Lycra sleeveless tee. Saturday afternoon I went to the grocery store and bought the best merlot I could find, a dozen white roses, and some lube. I'll get to that part later!

It was nearing 8 o'clock that night, and I was psyched, waiting for May to arrive. Just then I heard the buzz of the intercom. I pressed the "answer" button and said hello.

"It's May. I hope you're ready not to disappoint me."

I just chuckled softly and buzzed her in. When I opened the door, May was wearing a long black leather coat, which was strange, considering it was the middle of August. I saw she had on her MOTHER/FUCKER T-shirt underneath.

"I see you've done as told," I said, pointing to the shirt. She came into my apartment and closed the door behind her.

"Yeah, well, I hope you don't mind a little artistic license," she said, opening the coat to reveal that she was wearing *only* the T-shirt underneath—as well as a pair of black high heels. Damn!

"Great minds think alike," I told her, and she was raring to go, because just then she pressed me up against the living room wall, mashing her full lips into mine. Her tongue was like an agile snake exploring the wild. Ten seconds of this and I didn't care if I *ever* saw Brian again. What had I been thinking?

May pulled off her shirt, and I took off mine. Since I don't usually wear a bra, we were breast against breast, hot skin against hot skin. "Oh, baby, you're so sexy," she said. "I wanted you from the moment I saw you."

"You just wanted my lamp shade," I laughed, but not for long, because May's hot mouth quickly shut me up. Then she grabbed my crotch and moved her hand up and down, kneading my cunt. "I'm going to make you so wet you're going to soak through this leather," she said. She slid her hand down my pants and felt how wet I already was. "Jesus," she whispered in my ear. "It's like Raging Waters down there." (That's a cheesy water park in L.A. I know, I know, it doesn't sound sexy, but I like a gal with a sense of humor.)

May slid her hand out, and then she helped me take off my pants and underwear. We were still standing against my living room wall. Then she got on her knees and buried her face in my pussy, lapping me up like cream. I squatted slightly over her while she sucked and slurped me into ecstasy. "I swear to God," she said, pulling a way for a moment, "if I'm ever on death row and they ask me what I want for my last meal, I'm going to tell them 'pussy.'" Again I cracked up, but when May started tongue-fucking my hot hole, I shut my trap.

"Oh, you're fucking good," I told her. "You are a motherfucking artist."

Just when I thought I couldn't stand it anymore, May brought me to the edge and I came in huge waves, my engorged clit feeling like it was going to explode. After the first time I came, she went back in for more. "Come for me, baby," she said. "Come on, let's make you come again." And I did...two more times.

But I was ready to please her now. "OK, you didn't disappoint," I laughed, "so now I won't. Stay here. I'll be back in a second."

I went into my bedroom, got the dildo I'd never gotten to use on Brian, put one of his condoms on it, grabbed the lube I'd just bought, and came back into the living room with my hands behind my back. May was sitting on the couch, legs spread open. "Like what you see?" she asked.

Jesus Christ, she was gorgeous. "Fuck, yeah!" I said. "Do you?" I held out the eight-inch strap-on.

May's eyes bugged out at the sight of the mammoth cock, then a huge grin spread across her face. She helped me put it on, then asked. "How do you want to do this?"

"From behind," I told her, and she turned around, propping herself on the couch cushion with her hands. I lubed up the cock and gently placed my hands on her plump ass cheeks, then entered her pussy from behind, letting her take it in slowly.

"Oh, fuck yeah," she said, even though I'd hardly begun.

I built up speed, not thrusting full force yet, but getting there. As I did, I slapped her ass gently. May moved in time with me, meeting each thrust with her hot, juicy pussy, her beautiful ass meeting occasionally with the leather harness I was wearing. "Come on, baby...harder, harder," she cried. "Faster." I was pounding this hottie full force now, and eventually she screamed out in pleasure and rode a huge orgasmic wave.

May and I fucked many times that night, in between glasses of merlot and several cigarette and snack breaks. I lay on the couch and had May sit on my face as I ate her out; we had sex in the shower and on the living room floor; she fucked me hard and fast with the dildo, as I'd done with her. You name it, we tried it. By 4 A.M. we were wiped out and fell fast asleep.

I woke up with her tongue in my ear. "Hey, sleepyhead," she whispered. "It's almost 11. Wanna get some breakfast?"

"Yeah!" I said, then slid down and buried my head between her legs.

May erupted in laughter. As I said, I like a girl with a sense of humor.

May and I still sleep together semiregularly, but we're not monogamous, and I've mostly been dating women. Sometimes we have three-ways with one of her more-than-willing female friends. She never fails to surprise me. I occasionally date guys, but I *refuse* to let them go down on me anymore. You can't switch to spam once you've had caviar!

When I told May later that she was my first female lover, she was incredulous, wondering how I could have known exactly what to do. I just said that I had promised her I wouldn't disappoint and that customer service is always my priority!

Bush

K.T. Fisher

We met after the Bush fiasco in a mothball hole in the wall off
South Street. I was buying the HE'S NOT MY PRESIDENT T-shirt;
she was buying the GOOD BUSH/BAD BUSH T-shirt with a picture
of a cartoon chick lowering the front of her bikini bottoms, jux-
taposed beside President Bush in his typical "Did I just say
somethin' stupid?" pose.

"Yeah, I almost got that one. I'm still torn," I said, examining
the nuclear-orange of her shirt next to the flat black of my
choice. I thought maybe I should have gone with the orange.

"I like yours too," she said. "But I thought this one was funnier."

Maybe, I thought, I'm just too serious for a nuclear-orange
bush. My T-shirt suited me; I'm more the bold-black-letters kind
of girl. Practical. Sandals with socks. Hats on hot days. Turn off
the lights you're not using. Call before 5 P.M. on Sunday for the
cheap rate. Decaf.

"But there's nothing wrong with being more serious…" she
said as if she'd just read my mind. "I've dated a lot of serious
girls, and it's good to attack an issue with humor *and* gravity,
you know?"

"Flank 'em."

"Yeah," she grinned, holding her shirt in front of her and the
mirror. "Flank 'em."

I didn't hold mine up since I was wearing three sweaters and
didn't feel like shedding in front of this beautiful girl, so I
checked the tag for size and followed her to the register. Hair in
my eyes. Head down. Geek.

The counter guy blew his nose into a well-used hankie and
asked if these two items were together. If they were, he mumbled, one is half off.

"Well, then they are," nuclear girl said as she tossed my sensible shirt on the ink-stained pea soup–green countertop. "My treat."

"Then how about I buy us coffee?" I asked, surprised by my bravado.

"Make it tea and you're on..."

Since I was only in the Philadelphia area for three more days (and one of those would be blown shooting a film for a friend working on his MFA), I had decided to try to be adventurous. And yes, asking someone out for coffee is adventurous, for me.

That's what I told her over tea, and she seemed flattered that I chose her as my adventure. Her: Heidi. Heidi, who looked nothing like I'd imagine a Heidi to look. Heidis should be pale farmer's daughters. She had short black hair, dark skin, and black eyes. Nothing pale about her except her nail polish, which looked like Saran Wrap. Black motorcycle boots. Tight blue turtleneck. Her mind and body were both well-rounded—interested in many topics, I hoped.

Heidi and I had four key things in common: One, she also worked in film (as a set designer with a huge warehouse of props at her disposal); two, she was a vegetarian; three, she was secretly addicted to Funyuns; and four, she also hated Kate Bush almost as much as President Bush. I was hooked. I asked her if she'd work on my friend's film with me. Most of the shots were indoor and in need only of a "gothic touch": red velvet drapings, maybe some high-backed wooden chairs.

"I...I mean, we could really use your help. I'll pay in Funyuns," I added.

"In that case...sure!" she said.

Heidi and I swapped info and took off in different directions. She headed back to her job in West Philly while I caught the Orange Line south where my friend Johnny lived. Johnny, who wants to be the next Ken Russell.

Two days later Heidi met Johnny and me for breakfast. Her hair was pulled back to a messy sprout. She sucked down three cups of green tea like she hadn't had liquids in days. Her ladybug blouse was on backward. Morning was obviously not her best time of day.

"I'll be OK," she repeated over and over until Johnny mouthed, "Is she really OK?" to me. I nodded weakly.

But after the grease and caffeine set in, Heidi was back to the girl I'd met in the clothing store. Feisty, witty, intriguing. She knew some guy who swears he fucked Ricky Martin; she's watched the sun rise over the Nile; she had a bit part in *The Bone Collector.*

"Really?" Johnny leaned forward, finally interested in the conversation. His wool hat smelled like yesterday's ashtray and tomorrow's thrift-store item.

"Yeah, sure."

"Want a bit part in my movie?"

"Sure…"

"I like to have action behind the scenes that doesn't necessarily go with what is happening in the foreground, you know?" Johnny leaned in closer. "So how about you and Jen here stand in the back corner and have a side scene during this main monologue…" He pulled out his 15-page script and flipped directly to the two-page monologue. "This part here is a bit long, but it's the climax. I'll be cutting in other shots and stuff to keep it moving."

Heidi agreed, pulled in like everyone else by Johnny's passion, and three hours later we were being "staged" in a loft that one of Johnny's friends lent him for the shoot. Three hundred square feet of hardwood and cinder block ready for molding. Johnny threw his cigarette out the window and pulled us over to our corner of the shot.

"The main guy here, TomCat Jones, is on his last leg. Shooting dope, drinking booze, too flaccid for dames. He's sitting in the corner of the bar." The "bar" being the left-hand side of the loft. Heidi and Johnny set it up beautifully. A few bar tables and chairs under dim lighting shot to the wall to solve the dilemma of not having an actual bar in the bar.

"He's over there thinking of things about as dark as you can get without everything turning black…" Johnny was drama director extraordinaire. "And in the background he sees you two ladies enjoying life and each other. He gets a stirring of his old passions. Then he starts to think that maybe things aren't all that bad. The world can't be so bad if pure happiness like this is allowed to thrive in public—"

"In a public bar," Heidi corrected him.

"Yeah, but see, that's the only public he cares about."

"Right," she smiled at me, amused and loving the ride.

I set the shot up through the viewfinder with Heidi sitting at our intimate table 10 feet behind TomCat who was frantically rehearsing his lines, then Johnny took over the camera so I could join Heidi.

"K.T. and Heidi, start talking to each other quietly, closely. You're on a first date. Came in for a drink after the movie. Flirt. Make a lot of eye contact. Play with your drinks. Then kiss. A nice, long kiss. OK, ready? Sound?"

"Check," the sound guy shouted from the back.

"And action…"

Kiss Heidi? I was so nervous about kissing Heidi. I didn't know how actors were suppose to kiss—tongue or no tongue? And was this acting? I really wanted to kiss her…but I didn't know if she was playing around or serious. My guess was, she was playing around.

"Do you feel awkward?" she asked, oblivious to TomCat's rantings and the camera rolling.

"Yeah, a little. But it's fun…"

"Have you ever acted before?"

"No…uh, how do you playact a kiss?"

"No tongue," she answered. "No tongue and more head-moving than usual."

"Oh…got it."

"Your lower lip is full," Heidi said while brushing her finger along my lip.

"That means you're very sensual."

"Huh…really…" I lost all my word banks suddenly.

"Yeah…and remember, I'm not scripted," she laughed.

"Just making it up as you go along, huh?" I looked down.

"Yeah…just pretending we had our first date and I want to kiss you."

"Oh…" My disappointment showed.

She took a sip from her drink. "No, no. What I mean is that I'm imagining how it might be after we have our first date."

"Have?"

"You only live in New York, right?" she asked.

"Yeah..."

"So I could come up for a date. I mean, if you were to ask me."

Adventurous didn't get much easier than this, I thought. "OK. How about a date?"

Johnny walked up behind Heidi, still a few feet from camera range, and gestured that it was time for the big kiss. TomCat was hitting the point when he could change his life around if only he could live for individual moments, etc. Johnny gestured to TomCat to turn around and look at us.

We hit the cue perfectly. Just as TomCat turned around, I leaned in and kissed Heidi. With tongue. A long, hesitant kiss that worked its way up to a passionate meeting. I felt Heidi throughout my body like she'd heated the oxygen I breathed. Her fingers danced in my hair.

I'm sure Johnny was in heaven.

We finished the short film that day, a feat I'd never accomplished before, in part because the monologue scene was so long and our kiss turned out fine the first time it was shot. Fortunately, we did the scene again as a backup and kissed for a few close-ups that Johnny would cut in during editing.

I walked Heidi to the subway. She turned to me and said, "Yes."

"Yes to what?"

"Yes to the date...and whatever other questions may be dancing around in your head."

"New York is a long way to travel for a date..."

"Well, then," she grabbed my hand, "we should have our date now. Or maybe just finish it."

Heidi's apartment sat near Drexel University. It was loud and a little scary but full of life. Floral pillowcases hung from bamboo rods subbed as curtains. Dried roses dotted the walls. She had candles set in perfect spacing. "I hate artificial light."

"And morning light."

"Yeah," she laughed. "Guess I'm a night creature."

The conversation lulled. I fidgeted with the ice cubes in my vodka-cranberry. Wondering if I should kiss her again. Knowing the likelihood of her coming to New York was slim to none.

"Where are you?" she asked.

"Ah…"

"In the future, huh? Well, we'll have none of that." Then she pulled me to her by my belt loops and kissed me. I set my drink on the stove top and stepped forward to press her against the kitchen wall.

She reached under my sweaters and T-shirt. I took a breath in, telling myself to relax. Relax and let her touch me without the usual self-deprecation. It's such a turnoff, really. Relax.

And I did. She kissed my neck and moved her hands slowly toward my chest. "I love breasts like yours. Firm, small. Otherwise I get a bit overwhelmed and don't know what to do with them."

I held my finger to her lips and she kissed it, taking it slowly into her mouth. She squeezed my nipple hard as she bit into my finger.

"Come with me," she said, pulling me to her overstuffed, overcushioned sofa. I sat down, and she climbed on top of me, pulling my sweaters off one at a time. I felt candle warmth on the back of my neck from a row of vanilla posts burning on a thin wood table behind the sofa.

When she got to my last layer, the T-shirt, she pulled it up and over my head, then wrapped my hands tight inside and pulled them down behind my back so I was secured in place. Heidi stood up and took her clothes off slowly. She licked her fingers and slid them into her blue silk panties, then moved her hips slightly up and back against the circular motions of her fingertips.

I leaned forward to kiss her belly, desperate to be a part of the show, but she waved her finger back and forth and told me to wait. I held back and watched while she inserted her fingers deeper inside, fucking herself slowly.

"I want you to suck me off," she whispered as she propped herself by pressing her left hand into the couch just over my shoulder. I was five inches from her pussy, so close I could almost make out her exact movement through the silk. The rotation of fucking and rubbing. The damp heat.

"How do you feel about me shooting a load into your mouth?"

"Yes…"

She took off her panties, threw them on the floor, then propped her left leg up under her arm so her knee was next to my ear. "Lean in," she instructed. I dove into her, grinding my tongue into her swollen spot until she was bucking against my face. "Stop…stop."

"Is everything OK?" I asked, nearly panting.

"This is the buildup I like if I'm going to come hard."

"Let me fuck you."

She stood back, surveying the options, then untangled my arms. We went into her dim, maroon bedroom. "Lie down."

I lay on her tall, soft bed, resisting the urge to touch myself while she rummaged through her toy bag under the bed. "Ah…here she is."

Heidi handed me a seven-inch black dildo. "Stay still. Stay right there. I want you to fuck me while you're getting me off." To this day, every time I think about how she looked and how she sounded when she said that, I get so hot I usually have to excuse myself for a moment.

She climbed on top of me again, her hands gripping the black wrought iron of her headboard. The shapes of flowers and vines. She lowered herself on to my mouth. I reached up from behind and gently slid the dildo into her tight pussy.

Heidi moaned and pushed back onto the dildo, as if she couldn't get it far enough into her. I followed with my mouth. Then she slammed herself down on the prick; I felt her juices on my hands. Tasted her in my mouth.

"Oh…fuck. I'm gonna shoot in your mouth. Keep fucking me. Harder. Push harder. There…oh yeah, there."

She sat back a little and took the dildo from me. I watched her fuck herself, taking it all in with powerful slams. She pounded faster and faster, then finally came in a short stream of hot liquid that hit me on my neck.

She flopped down, recovered her breath, then leaned up beside me, her fingers moving into my dampness. "Close your eyes," she said. "Your turn."

"Now," she continued, teasing me a little harder, "there's this guy watching us. He's a friend who stopped over to see what I was up to. His dick is hard. I can see it through his pants. He wants to fuck us, but I shake my head no. You're mine. But he can watch."

Her fingers pushed inside me slowly then back out to my hard clit. "He's unzipping his pants. I nod that it's OK. He pulls out his cock. It's huge. He strokes it slowly until it's fully erect, stretching out." She started fucking me in time. "He strokes up and down, wanting to fuck you the way I am now. He's moving faster..."

Heidi slid down and licked me while her fingers kept diving inside. I imagined her friend standing against the wall, jerking himself, kneading the head of his cock to slow himself down, wanting to slide his dick inside Heidi's upturned pussy. Or her ass, depending on his style.

I saw him speed up and fall against the wall just as Heidi plunged hard into me and pressed her hot tongue in just the right spot until we came together. Then he slipped out the door as she moved back up beside me. I opened my eyes.

Heidi kissed me, then made us some tea and we fell asleep.

When I got back to New York I found she'd hidden her T-shirt in my bag with the words K.T. IS scrawled above the nuclear-orange GOOD BUSH. She never visited. Johnny told me a few months later he had run into her and that she was planning to move to Los Angeles to study acting.

I wonder if I was her first attempt at method acting. If I was, she already had more than enough talent to make it.

A Contribution to the Arts

L. Dewlap

When I was in my early 20s I fell in love with the idea that sex was about having great adventures, and believed myself to be a real Christina Columbus. I liked to label my lovers and proudly collected these labels like the flags of plundered foreign countries: the "debutante," the "welder," the "bank teller," and so on. It never occurred to me that I was the one being plundered, but anyway—that said—my lover's best friend, Cassi, a painter, was a "leftover from the '60s," an "Amazonian art-punk" who was once a real-live "street whore" and a "postmodern neofeminist." Several flags all rolled into one.

For my birthday, she drove me out to Sauvie's Island—a grimy little nude beach on the banks of the Columbia River in Portland—and for a half hour the sun baked our two nude hides to a delicious crisp as we lay facedown on a giant patchwork quilt. What a great feeling, as my skinny white ass plumped and ripened under the friendly caress of the Oregon sun! From under the quilt, soft, cool sand divots soothed my knees, belly, and toes. I was as happy as a 21-year-old up-for-anything baby dyke could be.

Cassi's slick calf pressed against mine, an innocent press implying a less than innocent intention—if only I would press back. Some people you just knew would fuck you silly. Cassi was one of them. She was my lover Rose's ex, and (according to Rose) an incredible fuck. "You can tell she's an artist," Rose had once wistfully told me. "Because she fucks like an artist—a fuck artist."

Rose was out of town at the moment.

Cassi sighed as she nudged me with her elbow.

"Why are you wiggling your feet?" she asked crankily in reference to my anxious habit of foot-pumping. It was no big deal, really—I was just working my toes back and forth in the sand.

"Sorry, it's just something I do…"

"Well, stop it, man, it's driving me crazy."

Cassi had a die-hard habit of calling women "man." I emulated her, so whenever I was around her, I did it too.

"OK, OK, man."

I stopped foot-pumping. My body tensed and could not relax.

Cassi flipped over to reveal the perfect 37-year-old body of a sun-ripened goddess. Her taut abs, thighs, and shoulders had been gained by genetic good fortune and years of hedonistic depravity, by alcohol and coke and crystal and sex and surfing, and a long hospitalization once, and a hysterectomy, plus organic food, vitamins, and meditation. In short, she was toned by the art of living. Her bronzed, flat stomach glistened in the sun. Her youthful golden breasts stood like plump upside-down funnels, the nipples relaxed, conical, and mocha brown. Every muscle seemed to quiver with a practiced sensuality, especially her thigh muscles, which were great, arching, and full of energy. A short mop of curly black hair made her look like a devilish cupid. Cassi was dangerous; she'd been to hell and back again, and I wanted to get close to that.

"Flip over," she said. "You'll get burned that way."

I flipped over and exposed my anxious tits to the sun.

"Here, put some of this on."

A bottle of all-natural sunscreen landed between my legs.

Self-consciously—perhaps even narcissistically—I sat up and began to smooth small dabs of white goo over my neck and collarbones. I had a long athletic body and was in training for the National Handball Tournament. My shoulders were nice and cutely muscular. My breasts were large and girlish.

"No, not like that, stupid! Here." Cassi took the bottle out of my hand. "Here, lie down." Shaking and squeezing the almost empty bottle so it made atrocious sex sounds, Cassi smoothed the lotion over my breasts. "I like your tits," she said playfully, stirring them as a painter mixes colors on a palate, pinching them as a potter tests the texture of the clay. "They're the perfect size and the nipples get really hard. You know, we should fuck sometime."

I tucked a hunk of my short blond hair behind one ear. "You mean, like you just fucked my girlfriend this past week?"

"She told you?" This was spoken casually, but Cassi must have felt guilty because she immediately moved down from my "perfect-size tits" and began to massage the lotion on my unremarkable shins. "Aw, man, she told you?"

"Of course she told me. What did you expect?"

"Aw, man…I'm sorry."

"You should be," I replied. "You broke your promise. You told me you'd never sleep with my girlfriend unless…" I trailed off, blushing.

"I know, I know, unless it was the three of us together, but you know, she's just such a tart, man! And we were just hangin' out one night and I couldn't resist. Anyway, I can't help it, I just love to fuck my old girlfriends, especially Rose—couldn't be in a relationship with her, but I love to fuck her."

"Well, you fucked me over."

"I know, man, I'm sorry, man."

"Aw, that's OK."

"So, let me make it up to you," she said moving up from my shins. Then she bit my nipple so hard I thought it was going to come off.

Cassi spent the next half hour pleasing the hell out of my tits. She gnawed, licked, and sucked things out of me I never knew existed. Sounds I never knew I could make, I made. Weird writhing postures took over my body. Bittersweet tastes came and went inside my mouth. It sounds dumb, but the way she sucked my tits transported me, like I was tripping on mushrooms or something. Maybe the sun caused some of my dizziness. But, no, it was mid afternoon by then and a breeze had kicked up. I shook a little and my teeth chattered. Was I cold or just nervous?

Cassi rolled me up in the quilt where, still sucking my tits, she proceeded to finger me roughly. I had never been handled like this by a woman before. All my previous lovers had been fairly gentle with me, well, sort of "gooey-gooey" you might say, and I'd just thought it went with the gender orientation. Suddenly I knew there was another choice. Cassi jabbed two fingers up my crotch, then she pulled out and jostled my clit till I came. When

I tried to push her hand away she pinned my wrist between her knees and clasped my other one over my head with her free hand. Never once did she stop jostling my clit, jabbing into my crotch, and I came and I came and I came with sand getting in my hair.

"Wanna take you home, sweetie," she murmured in my ear before she chewed viciously on my lobe. "Wanna take you home and get my cock up that hot little snatch of yours."

Why do people wear swimsuits on the way to nude beaches? I faked a nap on the drive back from the riverbed, curled up against the car door with the quilt as a pillow and my left hip rotated out to allow Cassi's hand inside the crotch of my sporty nylon bikini bottoms. It reminded me of my high school years when I was a typical bad little Catholic girl cruising around town with my boyfriend. Cassi was a great one-handed driver, and she was gentle but sure-handed as she lazily played with my aching wet lips. She pinned me open with her thumb and middle finger, circling my clit with her index. As the car rounded a corner, I came on the softest tease of the tip of her finger—with a quick, urgent pounding in my cunt.

Cassi's place was decorated with her own postmodern collage paintings: skeletons and sets of animal eyes floating in a swirl of hieroglyphic symbols, spirals, and question marks. It all seemed so raw and surreal. You know, evil, but very tongue-in-cheek. I was in awe of her. One particular painting I could have studied for hours—a confused and trembling demon dog trapped inside a gold leaf pentagram that dripped with blood.

"What are you doing?" Cassi grabbed me from behind, nibbled and licked my neck.

"Sorry," I replied, swooning and gesturing toward the piece. "I was just appreciating."

"You want it?" she said. "It's yours."

She led me by the hand upstairs to her black-walled bedroom. A big drawing table with a pencil sketch in progress held court in the center of the room. An empty Scooby-Doo coffee mug rested on a nearby stool. In one corner, under a sunny window shielded by a tree's green leaves, an immaculately made futon with a brown quilt and black pillowcases waited on the floor. There was an exotic charcoal-perfuminess to the room. "What's the smell in here?" I asked her.

"Incense," she answered. "Nag Champa."

I was learning a lot, the answers to great mysteries, I believed.

"Why don't you go in and use the shower," she suggested, indicating a small bathroom off at one end of the bedroom. "You're all gritty. I don't want sand in my sheets."

I took a long and fastidious shower. When I came out all wet-haired and expectant, looking like the snub-nosed southern Oregon farm girl I was, she was already naked under the blanket on her futon. Having taken a quick rinse herself downstairs, she'd had time to light up a stick of that sweet churchy incense, and the whole room now reeked of a high Catholic Mass. Plus an electronica version of some chanting monks drizzled out of the massive boom box she kept on her drawing table.

She had a steel flask from which she took a swig of Jack Daniel's. "Come here," she said.

And I took a swig myself.

There wasn't much of a need for a lot of foreplay at that point.

She held my legs up high, and my knees shook and jumped around my ears as she thumb-fucked me with great earth-shaking thrusts, rapid-fire piston-like thrusts as her hot juice boiled out and flooded over me again and again. Her fist balled up against her clit, her hips pushing and pushing her crazy freak-ass thumb into all my craziest freak-ass spots. I thrust back at her, my awed pussy open and begging for more. Her breasts and abs, slick with sweat, rained down on me. Over and over her nipples landed and slid across my own. Each time her hot cum washed over my cunt lips and ran into my hole, her body stiffened and she emitted a whine that reminded me of the sound my old Volkswagen hatchback made when all its gears clashed and the engine fell out on the freeway. And that loud, staccato whine was like fucking transcendence, man. I closed my eyes and saw stars. Then she went down, her hand worked in, her tongue softly tor-turing in ways I'd never experienced before and I never have since. I knew I was way too worked up now to cum. I told her so. "Stop, Cassi. I think I'm all cummed out."

Cassi looked up at me with her ferocious black eyes. "Bullshit," she growled. "Not with me, you aren't."

She put my clit in a lip lock, sucking and pulling away with audible slurps.

"That hurts…a little," I said.

"Tough," she replied before enveloping my clit again, sucking and biting, and wrenching a deep shuddering scream out of me. I had no choice but to ride it out madly with my fingers tangled up in her black curly locks.

I kind of wanted to be held after that, but Cassi just rolled away from me, then lay on her back, lit up a joint she'd grabbed when she rolled away and took a deep long toke. "That was cool," she said, and chuckled. She seemed very impressed with herself. She put one hand under my ass and kept it there.

I had never slept with a woman like her before—the indifferent type who did not want to get fucked herself. But I was too young, too fresh to be annoyed by her arrogance. It was probably my innocence that brought Cassi's guard down, because when I rolled into her, ran my tongue down her taut abs, and began to worshipfully kiss her buzz-cut bush, she moaned and did not put up much resistance other than to say, "What do you think you're doing?"—as if I had no idea.

I was young and anxious but bold. I had come for a lesson, but intended to teach one too.

She chuckled and acted like I wasn't worth her time for the first couple of minutes that I softly licked at her, but then it was all over. She bucked and grabbed the back of my head and yelled, "Oh!" and I was off. She was beastly as a bottom—and a shouter from the get-go. I could barely keep up, chasing her around with my hand buried in her soft, juicy twat as she crawled across the floor on all fours. I held on for dear life as she knocked the Scooby-Doo coffee mug off her drawing stool, hauled herself up on it, spread her legs wide, leaned back on her hands and lowered her burning clit to my mouth.

I adored the exposed underside of her jawline, her raised, shuddering shoulders. Her tanned breasts and erect nipples thrust themselves up and up into the room's hazy chaos while my tongue flicked and teased her engorged clit. I prayed I was doing it good. I was, thank God, and the drops of saliva-laced cum falling off the low rung of the stool was my proof. Next we staggered around the room, kissing and hand-fucking each other, and groaning into each other's mouths. My foot landed on someone's wet spot. Whose would be hard to say.

Later that afternoon, Cassi smeared my tits with red acrylic paint and we made multiple prints for one of her art pieces. She also let me paint her twat lips, and I watched in wonder as she performed a series of kneeling splits—like a broken-winged butterfly—over the paper. I got to view the final product at a neighborhood art auction months later. The proceeds went to AIDS research. It was titled: "Nice Tits With Blue Twat Prints," and it fetched a pretty penny from an anonymous collector.

Double or Nothin'

Holly Franzen

A few years ago I was working the 3:30 to midnight shift waiting tables at a chain restaurant. I'd been single five months and hadn't had sex since my girlfriend Claudia had broken up with me to go out with a guy she knew from work. I'd get home around 12:30, stay up and watch a few talk show reruns, go to bed around 3, then get up and do the whole thing all over again. I'd get to see my friends only on the weekends, since all of them worked days. Even then, I'd spend many weekends alone, since nearly all of my pals were coupled up and didn't want to hit the lesbian bars with me. Sure, I would have loved to have a girlfriend, but I really just wanted to get laid. That was my number one priority. And I didn't like going to the bars alone. It felt too desperate.

A couple times a week I'd stop by the local gas station on my way home and pick up some cigarettes. Usually there'd be this scruffy-looking guy in the booth. I'd slide him 10 bucks in the silver drawer, and he'd give me three packs of Camel Lights. Occasionally he'd say, "Have a nice evenin'." But one night he wasn't there; in his place was the most beautiful butch woman I'd ever laid eyes on.

"Three packs of Camel Lights," I barely squeaked out.

"No problem," she grinned. She had short dark hair and looked to be in her mid 20s. She dropped my change and the cigarettes in the drawer and pushed the little lever forward. And then, I swear to God, she winked at me.

I was too flustered to say anything other than "Thanks" before darting off toward my beat-up Honda.

That night, though, as I lay in bed, I couldn't stop thinking about her. She had the whitest teeth, the most sparkling green eyes, high cheekbones, and a strong jaw line. In fact, she was on my mind so much that I dreamed about her. In the dream I walked up to the gas station booth, slid the $10 in the drawer, and said, "Three packs of Camel Lights," but just as I was about to withdraw my hand, Beautiful Butch grazed the top of my fingers with her own. "Not so fast, sweetheart," she said, then licked her lips. She motioned for me to come around to the side of the booth, where she opened the door and let me in. In no time her strong hands were all over me, sliding over my tits and down my stomach. She quickly unfastened my belt and shoved her hand down my jeans, my sticky come covering her fingers. She massaged my swollen clit in little circles, as sweet sensations flooded my body and... Just then the alarm clock went off. Doesn't that always happen? I couldn't even get laid in my dreams.

For the next few days I couldn't keep my mind off her. But I didn't need any smokes and my gas tank was nearly full, so I just had to wait it out. Finally, when I was down to a few cigarettes, I stopped by the gas station one night after work. There she was, sitting in the booth, reading a copy of *Sports Illustrated*. As I approached, she glanced up from the magazine and gave me a grin like the Cheshire Cat. You know how there are certain moments in your life you remember in vivid detail? Like losing your first tooth or going to your first party or kissing someone for the very first time? Well, to this day I remember in distinct detail feeling myself get wet at that point. I don't think I've ever been so absolutely attracted to a complete stranger in my entire life.

"I've seen you before," Beautiful Butch said with a smirk on her face.

"Well, I come here once or twice a week," I told her.

"No, someplace else. Like maybe at Rose's?" Rose's is one of the two lesbian bars in my town.

"Yeah, I go to Rose's every once in a while."

"Thought so," Beautiful Butch chuckled. "It's been a long time, though, huh?"

"Yeah, well, it's hard to get my friends to go anywhere anymore, now that they're all practically married to each other. I'm Holly, by the way."

"I know," she smiled, running a hand through her dark brown hair. "Word gets around. I'm Pamm—with two m's."

"Nice to meet you."

"So...whaddya say? Wanna meet me at Rose's Saturday night?"

Oh, my God! I couldn't believe this hot woman was asking me out—and she knew who I was! "Um...sure," I stammered, feeling myself get wetter by the second. "Ten o'clock? It usually doesn't get crowded until then."

"We don't need any crowds, hon. Make it 9."

I bought my cigarettes and left, smiling all the way home.

For the next several days, I was nervous as hell but excited too. As I said, it had been many months since I'd had any action, and I felt like my body was going through a complete metamorphosis, like Kafka's cockroach man, but in a much sexier way. At work I flirted with all the customers—even old men—and I felt like my skin was glowing. If this is what I felt like *before* having sex with Pamm (which I knew in my gut was inevitable), then imagine what I'd feel like during and after!

Saturday night, I arrived at Rose's at 9:05 (I didn't want to look desperate), and as soon as I walked in the door, I spotted Pamm at the pool table with a couple of older butch women. She was by far the most attractive of the lot; she was wearing a black tank top, black jeans, and black boots, and her hair was slicked back with some kind of gel. She also had a long chain running from her belt loop to what I assumed was a wallet in her back pocket. She looked totally cool. Even though I'm a sucker for butches of all stripes, most of the other women were a little too pudgy and out of shape for my taste—plus a couple of them had mullets, which are as omnipresent in dyke bars as hamburger in a butcher shop. I pass no judgment, though: I once wore a bolo tie every day for a whole year.

I went up to the bar and got a soda. (I had stopped drinking two years before after a nasty fall through a friend's glass-topped coffee table. I still have an ugly scar on my hand, my personal war wound.) I just stood there for a while smoking a cigarette and watching Pamm make all these excellent shots at the pool table. She was up against this amazingly sexy butch woman who had beautiful mocha skin and bulging biceps. I thought I would pass out from just looking at her, but she wasn't my date—Pamm was—so I went over to the pool table, hoping I wouldn't make a fool of myself.

"Hey, gorgeous," Pamm said, and gave me a sweet kiss on the cheek. And like any person with manners, she stopped the game momentarily and introduced me to her friends. Two of them were named Pat.

"Lemme finish up this game," Pamm said. "Ten seconds, max." She just had the eight ball left, and I watched her squat down, quickly survey the shot, then rise up, aim the stick, and sink the ball like Minnesota Fats. The whole scene was sexy as hell. The only thing hotter than a butch woman with a pool stick is a butch woman naked in bed…or fixing a car…or naked fixing a car.

"Damn! That's the third time in a row!" her gorgeous rival practically yelped.

"Double or nothin'. You promised. Pay up," Pamm said with a quiet laugh.

The beautiful woman extracted a $10 bill from her wallet and handed it to Pamm, then shook her hand.

"The table's all yours, ladies. I've got someone to attend to," Pamm said.

"Thank God," said Pamm's opponent.

"For real," someone else piped in.

Pamm threw her arm around me and led me to a table in the corner. Janis Ian was playing on the jukebox. It wasn't that crowded in the bar, and the atmosphere was mellow. From across the table I could smell Pamm's CK One, and it was intoxicating.

"Can I get you something to drink?" I asked.

"Nope. Don't drink."

"Really? Neither do I…I mean, I drink beverages, just not alcoholic ones." I was already making a fool of myself. That didn't last long, though, because Pamm's warm smile and kind face put me at ease as we talked about all kinds of things, ranging from movies we'd seen to books we'd read to our favorite TV shows of all time: her, *21 Jump Street* and *Law and Order*; me, *Deep Space Nine* and *Murphy Brown*. We sat and talked for at least an hour, and to me, it seemed like a minute. She was that good at putting me at ease and that good of a conversationalist. At one point she put her hand on my leg and I thought I was going to faint—or drown in my own wetness.

"Excuse me for a minute," I told her. "I have to go to the restroom."

"Don't be long," Pamm smiled.

I went to the restroom—which was this tiny room with one toilet and a sink—and did my business (which was to check how wet I actually was). When I opened the door, there Pamm was, grinning from ear to ear. "Mind if I step in for a moment?" she asked. I thought that grin was going to swallow her head, it was so big.

"Why no, of course not," I smiled back.

I backed into the restroom, and Pamm walked in and locked the door. Immediately she leaned into me for a long, sexy kiss. Her sweet tongue made its way into my mouth with graceful agility. She had her strong hands on either side of my face, and occasionally she slid her right hand behind my head and through my long brown hair. "My God, woman, you are stunning," she breathed into my ear. "I've been wanting this since the first time I saw you."

I was speechless, so I just kept up with her, my tongue roaming her mouth as if it had a mind of its own. I love women so much, sometimes I think it does.

As Pamm continued to explore my mouth and nibble gently on my lower lip, she moved her hands down to my breasts and cupped them forcefully, kneading them through my T-shirt. I grabbed one of her hands and shoved it under my shirt, letting her know it was OK for her to get a little closer to the real thing. With that cue, she lifted my T-shirt over my head, unclasped my bra from the front, and circled one of my hard, pink nipples with her tongue. She licked lightly at first, making little flicks, then put her entire mouth over my nipple, as though she were drinking me in. "So beautiful," she mumbled as she kept feeling me up. "So beautiful."

"You're the beautiful one," I said back, so turned on now I didn't care what I said. She had me in absolute heaven.

"Butches can't be beautiful. We're good-looking," Pamm

laughed as she continued to lick and suck my breast.

"Nope. You disprove that theory 100%. Like it or not, you're a beautiful butch, baby."

Pamm just laughed again and made her way down my stomach with hot, wet kisses. She got down on her knees, tugged at my skirt, looked up at me, and said, "May I?" I assumed she wanted to go in for some honey, and I was raring to go. I was so wet and horny I wanted her mouth right on me. I just nodded.

Pamm lifted my skirt, and I held it up as she buried her face into my crotch. Through my panties she licked my clit, then moved her mouth up to nibble at the top of my panties where a few tufts of pubic hair stuck out. "Fuck! This is it! This is it!" Pamm said. "You smell so good. Now I want to see how good you taste." She pulled my panties down until they were at my feet, then shoved her face into my pussy. Graciously I spread my legs a little wider to give her some room to work her magic. She dragged her tongue over my lips and ran it over the hood of my clit. Just then she took my whole clit into her mouth and sucked and licked me into ecstasy. She fixed her warm, wet lips to it, and I felt her tongue lick gently under the hood. Man, she had a mouth made for sucking on a rock-hard clit. "You taste so sweet," she practically sang. "And you're so wet."

Pamm's cunt-lapping took on a new intensity as she built up in rhythm and speed. "Fuck! Oh, my God! Fuck! You're so good," I cried out, not caring if the whole county, let alone all the women in the bar on the other side of the door, heard me. Just then there was a knock on the door, and Pamm yelled, "Use the men's room!"

"Get a room of your own!" we heard a gruff voice bellow, and we both laughed.

Again Pamm buried her face into my hot, drenched pussy, and this time it was no-holds-barred cunt-slurping action. When she slid two fingers into my aching hole, I knew she was going to take me all the way home. In and out she slid, first slowly, then more quickly, as her tongue worked on my clit faster and faster. I felt my vagina contract at her touch, then clench her fingers. I felt the fluids inside my pussy pulsing, practically squirting out of me and onto her hand. When she hit my G spot, her fingers stopped sliding in and out, and she massaged it as she ate me out fast and furious.

"You're so good, sweetheart, so good...Oh, God!" I cried out as I felt my knees go weak and wild electric sensations fill the entire lower half of my body. "Oh, God!" I said again, but this time it was a scream, one so high-pitched and loud I was sure it would break the bathroom mirror. Just then I rode the wave of a massive orgasm, and I felt my entire body go limp. I ran my fingers through Pamm's beautiful brown hair, and she looked up at me with a big ol' pussy-eating grin. When she stood up, she kissed my neck gently, then moved to my mouth and planted a long gentle kiss on my lips. Her face was covered in my come, and I tasted myself on her lips. She was right: I did taste sweet, like honey from the hive. After a few minutes of kissing—which got me excited all over again—we got ourselves together and opened the bathroom door.

Well, who was standing there but Pamm's opponent from earlier in the night. From the huge smile on her face, it was clear she'd heard at least part of what went on. "Double or nothin' you can't make her scream like that again," she said, half joking.

"I'll take that bet," Pamm smiled, then led me into the bathroom for more.

Great Minds Think Alike

―――――――――

Justine Moss

Being a graduate student is sexually frustrating. One of the main reasons I want to finish my dissertation is so I can stop working 24 hours a day and have a normal life. And a normal life includes sex. I've been thinking thoughts like this for the past four years...a very dry four years. When I started graduate school, I was in what I thought had been a happy and fulfilling relationship. My girlfriend Terry loved me so much she was willing to relocate from cloudy Portland to sunny San Diego, where I entered a Ph.D. program in cultural anthropology. To say the least, it was a rude shock to me when, after we had barely even been there a year, she informed me, "We haven't had sex in eight weeks!" She was sick of it, and she had gotten herself involved with a nurse at the hospital where she worked who *was* giving her some, thank you very much. She wanted to break up—immediately.

I dealt with my disappointment and loneliness by burying myself in my studies and suppressing whatever sexual urges I might have had. Unless you count when I went to Japan to do a year of dissertation research. There I rented kinky pornographic videos every night and held the vibrator between my legs until I was exhausted enough to sleep. It was a pity, really. I'm actually a very attractive young woman, in the prime of my life. I have a slender body, but with good-size tits, ripe for the touching. My hair is smooth and dark, cut in a trendy bob. My features are regular. In short, I'm pretty. But the looks and attention I received from others was wasted on me. I had been burned once. I was not going to get involved again. Instead I studied, studied, and studied.

It shouldn't have been different when I started taking Tracy

Bateman's class. But Professor Bateman snapped me out of my spell. I should have seen it coming…I was close to finishing my dissertation and filing for my Ph.D. She was a professor in the history department and offered a class on historiography that was popular with students in other disciplines. Later I realized exactly why she was so popular, but when I E-mailed her asking if I could enroll in the class, it was because I needed some historical background on Japan and wanted to make sure I did a thorough job—I was that dedicated to my studies.

I had repressed my sexual urges so successfully that I barely noticed something very important when I walked into that classroom on the first day of the semester: Professor Tracy Bateman was hot. She was in her late 30s, tall, with green eyes and smooth, sleek blond hair. Unlike most female professors of that age, who draped themselves in dowdy matrons' garb and slunk around with poor posture, Bateman stood up straight and dressed stylishly. The confidence and humor she exuded were appealing, something I noted in my subconscious. Consciously, I was just very concerned about my academic performance. I worked very hard in her class. It was kind of intimidating for me because most students were in the history department and were already familiar with a lot of the debates and methodology she used. Unlike in my anthropology classes, where I was a bit of a gasbag, I mostly kept to myself in her class. So, when she sent me an E-mail inviting me to visit her during office hours to discuss my "performance," I was rather surprised. As I understood, my performance was good. In any case, I was doing everything she asked of her students.

"Come in, Justine," she smiled. This was the closest I had ever gotten to her, and I noticed for the first time that her lips were luscious, full, and red. Her teeth were very clean looking too. I blushed, although I wasn't sure if it was because of her lips or my intense nervousness about why she had summoned me in the first place. She patted the leather seat across from her; I sat obediently, looking, I imagined, expectant and apprehensive. She appraised me, I thought, just a moment too long.

"You're probably wondering why I called you in today." She smiled again.

"Well, yes, I am," I admitted. "Is something wrong...? Did the last paper I handed in have a prob—?"

She interrupted me quickly. "Oh, no! On the contrary, I thought it was really good. In fact, I'd be interested in collaborating with you. You see, I'm putting together an edited volume on colonialism in the postcolonial context. I think your paper on subaltern metanorms in Japan would be a very good addition."

I was surprised. I thought my paper was good enough, but I didn't think it merited this kind of attention. "S-sure," I stammered. "Um...I mean, what should I do?"

She laughed again, cocked her head, and looked at me. This time, I noticed there were some fine lines forming at the edges of her eyes, that were, quite frankly, very sexy. "You, my dear, are really shy, aren't you? That's cute."

I wasn't sure how to react to this. Certainly no professor had ever told me I was cute. And no professor had ever given me such hot looks as Professor Bateman was giving me now.

"Seriously, Justine, why don't you take this abstract that describes the volume. And take these drafts of papers I plan to publish in the book."

I was confused. One moment ago, I swear to God, she was flirting with me. A moment later she was all business.

"Oh—and here's a draft of the preface I'm working on. Can you take these home and read them? Then maybe we can talk about them and how we can fit in your contribution. Hmm....this is a busy week. How about you come over to my house this weekend for dinner and we can talk? Will Saturday work for you?" At this she looked right at me with those green eyes. I was surprised, but under her green gaze my crotch burned and my panties dampened. "Or do you have something to do that night?" She blinked slowly and my nipples tingled. I could tell she knew my Saturday nights were free. And if they weren't, I would make them free.

Before I left I noticed a picture sitting on her desk of a blond child wearing glasses. She noticed me looking at it. "My daughter," she smiled. "She's spending the year in France with her father. He's doing research there, and we thought it would be a good idea to expose her to a foreign culture and language.

Oh…we're divorced," she added. I was puzzled as to why she would include that last bit of information but also pleased. I found myself blushing again and smiling like a fool. "She's really cute. She looks just like you." I was embarrassed at this, but she just grinned and I left.

That conversation took place on Wednesday. It was hard for me to make it until Saturday. For the rest of the week I tried to be professional, reading the stuff she gave me and making some notes. But I kept thinking about things that were, well, unprofessional. Like Tracy's (I was calling her Tracy in my head now) long, smooth blond hair and that beautiful mouth. Why was I doing this? After all, I scolded myself, she just wanted me to work on my paper for her volume. Nevertheless, on Saturday I was a nervous wreck. I kept putting on and taking off outfits, finally settling on a tapered light blue button-up shirt and a pair of black hip-hugger jean pants. At the last minute, I threw caution to the wind and applied some mascara and some glittering eye shadow. I thought I looked sexy. I wanted to look sexy…

When I got to Tracy Bateman's house, I drove around the block several times to quell my nervousness. Besides, I didn't want to be early and reveal my eagerness. Finally, though, at five minutes after 7, I took a deep breath and rang the doorbell.

"Hi, Justine." Professor Bateman smiled, and my stomach dropped to my feet. She looked gorgeous in her white silk wrap-around shirt and black silk pants. "Thank you so much for coming…Oh, you've brought some wine. How sweet!"

I awkwardly held out the bottle of cabernet I had purchased on the way over, and she took it gently. I followed her to a sunken living room that was tastefully furnished with Chinese scrolls and potted plants. Ambient lounge music emanated from the speakers. She gestured to a white sofa and I sat down.

"Would you like some wine?" she asked. "I have red or white. Or perhaps a beer?"

"Wine is fine." I answered quickly. And then as an afterthought, "white."

"Great minds think alike." She laughed. "That's what I'm having too. *And*…that's *exactly* why I want you to work with me on this volume."

"Oh…" I felt awkward. "I read all the papers you gave me…"

She put a finger to my lips, and I felt something in my crotch again. Something like a slow tingle and burn. "That can wait," she said. "Let's eat first. Are you hungry?" The words *I'm only hungry for you* popped uninvited into my head. I quickly suppressed that thought and just said, "Sure."

Dinner was good, and although I didn't eat very much, I found that I really enjoyed talking with Tracy (which she told me I should call her outside the context of class because we were "practically colleagues now"). After our meal, when she suggested I follow her to the living room, wineglasses refilled, discussing academic papers was the furthest thing from my mind. When I sat down, I was bit startled when she didn't sit next to me, but rather leaned back into the sofa just in front of my feet until the back of her head was touching my leg slightly. I was even more startled when, to my mortification, my hands somehow found a life of their own and began to wend their way through her soft blond hair. I held my breath and looked straight ahead. My whole body was shaking, my legs burning and jumping with little tremors and my hands continuing to stroke her hair.

When I finally dared to look down at Tracy Bateman, I saw that her eyes were closed and that she had a rapt expression on her face. "Is, is it OK?" the hoarseness of my own voice startled me. "Justine…" she murmured, as I traced my finger gently along her eyebrow. "Will you kiss me, please?" Finally her eyes opened and she turned to face me. I nodded mutely, and she sat next to me on the sofa and took my hands. I leaned forward, trembling, while she brushed her lips against mine with the lightest and most feathery touch. Our mouths were slightly open and I could smell her sweet breath. When she slid her tongue into my mouth, I welcomed it eagerly. Oh, it had been so long! We kissed for a long time, taking our time, exploring each other and feasting upon each other's mouth. I was in a trance as I lost myself in her intoxicating kisses.

Eventually she slid me onto her lap and ran her smooth hands down the front of my shirt, cupping my breasts and sliding over the fabric. I moaned and clasped her waist with my legs. I was aching to feel her hands on my bare skin, and I frantically wriggled out of my shirt. She didn't make me wait, expertly unclasping my bra and rubbing her cheeks along my eager flesh. My nipples were singing and they were as big and hard as grapes. Tracy pushed my boobs together and put first one nipple and then the other in her hot mouth. She went back and forth from one to the other until I thought I would explode right there. "I need to feel you, all of you, now." I leaned against her and muttered dizzily, "Me too, honey."

Her gaze was soft and unfocused. Her lips looked especially puffy. She watched me as I stepped out of my jeans, leaving them in a pile on the floor. Then, mercifully, she removed her blouse and her gorgeous tits came popping out. Then her pants came off. Wearing nothing but panties, we clutched each other and rubbed our bodies together, falling down onto the sofa. From my position on top of her, I kissed a line from those luscious tits down to her soft golden belly and then flipped my body around so my head was facing her feet. I ran my finger along the outside of her panties, tracing the sweet cleft of her pussy outlined under the fabric. She moaned and spread her legs. I teased her like that a bit more, this time using my tongue until she was practically begging for it. "Please, baby. I want you so badly. I want to feel your tongue on me so badly." With that I slid her panties down her thighs and pulled them off. Her pussy lips were beautiful—full, red, and glistening with wetness. I buried my face in her hot snatch and ran my tongue over her entire vulva, up and down, up and down. She shuddered and moaned.

Meanwhile, Tracy had started to do the same to me, grabbing my ass with her capable hands, burying her face in my hot, yearning snatch and probing with her soft wet tongue. We were now engaged in a full-blown, hot and heavy sixty-nine. I wasn't sure if it was because I hadn't had sex for so long or because of the improbability of the situation, but this was blowing my mind. Tracy expertly tongued my clit, creating waves of pleasure throughout my body, taking me to places I hadn't been in a long time. When she rotated her finger gently and maddeningly around the outside of my opening, I lost it. I screamed with the intensity of my orgasm, and my legs clutched her head. She followed, her breath hard and fast and her hips bobbing up and down under my tongue.

We just lay toe to head and head to toe like that for a few minutes, stunned and spent. In a little while though, I crawled into her arms and we kissed passionately. I licked my juices off her face and then rested my head against her collarbone and sighed.

"So is this the real reason why you invited me over here?" I asked Tracy mischievously.

She laughed. "I invited you over her because great minds think alike."

Fifteen Years

Julie Jacobs

For weeks—well, months actually—I'd been a nervous wreck. My 15-year high school reunion was coming up, and all I could think about was Debbie Neiman. She was my first girlfriend, when I was 17 and didn't have a clue about how cruel women could be. We didn't tell anyone about our torrid affair, of course, since it was the early '80s and, well, that kind of behavior—especially in the suburbs of Columbus, Ohio—wasn't as accepted as it is today. Plus, we both came from fairly conservative Jewish backgrounds (our parents made us go to synagogue every Friday night *and* Saturday morning), and there's no way our families would have understood, let alone condoned, such a *meshuggeneh* relationship.

Back in high school, Debbie had long curly brown hair, sparkling brown eyes, and the sweetest smile I'd seen in my life. We had met originally in 10th grade in orchestra class—she played the violin, I the cello—and had become fast friends. Eventually we both revealed our feelings for each other at the end of our junior year, and that led to a beautiful relationship that lasted throughout the summer. But when school started again in the fall, she dropped me like a hot potato. I didn't understand it, and I was crushed. Looking back on it now, though, I realize that it was one thing for us to have a summer affair, quite another for us to continue our relationship while we were both in high school. Clearly she was afraid our classmates—and quite possibly our parents—would find out about us. In October she started dating this guy Eric from the swim team, and whenever I saw them together my ears burned with jealousy.

Over the course of our senior year Debbie and I grew distant, just talking on the phone maybe once every two weeks or so, and though we promised to write each other from college (she got accepted into Brown, I enrolled at Stanford), we never did. I was still in love with her, and the thought of not being able to be with her drove me crazy. I couldn't go through that pain.

I had planned on going to my 10-year reunion, but I couldn't muster the courage, since even after all those years a piece of my heart still had her name on it. But after a few years of therapy and a lot of positive self-talk, I was determined to go to the 15-year reunion and see Debbie. Plus, I looked damn good. I'd been working out regularly, and my calves and biceps were fit and toned; my short dark hair was cut in a chic wavy bob; and I had the perfect little black dress to wear. So, even if Debbie was married to a nice Jewish boy and had a ton of kids, maybe I'd find some other hot woman at the reunion to hook up with. Sure, that's what I told myself. But secretly I wished Debbie had turned into a big ol' alcoholic bulldyke who'd been pining for me for a decade and a half. I guess I could have used a bit more therapy.

The day of the reunion, I'd flown in from San Francisco and gotten a room at the hotel where the event was being held. I would have stayed with my parents, but I hadn't even told them I was coming into town. This trip was already traumatic enough for me; I didn't want to make it any worse by having to spend time with my neurotic mother and my chain-smoking dad. When 7 P.M. rolled around, I took one last look in the mirror and headed downstairs, my stomach nearly in my throat.

When I got to the table with everyone's name tags, I secured mine and made some idle chitchat with a couple of former classmates I'd recognized. I told them a little about my life in San Francisco, that I was an independent filmmaker, etc. One of them, a fairly prim woman I remembered from biology class, asked me if I was married. "Well, if there weren't so many bastard congressmen in support of DOMA, maybe I *could* get married," I said. From the look on her face, I was fairly certain she had no idea what I was talking about.

I entered the ballroom where the reunion was taking place. It was fairly crowded, even though it was early. I hadn't spoken to anyone from high school in 15 years, and I really didn't want to start now. The only thing on my mind was Debbie. Plus, it's kind of a harsh thing to say, but most of these people were major dorks who had never left Columbus. As I stood in the corner nursing a gin and tonic, I overheard dozens of overweight men discussing their "hot jobs" in the pharmaceutical industry. The women spoke about their children mostly and reminisced about cheerleading and the clothes they wore back in the day. Several of them discussed that day's episode of *Regis and Kathie Lee*. It was pretty sickening.

After about 45 minutes of taking this in (and scanning the room constantly for anyone who vaguely resembled Debbie), I saw her enter the room. She was even more ravishing than I had remembered. She was wearing tortoise-shell glasses and was a little rounder now (in all the right places), but there was no doubt that she was gorgeous. And there was no doubt that she was a full-on lesbian. After living in San Francisco for so many years, I was certain my gaydar was in working order. Man, was she beautiful. Man, was she absolutely *gay. And* she was without a date.

I just stood there for 10 or 15 minutes watching her: watching the way she walked across the room, watching the way her fingers grazed the sides of the glass in her hand, watching her smile at everyone. This was the kind, loving girl I'd fallen in love with all those years ago. This was my very first girlfriend. But *now* she was a woman.

I decided I'd looked at her long enough, so I bolstered myself and approached her. "Debbie?" I said as she reached for an hors d'oeuvre.

She looked up at me, and I could tell she was speechless. In her eyes I saw a look of pure love—that's the only way I can describe it. Immediately we embraced for what seemed an eternity. "Julie, oh, my God, I can't believe it. You look spectacular," she said, and as she did, her voice cracked a little.

"Yep, it's me. In the flesh." My nervousness was quickly turning into serenity, the kind of serenity you feel when you're with the woman you love. The kind of serenity you feel when all is right with your world. "You don't look so shabby yourself, kid."

Debbie and I took a table near the bar and caught up with each other's lives. I learned she was living in Los Angeles and teaching law. Somehow that didn't surprise me, since her father had been a lawyer and had always encouraged her to follow in his footsteps. I told her about the indie films I'd been making, several of which had screened at places like Sundance and various gay and lesbian film festivals. And I told her about the small production company I ran. She was clearly impressed and said she was proud of me, since even back in high school I had talked about wanting to become a filmmaker. It was my lifelong dream come true.

"And, of course, I'm perpetually single," I smiled.

"Yeah, me too. The women in L.A. are a bitch." There it was! The proof I needed! (As if I really needed it.) "Listen, Julie, I want to apologize to you…" Debbie began. She looked a little pitiful.

"For what?" I knew for what.

"You know, for treating you like I did. For giving up on you. It was a mistake. I was just a kid. If I'd had an ounce of sense, I never would have let you go. I've thought about you so many times over the years. Thought about getting in touch with you, finding out how you were, but I was afraid you wouldn't want to talk to me."

"And I was afraid you'd be married with eight kids," I laughed.

Just then, Debbie and I both looked up, and who was ambling over to our table but Eric Geary, the guy Debbie had gone out with our senior year. "Hey, girls," he said as he approached us. He had a fairly large gut now and his hair was thinning. "It's been a long time."

"Yeah, it has," I muttered. Even after 15 years, his mere presence still pissed me off.

"Hey, Debbie. Beautiful as ever," he said.

"Hi, Eric. Good to see you." Debbie was being very sweet, as usual.

"So, no date?" he asked her.

"Sure, I've got a date. She's right here," she said, and grabbed my hand.

Eric was visibly stunned. He mumbled something, then took off for the bar.

Heh, heh, I said to myself. *Who's got the girl now? Who's got her now?*

For the next couple of hours, Debbie and I talked, reminisced, learned more about each other. And over those couple of hours, she held my hand the entire time. I realized then and there that she was my soul mate, that maybe those 15 years apart were for a reason. We were both mature women now who knew what we wanted. And I knew for a fact that I wanted her in my bed that night—and quite possibly for the rest of my life.

I eventually got up the nerve to ask Debbie to come up to my room for a drink. She told me she was staying at her parents' place but said she'd call them and tell them it would be a late night. We both laughed at her having to phone her parents and tell them she'd be late, especially since she was over 30 now.

When we got to my room, I turned on one of the table lamps, and we opened up a bottle of merlot from the mini bar. We took a seat on the edge of the bed, and Debbie proposed a toast. "To never going another day without doing what you should have done years ago," she said.

"*L'chaim!*" we both exclaimed, then clinked glasses and swallowed a gulp of the bittersweet wine.

"To kissing you right now!" I said, and we clinked glasses again, but this time we didn't drink. Instead, Debbie put her glass down and placed her hands on either side of my face, pulling me in for a kiss I'd waited nearly half my life for. Slow, sweet, sensual. Our tongues intertwined. I explored her with my curious mouth, my eager lips. She closed her eyes, and I kissed her forehead, her cheekbones, her chin, her neck. Softly, tenderly, with more love than I'd felt for anyone in my entire life.

I placed my glass on one of the end tables and lay on the bed. Debbie straddled me, sitting upright, her hands roaming the length of my body. "I can't believe this," she whispered. "I can't believe it's really you." She ran her fingers through my hair, traced my lips with her fingers, ran them over my face, down my neck, over my breasts. The mere touch of her fingers on my breasts sent shivers down my spine and flooded my mind with sweet memories of our summer nights together when we were teenagers. She continued to touch me like that, caress me through my dress, for quite a while. "Your body is so beautiful," she said. "So compact and firm. My God, you're gorgeous."

Somehow we wrangled ourselves out of our clothes—me out of my little black dress, Debbie out of her black rayon shirt and stylish gray slacks. We were still in our bras and underwear, but now we were skin against skin. Her curvy, smooth body felt like an old friend returning. I took Debbie's glasses off and set them on the end table. Her chestnut-brown eyes sparkled in the lamplight.

Debbie leaned over me and with her full lips placed tiny, gentle kisses on the part of my breasts that my bra didn't cover. She ran a finger down my cleavage. "So beautiful," she whispered. I reached around and took off my bra, and she just stared at me, taking me in like a long swallow of expensive wine. Then she put her luscious mouth to one of my nipples, circling it with her wet tongue, while kneading my other breast in her hand. The combination of her warm breath and wet tongue on my nipple drove me crazy. I quietly moaned, then whispered, "I love you."

Debbie looked up at me and smiled. "I know, sweetheart," she said, then continued down my body, caressing and kissing me, until she got to my panties, which I removed before helping her out of her lingerie. We were now both completely naked. Her skin was like alabaster. A lamppost outside sent light streaming in through the window and made her skin glisten; she looked like an angel. I put my hand between her legs and gently grabbed her short, trimmed pubic hair before spreading her lips with my fingers and running them lightly over her clit and vulva. She let out a small moan when I did this. She was so gorgeous, so loving, so clearly excited. I wanted to eat her up.

I covered Debbie with kisses from head to toe, touched her zaftig body all over, then spread her lips and buried my mouth into her crotch. I kissed her bright pink outer lips, ran my tongue over them, tasted the tangy sweetness of her cunt. My mouth quickly found her clitoris, which was hard as a bead. I felt it swell and harden even more in my mouth. I alternately sucked and licked, pausing to circle the hood or lick the slippery entrance to her vagina. I inserted two fingers in her and slid them in and out as I continued my rhythm on her clitoris. "Just like that, baby, just like that," Debbie moaned.

I kept it up, my face wet and sticky now. "Faster," she panted. "Faster." I did as instructed and picked up the pace. Several times I thought about how although Debbie and I had had a sexual relationship in high school, we'd never gone down on each other. I guess it was a little scary for us back then, but now I was making love to her as a woman, and I even though it was bringing back a flood of memories for me, I was making even more beautiful memories with her now—hopefully, ones that would last a lifetime.

Debbie cried out in orgasm, her tender hands grasping my shoulders as I brought her over the edge. Her entire body shook, her face was flushed and sweaty, and she'd never looked more gorgeous than right then. I climbed up beside her and held her for a while. We didn't need words now. We had each other.

We made love several times that night, and it was like some crazy dream come true. After that night, Debbie and I began a long-distance relationship, and one or the other of us would drive up to L.A. or down to S.F. every other week. Eventually I got up the nerve—and money—to move my production company to L.A., and Debbie and I moved in together. I love her more and more with each passing day, and this ending couldn't have been more magical if I'd written the screenplay myself. But really, it's not the ending—it's just the beginning.